Muddy Waters

Muddy

Waters

A HENRY "WHISPERING" SMITH MYSTERY

Book 1

Candace J. Carter

An Imprint of ABSOLUTELY AMAZING eBOOKS

WHODUNIT MYSTERIES
is an imprint of
ABSOLUTELY AMAZING eBOOKS

Published by Whiz Bang LLC, 926 Truman Avenue, Key West, Florida 33040, USA.

Muddy Waters copyright © 2018 by Candace J. Carter. Electronic compilation/ paperback edition copyright © 2018 by Whiz Bang LLC.

For information contact:
Publisher@AbsolutelyAmazingEbooks.com

ISBN-13: 978-1949504149 (Absolutely Amazing Ebooks)

ISBN-10: 194950414X

Muddy Waters

PROLOGUE

Colorado Plateau
Late Spring

Henry Smith paused in the sparse shade of a juniper. He recognized the truck parked below in the isolated canyon, and that bothered him. The attached stock trailer and makeshift loading chute bothered him even more. He followed a deer trail down the slope and circled the vehicle, examining tracks in the soft ground. Someone had unloaded a horse and ridden out of the canyon to the west. Glancing toward the late-afternoon sun, he pushed back his Stetson and wiped his face with a faded bandana.

It was cooler here under the cottonwoods, but that wasn't saying much. Spring had been unseasonably hot and dry on the Colorado Plateau. Clumps of gray-green sagebrush stretched to the purple horizon where dancing heat waves melted cloudless sky into parched earth. This small canyon was a refuge from the drabness. The bright patch of green by the spring stood out like an unexpected splash of color in a monochromatic photo.

Henry returned to his horse tied near the spring. He found a half-melted Snickers bar in the saddlebag and wrestled with the sticky wrapper, his thoughts on the pickup. The faded Mesa State license plate frame brought back images of a grinning Aubrey Miller, whom he'd known since they were kids growing up in North Carolina. A day after graduation from college, Aubrey had stopped by to show off his brand new F-250. Aubrey was still driving that same truck last year, vowing to keep it until he ran it into the ground. Henry had laughed. He wasn't giving up his 1965 Chevy any time soon.

Friendship wouldn't make a difference to the ranchers who paid Henry to take care of stock thieves. It wouldn't make a difference to Henry, either. After ten years as a range detective, he wouldn't allow a friend's transgression to tarnish his otherwise spotless record.

Henry licked chocolate from his fingers before wiping them on the bandana. He swallowed a mouthful of lukewarm water from the canteen, grabbed his rifle and settled down in the lengthening shadows near the trailer to wait. Around dusk, the roan twitched his ears, listening. The distant shuffle of hooves grew louder, echoing off the canyon walls. Henry placed his hand over the roan's nose to keep him from whinnying.

A rider emerged from the shadows, herding the small group of yearlings toward the loading chute. The cattle were urged forward until they clambered inside the trailer. When the rider leaned in to close the door, Henry's suspicions were confirmed.

Henry stepped forward. "I'll get that for you, Aubrey."

"Damn!" Aubrey jerked the horse's reins.

Henry swung the door shut and leaned against the trailer, cradling his rifle in the crook of his left arm. An owl hooted somewhere near the spring.

"They don't call you 'Whispering Smith' for nothing." Aubrey dismounted. "How long you been out here?"

"Long enough." Henry could see dust covering Aubrey from his battered cowboy hat to his boots. He'd put some effort into stealing the cattle. "These Lazy K steers look good, despite the drought. Only problem is, you don't work for the Lazy K."

Aubrey twisted the reins in his hands. "So what happens now?"

Henry stared at Aubrey. What did he think happened to rustlers? He clenched his fists, wondering if it really was possible to knock sense into someone. "What were you going to do with the cattle?"

Aubrey shrugged and tied his horse to the trailer.

"Wouldn't have anything to do with your friend Connor, would it?"

When Aubrey didn't answer, Henry took it as a yes. Connor was a nasty piece of work, but good at getting rid of stolen cattle quickly. He'd been lucky at staying a few steps ahead of range detectives across three states. That luck might be turning.

Henry moved away from the trailer. "Where were you meeting him?" He shifted the rifle to his right hand.

Aubrey licked his lips. "You know I can't tell you that."

"Maybe you'd better think on saving your own skin." He leaned against the trunk of a cottonwood.

Aubrey dropped his head and kicked a stone.

Henry watched the stone bounce, realizing Aubrey's boot hadn't made the tracks by the truck. When a slight rustling near the spring caught Henry's attention, Aubrey rushed him and they both hit the ground with a force that knocked the rifle from Henry's grasp. A bullet ripped bark from the tree he'd been leaning against.

Aubrey grabbed the rifle. Henry's first impression was that Aubrey was about to shoot him, followed by how quickly he could draw the holstered pistol at his waist.

"That idiot," Aubrey hissed. He pointed the rifle toward the brush surrounding the spring. "If I'd any idea he was going to pull a stunt like this, I'd have told you he was out there."

Hands shaking, he passed the rifle to Henry as a second shot slammed into the trailer. Pinpointing the muzzle flash in the darkness, Henry fired three shots at the flash then dropped to the ground a few feet away. He watched the shadows for movement. The cattle inside the trailer were bawling and thumping the trailer walls, making it impossible to hear anything else.

"Let those cows out," Henry snapped.

"Do what?"

"And keep your head down."

Aubrey swore as he untied his panicked horse. It reared, then wheeled and kicked at the trailer before running into the gloom. Seconds later, Henry heard the clank of the latch and the groan of the metal door on its hinges. He saw Aubrey jump away from the cattle and flatten himself on the ground near the trailer. The cattle scrambled over each other in their haste to escape, stampeding through the brush and out of the canyon.

Silence enveloped the spring.

"I'm a range detective for the Colorado Plateau Cattlemen's Association." Henry's voice carried in the stillness. "It's best if you come on out now, before things get out of hand."

A bullet scattered dirt a few feet to Henry's right. He spaced three more shots at the muzzle flash before shifting to his right, then studied the shadows. With his foot, he pushed the trailer door in hopes the squealing hinges would elicit another shot. Nothing. After several minutes, he crawled to the rear of the trailer and got to his feet behind the door. Henry leaned the rifle against the trailer and drew his pistol. Signaling Aubrey to stay put, he peered into the darkness.

"Connor! If I have to come after you, one of us won't make it through the night. I'm figuring that'd be you."

Connor's next bullet ricocheted off a rocky outcrop on the slope behind the trailer. Henry determined the location of the muzzle flash, and firing twice, he slipped into the scrub beside the trailer. He edged quietly toward the spring, listening for movements in the undergrowth to locate his quarry. He found Connor hunkered beside the bones of a long-dead tree, tying a bandana around a blood-soaked leg. His rifle leaned against the trunk.

Henry used a large cottonwood for cover. "Move away from the rifle and keep your hands in sight."

Connor was quick. In one move he grabbed the rifle and fired. The shot clipped branches to Henry's left. He tried to chamber another round as Henry stepped into the small clearing, pistol aimed at Connor.

"Drop it – now!"

Connor raised the rifle to his shoulder. Henry squeezed the trigger. His bullet struck Connor squarely in the chest. Dry limbs cracked as Connor collapsed against the decaying trunk. Henry kept the pistol trained on Connor as he approached, watching for movement. His boot on Connor's rifle, he leaned in and checked for a carotid pulse. Nothing.

The image of Connor's empty eyes burned into his memory. He took a few deep breaths and holstered his pistol. Above him, the moon shone through the tangle of cottonwood branches. Somewhere in the darkness a coyote howled. Cattle rustled through the brush as they slowly returned to the spring. Henry checked the handcuffs on his belt. He fished in his chest pocket for his Miranda card while walking toward the truck to arrest an old friend who'd just saved his life.

CHAPTER 1

North Carolina Mountains
Early Summer, One Year Later

The Parsons Gap city limits sign loomed ahead, dappled sunlight offering a more welcoming impression than Henry believed was deserved. He slowed the old pickup to meet the speed limit, unexpectedly attracted to the dense greenness absent in northwestern Colorado. Summer had always been his favorite time of year growing up here. Now it seemed cold and uncertain, like he was about to dive into muddy waters. When he'd left his North Carolina hometown fifteen years ago, he promised not to return. He'd never gone back on his word before. That was one of the few things his father bothered to teach him.

He pushed thoughts of his father aside before they brought on a hailstorm of unpleasant memories.

The municipal lot across from the Corner Café offered plenty of parking. He set the parking brake and climbed out of the pickup. The town had changed during his time away. The only thing he recognized was the faded, red-and-white café sign. The clothing store was gone. So was the gas station. A restaurant had replaced the bank. By the time he crossed the street to reach the café, he was nearly convinced this was the wrong town.

He pushed through the glass door, automatically removing his hat as he took in the café. The familiar aroma of bacon, hot coffee, and fresh-baked biscuits greeted him.

Muddy Waters

Nothing had changed here, from the red vinyl chairs and yellowed floor tiles to the faded photos of local high-school teams and athletes on the walls. Even the big picture window overlooking High Street wore the same grimy streaks. It was strangely comforting.

"I was beginning to think you got lost." Aubrey Miller grinned at him from a stool at the far end of the counter.

"I hope you've managed to stay out of trouble." Henry took the seat beside him. A year had passed since the arrest and it was good to see Aubrey again. After serving a brief probationary period, Aubrey had decided to leave Colorado and accept a job with his cousins back home.

"You look like you're in shock or something."

Henry glanced out the big window toward the street. "I barely recognize this town."

Aubrey laughed. "Things are different around here, that's for sure."

Henry found a menu wedged between the napkin dispenser and a ketchup bottle. "You order yet?"

"Yes, sir. I'm a working man now. Got responsibilities." A waitress in her early twenties appeared with a heaping plate of food. She placed the plate in front of Aubrey and winked suggestively before turning to take Henry's order. She ripped the order ticket from her pad, flipped her blonde hair and winked at Aubrey again as she returned to the kitchen.

"At least the service is good," Henry said.

Aubrey wasn't paying attention to anything but the waitress. She returned with a mug of hot tea, staring at Aubrey as she slid the mug to Henry. Henry moved to the edge of the stool to evade the hot liquid she was undoubtedly about to spill. The danger passed and Henry relaxed until she reappeared moments later with a steaming pot of coffee.

Aubrey shoved a forkful of scrambled eggs into his

mouth then stabbed a piece of ham. He shook the ham to emphasize his words. "Never thought I'd move back home."

"It's hard to say no to a fresh start."

"Ain't that the truth!" Aubrey chewed the ham and washed it down with coffee. "I never did thank you properly for what you did. Your testimony kept my sorry ass out of jail."

"You kept my sorry ass out of the graveyard."

"I hope that doesn't mean we're square." Aubrey picked at a chip in his coffee cup. "Henry, there's something on my mind. Something maybe you could help with, now you're here for a few days."

"What's that?"

"Rumors about the slaughterhouse. I think my cousins are taking in cows with questionable ownership."

"As in stolen?"

"Maybe I shouldn't say anything." Aubrey tapped his fork against his plate. "Seen your father yet?"

Henry shook his head. "I'm having supper over there tonight."

"You two finally going to kiss and make up?"

"It'll take more than one date for that." Henry stirred sugar into his tea and shifted Aubrey's attention. "Who's the girl?"

"What girl?"

"The one that seems to think you're the only person in the room." Noticing Aubrey's blank expression, he added, "The waitress."

A smile spread across Aubrey's face. "Oh, that's Alva Jean."

Alva Jean appeared to be Aubrey's latest love of his life. The ridiculous grin confirmed it. He'd only been in town a few months, but that was Aubrey.

"Looks like you've settled into this place quick enough. How's the job?"

"Never expected to be working this side of a cow, but I like it. My cousins want me to learn all about the business. Never knew there was so much to making steaks."

Alva Jean returned to refill the coffee. Aubrey nearly slipped off his stool trying to watch her walk toward the kitchen. His behavior made Henry seriously consider the possibility Aubrey had become a born-again adolescent.

"This ol' town ain't so bad." Aubrey re-centered himself on the stool. "It's grown into a nice little place. You ought to consider staying."

"The only thing I ever liked about this town was the fishing. You know I wouldn't be here now if it wasn't for Vernon's wedding."

"Why'd you come back for two weeks then? Only takes one day to be best man."

Henry looked out the big window.

"Boy, that's something ain't it? Your uncle getting married." Aubrey's expression grew serious. "You've been lucky so far, you know."

"Haven't met the right girl."

"Not that." Aubrey picked at a fingernail. "I've been thinking about a lot of things lately. They say life-altering experiences do that to a person."

Henry wondered if he meant being arrested for rustling or finding a new girlfriend.

"You ever think about a new profession? One of these times you may not come out in one piece."

Henry raised his eyebrows. "This may be a surprise to you, but I don't go into situations unprepared."

"I didn't mean it like that." Aubrey waved a hand as if erasing the words. "You're prepared all right. It's just that, well, you nearly got shot that night. Maybe it's time to find something a little bit safer."

"I don't track down dangerous people every day. Most days, the worst that can happen is a severe paper cut."

"What's so wrong with a new line of work?"

Henry shrugged.

"You must be thinking of that saying about old dogs and new tricks. It ain't true." Aubrey grinned and spread his hands. "Look at me."

Henry didn't mention his leave of absence following Aubrey's trial. Or the career change he was considering. They sat in silence until Alva Jean returned with Henry's breakfast. He tried to ignore the silly look on Aubrey's face when she was near. Something in the way they looked at each other made Henry imagine them settling down and raising a bunch of kids, all with names beginning with 'A'.

"You really like her, don't you?"

Aubrey grinned. "You know me. I fall in love every other week."

With Aubrey it was more likely to be lust than love, but this affliction seemed different. "You always did have good taste."

Happy to discover strawberry jam in the bowl of individual jelly portions, Henry split open a biscuit and meticulously coated the inside of both halves.

"Tell you the truth, I've got a feeling things could get real serious here." Aubrey waved his toast toward the waitress. "You don't recognize her, do you?"

Henry studied the waitress. "Should I?"

Aubrey stuffed a chunk of toast into his mouth. "Here's a clue, her big sister was your high school sweetheart."

"That's A.J.?" Henry barely avoided blurting something about her being all grown up. That was obvious. She'd been about to start kindergarten the last time he'd seen her. What was Aubrey doing with a girl fifteen years younger?

"Guess I never gave much thought to what the initials 'A.J.' were for."

"I ran into her the other day." Aubrey paused to swallow the toast. "Carlie, I mean. She's a doctor now. Moved back to town a few years ago and set up shop. Maybe you should look her up while you're in town."

Henry didn't comment.

"Say what you will, but I never did believe that story about her cheating on you." Aubrey waved a second slice of toast at Henry. "Even if she was the one that said it." He glanced at the clock on the wall, then tucked several crumpled bills under the edge of his plate. He got to his feet. "Better run. If I'm late, my cousins will kill me."

Henry stared at his plate. His mind wasn't quite a million miles away, just fifteen years in the past. He'd lost his appetite but still felt it a shame to waste strawberry jam.

CHAPTER 2

"I'm not looking forward to this." Henry stomped his feet into his boots. He glanced at his uncle, who relaxed in a threadbare recliner at odds with the rustic furnishings of the cabin.

"You act like you're going to have a root canal." Vernon Smith leaned forward and tossed the newspaper he'd been reading onto a table. "It's only supper. Just get yourself over there, and you'll see the 'Old Bastard' ain't so bad these days. He's changed."

"It's only supper," Henry echoed sarcastically. "More like round two."

He'd not spoken to his father since the fight, and he was growing increasingly anxious. How could Vernon be so calm? The orange cat curled in his lap seemed equally untroubled. Henry recalled Vernon hated cats. He also swore he'd never get married. Maybe he was right. People do change.

"Aren't you invited?" Henry shrugged into a dress shirt.

"Of course I am," Vernon replied. "Going to be fashionably late, that's all. Got to take care of a little business first."

"Wouldn't have anything to do with the future Mrs. Vernon Smith, would it?"

Vernon smiled.

"Della's not joining us tonight?"

"Her grandson has something going on up at the school, and she never misses an event."

Henry buttoned his shirt and tucked it into his jeans. He surveyed the cabin. "This is a nice place, Vernon. Didn't see any make-up or other female things in the bathroom. Why is it you two don't spend much time here?"

"She doesn't like the place." Vernon scratched the cat's head. "Too small, too dark, too plain, or whatever it is women don't like about bachelor pads."

Knowing his uncle's reputation, it might have a lot to do with the Ghosts of Conquests Past.

"She's got a place in town," Vernon said. "Not far from where she works. Decorated a little too frilly for me, but we're finding middle ground. It's an older house and I do like that. Needs work – minor stuff. Since I'm there most of the time, I've been taking care of the household maintenance for her." Vernon waggled his eyebrows. "There are fringe benefits, too."

"By that you mean her good cooking?" Henry pointed at Vernon's protruding stomach.

"She's a good cook all right." Vernon grinned and patted his belly. "It sure does feel good waking up next to her every morning."

Henry raised his eyebrows. Vernon's face reddened and he turned toward the window.

"Don't forget we're fishing early tomorrow."

"I never forget anything having to do with fishing." Henry grabbed his keys from the peg by the door. "Wish me luck."

Vernon managed a noncommittal grunt as Henry left the cabin. His uncle had always made it clear he enjoyed being unattached. This same lean toward matrimony appeared to be happening with Aubrey. Henry hoped it wasn't contagious.

He started his pickup and shifted into gear, not wanting to admit he was interested in seeing his childhood home. Through infrequent letters, Vernon had told him the house had gone through a major renovation. Said he wouldn't recognize the place. The irony of a homecoming to a strange house didn't escape him. He mulled over the packet of letters Vernon had found and sent. They'd been in the attic. Letters Henry's mother had written to her father but never mailed. Henry had read them all, along with Vernon's letter about his father's illness.

Henry's hands tightened on the steering wheel. Reconciliation had been the last thing on his mind before he'd read those letters.

The drive to the ranch was a short one, especially by the standards he'd grown accustomed to out west. He loosened his grip on the wheel when he reached the driveway. Stopping the truck, he studied the Bar T Ranch brand burned into the large beam suspended over the entrance, a bar above the letter T. It absurdly reminded him of the American Lung Association logo. As long as he could remember, his father had rolled and smoked his own unfiltered cigarettes.

Several smaller signs hung below, each announcing services available at the guest ranch. Bed and breakfast, guided trail rides, overnight horseback excursions, fishing, and just plain relaxing.

The curving drive led to a two-story house perched on a wide knoll. White paint gleamed in the late afternoon sun. Green shutters flanked the windows. Rocking chairs and hanging baskets overflowing with ferns dotted the new wrap-around porch. Nothing hinted at the unhappy place he remembered.

Henry parked near the old barn. Once a favorite escape from his troubled home life, it looked dressed for a party. Weathered wood had been replaced and painted to match the house. Split-rail fencing enclosed small corrals where horses milled around hayracks. He climbed out of the pickup and walked slowly toward the house, fighting the urge to turn and run. *Don't be an idiot. You've faced worse situations as a range detective.*

Henry stepped onto the porch and raised his hand to knock. The door swung open before he touched it.

"Henry!" His stepmother's warm smile greeted him. "It's wonderful of you to come."

"Sally Ann." Henry gave her a heartfelt hug, suddenly feeling guilty for not keeping in touch. The same dark, intelligent eyes he remembered regarded him from a weathered face. Streaks of silver accented the hair she still kept tied back in unruffled sleekness.

"You haven't changed a bit," Henry said.

"You know you don't need to flatter me."

"I'm sure you like hearing a kind word now and then." There was a trace of bitterness in his voice. He immediately regretted his words.

Sally Ann only smiled. "Come in. I'll tell your father you're here. He's anxious to see you."

She ushered him into a large, open room with beamed ceilings and a huge fireplace. This was obviously the reception area and lounge for guests at the ranch. Heavy wood furniture upholstered in brown leather flanked the fireplace. Framed prints depicting cowboy life hung along one wall and a small collection of antique rifles occupied another. Henry recognized a few of his grandfather's old guns. His eyes were drawn to the massive stone fireplace.

He loved that fireplace and was happy to see it had survived the renovations. The entire wall was natural stone with a wide fireplace in the middle. A rough-hewn mantle perched above the opening. In his mind he saw Christmas stockings hanging there, ones his mother made by hand.

His gaze lingered on the log fire before taking in the rest of the wall. Each stone, with its unique shape and variations of color, seemed familiar. A plaque centered near the ceiling bore the name of the original stonemasons, A.H. Moon &

Sons. The large Frederic Remington print, *A Dash for Timber*, had hung above the mantle since his earliest recollection. The action-packed depiction of cowboys and Indians still captivated him. His mother had given him a book about Remington for Christmas. Her last Christmas.

"Hello there, Henry." His father's voice echoed in the big room.

CHAPTER 3

Sally Ann had yet to reappear, and Henry felt absurdly alone in the huge room. Roderick "Rory" Smith strode to the fireplace, smiled and offered his hand. The smile even seemed sincere. Fearing the past might overtake the present, Henry placed a steadying hand on the mantel.

"Hello yourself." Henry shook the rough hand. His father's grip was still strong though the once-broad shoulders were slightly stooped, the face creased and leathery. Henry reminded himself the man had closed on sixty a number of years ago, and it had been fifteen years since he'd seen the Old Bastard.

He could think of nothing else to say and was grateful when Sally Ann entered the room with a pitcher of tea and ice-filled glasses on a tray. She placed it on the buffet, filled the glasses and passed them around. Ice clinked in the uncomfortable silence as Henry took a sip.

His mother's letters gnawed at his mind. Before she could gather the courage to send them, her father had died. Her father never knew his only daughter sought forgiveness for running away from her family in England to marry the handsome American soldier, Rory Smith. The guilt in those letters haunted Henry. While he was glad he'd read them, Vernon's intent was clear. Reconcile before it was too late.

"This is nice." Henry's words felt artificial, but he continued to force conversation. "You've turned it into a really beautiful place."

"Learned a lot about this house during the renovation."

Muddy Waters

Rory glanced around the room.

Like Sally Ann, his father was dressed casually. The couple wore matching jeans and boots. Henry imagined matching cowboy hats hung in the mudroom.

"There's history here that I knew nothing about," Rory said. "You know this place was once a general store? And before that, a stage station? The fireplace and this room is all that's original."

"Of course, Rory had to be coaxed into renovating." Sally Ann stuffed her hands into her pockets. "He wasn't convinced change was needed. Now I think he likes the place even more."

"Not that I'll let on." Rory grinned at his wife, and she smiled fondly at him. Henry wondered, certainly not for the first time, what intelligent women saw in the Old Bastard.

"The history is really fascinating," Sally Ann said. "The family that originally settled the place had three sons. The oldest died at a very young age. Later, when the parents died, the middle son inherited. It was a general store by then. This son was an adventurous fellow who didn't care for the sedentary life of a storekeeper, so he talked his younger brother into taking care of things."

It was obviously a rehearsed speech reserved for paying customers. Not that Henry minded. History interested him. Out West, he'd discovered a lot of information about abandoned cabins and homesteads, by listening. And considering some of the recent Smith family history, it was easier to talk about anything other than themselves.

"The middle son set out to travel the west, but didn't get far." Sally Ann paused to sip her iced tea. "The North Carolina gold rush was in full swing and mining towns were popping up everywhere. He was attracted to the easy money."

"I didn't realize North Carolina even had a gold rush." Henry finished his tea and declined Sally Ann's offer of a refill.

"It began with a sizable nugget found by a twelve-year old boy in 1799," Rory added, as if on cue. "No one realized it was gold until the early 1800s. That nugget started this country's first gold rush. Of course, things slowed here once gold was found in California."

Sally Ann took up the story again. "This wayward son found various ways to relieve miners of their gold, and did quite well for some time. Then he had the misfortune of killing a lawman during a holdup. He was eventually caught and hanged for his wrongdoing."

Henry raised his eyebrows. "That's quite a detailed history. How'd you discover it?"

Rory stared at Henry a second then abruptly walked into a room marked "office."

Henry stared at the floor, afraid Sally Ann would see the heat of anger he felt rising to his face. He remembered all too well how his father had infuriated him with this habit of ending a conversation by walking away. That old feeling of irrelevance resurfaced. More than anything, Henry was angry with himself for expecting anything different. He considered going into the office after his father, but that would only start an argument.

Just like it always had.

Rory reappeared with an old leather-bound book tied with a faded ribbon. Ashamed over his assumption, Henry fought to concentrate on his father's words.

"It came from this journal." Rory handed him the book. "We found it in the attic. Supposedly a diary kept by the younger son's daughter. That story is in there, and it overlaps the history of the area."

"In fact, we've spoken with the local historical society about its accuracy." Sally Ann gestured toward the diary. "We're planning to donate this journal to them. Not only do they have the expertise to preserve the journal, it will be available to people doing historical research."

Henry opened the journal carefully and read a few passages on the yellowed pages. Observations on the weather. Descriptions of daily activities. On one page, a well-written poem about the changing color of the autumn foliage. He couldn't tell whether it was an original work or that of a famous poet, and wished he had paid more attention in literature classes at college.

"The point of the story is this bandit accumulated quite a lot of stolen money that was never found," Rory said. "Apparently it's buried around here somewhere. Jimmy Lee and a couple of the wranglers have shown some interest in trying to locate it."

"Vernon was interested, too." Sally Ann glanced at her husband. "Though I doubt he'll find time for it now."

"Marriage has a way of doing that." Rory winked at his wife.

"Della is a wonderful person," Sally Ann said. "Vernon is smart not to let her get away. Rory tells me Vernon's not been this serious about a woman for quite some time."

Rory nodded as he gazed at Henry. "You were only a youngster the last time he went crazy over a woman. He planned on marrying that girl."

"Don't believe I remember that." Henry frowned. "What happened?"

"She died," Rory said flatly.

"I see." Henry wanted to crawl under the nearest piece of furniture.

"Vernon took it hard." Rory shook his head. "He'd just proposed. I expect that's why it's taken him so long to get around to asking someone again."

"I'm glad he's finally popped the question," Sally Ann said. "And I'm happy for them both, especially Vernon. At his age, it's time to settle down."

Rory laughed. "Women. Always trying to rescue us poor

men from ourselves."

The front door slammed, followed by Vernon's greeting echoing through the house.

"Speak of the devil." Rory grinned.

"Greetings, y'all!" Vernon joined them in the living room, sporting his usual mischievous grin. He kissed Sally Ann on the cheek then gave Rory a hearty slap on the back.

Vernon waved a hand to decline Sally Ann's offer of iced tea and headed for an antique cabinet near the office door. Opening it, he selected a bottle of whiskey and topped one of the ice-filled glasses with amber liquid. He replaced the bottle and turned to his brother. With a nod that Henry supposed was some sort of toast, Vernon downed half.

"You could at least offer some of my good whiskey to everyone else," Rory said.

"It's your liquor, so you should be the one to make the offer." Vernon smacked his lips and took another drink. "But since you're greedy and have a tendency to keep all the good stuff for yourself, I doubt you will. In the end, I guess you're right. It does fall to me." He cleared his throat theatrically. "Would anyone else care for a drink?"

Henry declined, and wondered what had gotten into his uncle. Vernon was usually quiet and reserved. Probably wedding jitters.

"Boys will be boys." Sally Ann slipped her arm through Henry's and guided him toward the dining room. "How about leaving them to discuss drinking etiquette while we check on supper?"

Over her shoulder she said, "You two can sit yourselves down at the dining room table when you're finished butting heads."

Outside the kitchen, she turned toward Henry. "Now tell me how you've really been."

"Let's just say I've been better."

"I certainly understand how you feel, but I'm glad

you're here. We're both glad you're here. I think you'll find things have changed for the better."

Henry was mystified by this unanticipated optimism where his father was concerned. How much could the Old Bastard have changed? There was quite a lot of room for improvement, and fifteen years wasn't nearly enough time to have accomplished it. He reminded himself he was doing this for Vernon and for Sally Ann. Pushing negative thoughts out of his mind, he followed Sally Ann into the kitchen where a mix of savory aromas greeted him.

"I want to tell you something about your father." Sally Ann leaned against the kitchen counter. "Don't say a word about it to anyone. Especially Vernon."

"Not a word."

"Rory has been meeting with the pastor of our church. He's been working through a lot of things, including his relationship with you. Or lack of."

Counseling. That's what she was saying, wasn't it? Henry leaned against the counter. He couldn't believe his father was capable of talking to anyone about anything remotely personal, let alone his own problems and shortcomings. Maybe it was his recent illness. Vernon said it was treatable, but a cancer diagnosis would have sobering effects.

Henry's lips moved but no words came out. All he could think about was the night he and his father stopped talking. He had been a senior in high school, arrogant and full of himself. Though he couldn't remember what the argument was about, he vividly remembered Rory's fist knocking the breath out of him.

"Henry?"

His mind snapped to the present. "Yes, ma'am?"

Sally Ann handed him a bowl overflowing with mixed salad greens and sent him to the dining room. Henry pushed through the door, stumbling through the fog of the past and into the clear, crisp air of the next room. A large window dominated the dining room, eclipsing rough-hewn log walls and a large, rustic dining table. Henry slid the salad bowl onto the table and found himself slowly crossing the room.

The view of the valley below was striking. Trees covered most of the hillside opposite, their brilliant-green leaves hiding many of the huge rocks that had tumbled down over time to litter the slope and stream below. Sunlight played on the water, giving the valley an enchanted appearance. He reluctantly turned away to help Sally Ann bring in the rest of the feast. Once food appeared, Rory and Vernon quickly found their way to the table.

Henry's gaze was continually attracted to the panorama outside the window throughout the meal. This was beautiful country. Something lost to him during his long absence. The golden glow of the evening light deepened, grew orange then red. It affected him in a way he couldn't define. Could he be homesick? The idea annoyed him. He made a concentrated effort to look away and pay attention to the dinner conversation.

"So far it looks like this will be a good year." Sally Ann passed the salad to her husband. "I've had a half-dozen calls today. We're nearly booked for the season."

"That's a good sign." Vernon rubbed his paunch. "Real good."

"How about the horseback trips?" Rory placed a small amount of salad in his bowl. He glanced at Vernon. "We may need to plan on hiring some extra stable help."

They were between dinner and dessert when a lanky young man shuffled into the big room. He tossed his cowboy hat onto a side table, apologized for being late, and flopped into the empty chair beside Vernon. Henry realized this was Sally Ann's son, Jimmy Lee. He'd been an obnoxious ten-year-old when Henry left for college. After a quick glance at his mother, Jimmy Lee pushed his long hair behind his ears and mumbled a polite greeting to Henry. He began filling his plate as he spoke to Rory and Vernon about cattle and weather.

"The weather is a lot different here than out west," Vernon said. "I suppose there's still snow in Colorado this time of year?"

Henry recognized the attempt to include him in the conversation. "In the higher elevations, yes."

"Beautiful country, I hear." Rory passed a bottle of salad dressing to Jimmy Lee. "I imagine you miss it."

Henry glanced at Vernon, who raised his eyebrows and gave him a slight nod of the head. Henry couldn't remember the last time his father expressed an interest in anything related to his life.

"I can only speak for the western part of the state. It certainly is an extraordinary place. Some even call it magical. I admit I'm missing the openness of that country."

"All these trees around here seem a little suffocating, I expect," Vernon said. "I certainly enjoyed those big, open skies when I was out there."

Henry recalled their fishing trip on the Green River with a grin. One of the few times his trophy trout had topped anything Vernon landed.

"It's deceptive. That wide-open country hides washes, valleys, and canyons. No wonder you've got problems with rustlers." Vernon chuckled. "They've got everywhere to hide."

"Rustlers." Jimmy Lee made a snorting sound. "I've heard some wild tales about you and rustlers. Aubrey Miller makes it sound like you're some sort of gun-packing hellcat."

Acutely aware that the attention of everyone seated at the table focused on him, Henry tried his most innocent smile. "I'm afraid it's like most stories. With every telling, the tale grows a bit more unbelievable."

"So what is it you really do?" Jimmy Lee folded his arms across his chest.

"I'm one of the range managers for an association of ranchers." Henry realized his family knew very little about him. Vernon knew more than anyone, but apparently had not shared much. Henry felt like the stranger he was.

"I thought you were working as a biologist." Rory looked up from his plate. "Killing weeds or something."

"There's quite a lot of that mixed in it."

"Where do the rustlers come into this mix?" Jimmy Lee's eyes narrowed.

"When problems come up," Henry replied. "That's when I take on some range detective duties."

"Problems like rustlers?"

"It doesn't really happen that often." Henry avoided Vernon's gaze, afraid he would see through the lie.

"A range detective. Is that so?" Rory's tone was familiar to Henry. His father's usual prelude to an angry remark. The room felt unnaturally quiet. Henry's fingers tightened on the arms of his chair.

Then Rory rubbed his jaw and smiled. "Does that mean you wear a gun, like an Old West cowboy?"

"Just about everyone carries a gun of some sort." Henry relaxed slightly. "Not six-guns in tied-down holsters, though. It's sometimes fifty miles or more between substantial towns. All sorts of potential dangers out there. Mountain lions, rattlesnakes, sometimes even elk and moose can become dangerous."

Henry paused to drink his iced tea. "I don't carry a gun when I inspect brands at stockyards, if that's what you're asking. Like many people, I keep a rifle in my truck. That's about it." Spreading his hands, he added, "Looks like I'm a bit shy of that 'gun-packing hellcat' label."

"You any good with a gun?" Jimmy Lee's words were

thinly veiled with skepticism.

Vernon answered for Henry. "I taught him, Jimmy Lee. You know he's good if he learned from me."

"There's some natural ability needed." Jimmy Lee eyed Henry. "Like riding a horse. Anyone can sit a saddle, but not everyone can ride."

The telephone rang and Jimmy Lee jumped to his feet. He darted into the kitchen, only to reappear a few seconds later, waving the cordless telephone in his hand. "It's for you, Henry."

Surprised, Henry took the phone and stepped into the kitchen.

"How's supper?" A familiar voice asked. "You about ready to gnaw your arm off to escape?"

"Very funny, Aubrey. What's going on?"

"I really hate to drag you away." Aubrey didn't sound very apologetic in Henry's estimation. "There's something I really need to show you. Tonight, if possible."

CHAPTER 4

Henry leaned against the trunk of a sprawling oak tree and waited, his fingers lightly drumming the smooth wooden grip of the pistol at his side. He peered through low, curving branches at the dark sky. A sliver of moon had appeared on the horizon. He picked out a few constellations. The cacophony of insects was nearly deafening, and he longed for the relative silence of the canyon country.

While apprehensive about the nature of the summons, he was grateful for an excuse to end the uncomfortable evening. Nothing had been resolved with his father, but the night wasn't a total loss. They hadn't argued.

Finally hearing the rhythmic sound of hoof beats, Henry spotted a shadowy figure on horseback move toward the old corral and pause near the rickety fence under the oak. A familiar whistle reached his ears. It was a pathetic attempt at imitating the call of a canyon wren. Henry stifled a laugh.

The rider leaned from his saddle to peer into the darkness beneath the tree. Henry appeared beside him. "Looking for someone?"

Aubrey cursed. "I wish you wouldn't do that. You scared the bejeezus out of me."

"Pay a little more attention to your horse. She knew I was here."

"How long you been here?" Aubrey dismounted.

"Long enough." Henry ran a hand down the horse's

neck and shoulder. "Nice horse. Where'd you get her?"

"Came by her honest." Aubrey seemed indignant. "Just to ease your mind, I'll have you know my cousins keep some horses in a barn near that lake below. The horses are a little rough, so they're happy enough to have me exercise them. They never seem to have the time, except for maybe Odessa and that boyfriend of hers. Anyway, sorry to get you out here at this hour, but glad you came. And I see you came loaded for bear." Aubrey pointed at the pistol.

"Told you I like to be prepared," Henry said. "What's on your mind?"

"Maybe I'm not be as sharp as you, but I do notice things." Aubrey fidgeted with the reins. "I think some cattle have been rustled."

Henry suspected there was more. He waited patiently.

"This sounds crazy I know. Do you remember my cousins, the McLeans?"

"I remember Hugh McLean. We played baseball together in high school."

"He's the oldest. Beaumont and Odessa are the others. When my uncle died last year, they took over their old man's slaughterhouse operation. Not long after that, the rumor I told you about got started. I don't put much stock in rumors, so I didn't really pay it too much mind. Until tonight."

"What happened tonight?"

"For a couple of months now, I've seen eight head of Bar T cattle out here. A few weeks ago I noticed someone's been feeding them grain. Tonight, I count six."

"You sure they didn't wander off? There's a lot of Bar T land around here."

Aubrey shook his head. "I took a good look around. Ain't seen hide nor hair of 'em. Can't help but think about my cousins having a butcher shop where they can sell the meat. Beau is like his father – always into making a fast buck. Without going into much detail, let's just say I wouldn't put it past him. I really hope there ain't nothing to it. I have to say I'm worried, though. Once my sordid past is known, I figure to be the subject of a lot of finger pointing."

"Maybe it's nothing." Henry tried to sound unconcerned. "Show me where you've seen the cattle."

Aubrey tied the horse to the corral fence and together they walked across a rutted dirt road. A stand of shadowy trees loomed ahead. Aubrey led Henry through them, stopping near an open area at the mouth of a draw. A light breeze teased the lower boughs and Henry caught a faint whiff of cigarette smoke. He scanned the surrounding area but saw nothing. A whip-poor-will called in the night.

"Here's where I first saw 'em." Aubrey's voice was almost a whisper. "Over there you can see a couple of buckets for grain. Next to that is a salt block."

Aubrey showed him where the cattle typically bedded down, at the edge of the pines. Henry barely made out their bulky shapes. He wanted to get a little closer, and he waved Aubrey to follow. The thick layer of pine needles littering the ground muffled their footsteps. As they approached the cattle, Henry expected them to jump warily to their feet and run. Instead they were content to chew their cuds, watching the two men with mild interest.

"Nothing like the open range, is it?"

"Not even close." Henry counted six head of cattle. He studied the open area beyond the trees then touched Aubrey's arm to signal he'd seen enough. Aubrey led the way back to the old corral.

"What do you think?" Aubrey checked the cinch before untying the horse.

"I'll look into it tomorrow. Something might stand out in the daylight." Henry regarded the night sky through the low-hanging branches of the big oaks. "What are you going to do if the rumors are true?"

"Haven't thought it through yet. Move on, I guess. I sure won't go to the police, if that's what you're thinking. I'll ask the same of you, Henry. I don't want my cousins getting in trouble with the law because of what I've told you. Besides being kin, I owe them something for taking me on after my stupidity back in Colorado."

Aubrey swung into the saddle and looked down. "Meant to ask how you fared at supper with your folks."

"Better than expected, I suppose. Jimmy Lee tried to start some sort of pissing contest."

"What about?"

"Something to do with gun-packing hellcats. Seems he's heard a few stories." Henry tried not to grin. "You wouldn't have any idea how that happened?"

"No idea at all."

"I'll bet." Henry patted the horse's neck. "Doesn't matter in the long run, I guess. I suspect that was only an opening."

"Piece of work, ain't he?" Aubrey strained to see the time on his watch. "Well, I'd stay and chat, but it's a Friday night in small-town America. I'm off to see a certain young lady."

"Don't go telling her any of your wild tales about me. She might forget all about you."

"Oh, she won't forget about me," Aubrey said. "Just in case, I'll be sure to come up with a story or two that doesn't shed such a glorious light on you."

"Good luck with that."

"There's that one about the old boy with the sheep wagon."

Henry groaned.

Aubrey laughed as he nudged his horse toward the trail. He twisted in the saddle, looked back and touched his hat before urging the horse down the rutted road toward the lake. Henry listened to the fading hoof beats until the sound of chirping insects once again filled the night. The yellow-green glow of fireflies danced above the small meadow beyond the corral.

He thought about the cattle and the real possibility of cattle theft in a place like Parsons Gap. The McLeans had the perfect place to dispose of stolen cattle. It occurred to Henry that Aubrey's cousins may have invited him here with a purpose in mind, to be the scapegoat. He already had a history of cattle theft, and his cousins knew it. Aubrey would never see it coming. He tended to think the best of people, even people like Conner. Henry guessed blood relatives would rank even higher on Aubrey's trustworthiness scale.

A slight breeze stirred the boughs of the oak. Henry caught another whiff of cigarette smoke. Noting the wind direction, he climbed the trail toward the road, certain he was being watched. He started the pickup's engine and drove toward the highway. Past the bend, he turned onto the dirt road toward the Bar T. Here he stopped the pickup, switched off the headlights and engine, and slipped out of the vehicle.

He waited until his eyes had adjusted to the darkness before proceeding quietly ahead. The mouth of the rutted lane from the lake came into view. He kept to the shadows as he descended. Loose rock slowed his progress and it took him several minutes to cautiously pick his way down the slope. Reaching the bottom, he crouched near a clump of brush. He made a thorough visual examination of the area. Once satisfied, he followed a cow path toward the spongy ground under the pines.

Cigarette smoke mingled with the scent of pine. Henry stopped and searched the darkness. Ahead and to his right, the orange tip of the cigarette glowed as it moved in a sweeping arc. He slipped silently through the trees, footsteps muffled by the soft pine duff. As he moved he kept an eye on the dancing ember. He froze when it bounced to the ground, listening to the crunching of pine needles as it was stamped out.

Henry was as patient as he was soundless. Eventually he reached a pine tree less than ten feet from his quarry. The cattle had bedded down less than twenty yards away, and Henry doubted the man's presence was a coincidence. The dark figure reached into a shirt pocket with a rustle of clothing. A jingle of change was followed by the rapid clicking of a lighter. A yellow flame illuminated a man's face as he lit another cigarette.

A loud beeping pierced the relative quiet.

The man swore as he unclipped a cell phone from his belt. It beeped again as he keyed the push-to-talk feature. "About time you called back," he growled.

"I was indisposed," the male voice replied.

The man cackled. "Not that redhead again, I hope."

"What's up besides your fascination with these new walkie-talkie phones?" The voice on the other end sounded annoyed. "Don't you know sound carries?"

"Ain't anyone around." The man exhaled smoke before he spoke into the phone. "Look, those cows are still out here, but our dear cousin has been here with that range detective friend of his."

"What for?"

"I don't know, maybe they're a couple." He took a draw on the cigarette. "They met at that old corral then walked over by the cattle."

"They see you?"

"Not possible." The man paused for another puff on the cigarette. "I know my way around the woods."

"Forget what we planned. Don't want to take any chances. And for God's sake, don't give Aubrey anything to get suspicious about."

"Don't know why you're so worried about Aubrey. He

understands family. You're the one always saying that garbage about blood being thicker than water."

"It ain't him I'm worried about. And it ain't garbage. You'd best not forget that. He might say something to that cowboy without thinking. That's someone we sure don't want to get suspicious."

"I can fix that. It's been a while since I whipped a cowboy's ass."

"Forget it. We can afford to lie low for a few days. He's only in town for a wedding."

The man closed the phone and jammed it back onto his belt. Taking a final draw on the half-smoked cigarette, he flipped the butt onto the ground. He stepped forward to crush it under his boot as he walked toward the road, passing within two feet of Henry.

CHAPTER 5

Heavy thumping roused Henry from a deep sleep. He glanced around the unfamiliar room, getting his bearings. The digital clock glowed 5:47. Vernon's cabin was still dark. His uncle's orange cat, which had been curled against his leg, bounded across his chest with what felt like five-pound weights on each of his paws. Henry got out of bed and followed the source of the loud banging to the front door. Looking out the window, he saw Vernon standing in the porch light. Henry swung the door open.

"You ain't ready?" Vernon grumbled.

"You ain't supposed to be here for another hour," Henry mocked. Behind Vernon, faint pink light was beginning to show in the eastern sky.

"It's never too early to fish. Besides, I couldn't sleep."

"Wedding jitters?" Henry asked.

Vernon grunted an affirmation as he shouldered his way into the cabin.

Henry looked at his uncle curiously. "Why were you knocking on your own door?"

"Last night after you left, Jimmy Lee told us a couple of the stories he'd heard about you and your antics in Colorado. I figured it would be safer to knock."

Henry wasn't sure if he was joking or not. "I'm betting whatever you heard was an over-exaggeration. I might have to kill Aubrey. Seems to be the only way to shut him up."

Vernon hooked his thumbs in his waistband and drummed his fingers against his belt. "I've got breakfast in the truck. All you need to do is get dressed and we'll go. I'll be outside."

Henry stared at the retreating back. These upcoming nuptials had obviously gotten under Vernon's skin. A laid-back morning of fishing might be the thing to ease some of his stress. The sooner they got out there, the better. Henry dressed quickly, brushed his teeth then grabbed his hat, boots and a pair of socks on the way out the door. Vernon was waiting in his pickup with the passenger door open.

"Where we going?"

"You'll see." Vernon handed him a homemade ham, egg and cheese biscuit.

"Did you make these?" Henry asked.

Vernon passed him a container of orange juice. "Della makes them for me all the time. She's really great, Henry."

Henry barely had time to slip on his boots before Vernon pulled to a stop in a small dirt lot. He grinned at Henry. "I figured an easy day at the lake would be best for starters. Kind of break you in slow."

Henry slid out of the truck. The quiet surface of the lake reflected the sun's orange glow. Wispy fingers rising from the water joined the thin layer of mist floating a few feet above it. He remembered the lake well. The trees were taller now, but the old trails skirting the shoreline were familiar. He'd fished here many times as a boy. A popular swimming hole was on the other side. There'd been many summers filled with inner-tubes and girls in cut-off jeans and bikini tops. He had spent some time with his high school sweetheart at this lake, too. Only they didn't do much fishing.

"I won't need any breaking in."

Vernon reached into the truck bed and handed Henry a spinning reel and a small tackle box. "Look here. Jimmy Lee's been talking a lot about how he's top dog at the Bar T. He's defending his territory. At the same time, your visit is important to Sally Ann and especially to Rory. Not that you'll ever hear him say it. What I'm trying to say is this. Tangling with Jimmy Lee won't sit well."

"I didn't figure it would."

"I know Jimmy Lee, and he'll push you. It's probably only a matter of time before he pushes you too far." A grin spread across Vernon's face. "Of course, part of me wants to see that fight. I'd have to put my money on you."

"You might lose. Aubrey's stories are earning me an undeserved reputation."

Vernon shook his head. "I doubt that."

"Speaking of stories. Have you heard anything peculiar about the McLeans?"

"Peculiar? Like what?"

"Just wondering if something I've heard about their business practices might have some basis in fact," Henry said. "Like cattle theft."

"You mean rustling? Here?" Vernon scratched his head. "Is that why you're wearing a pistol? You're on the job?"

The pistol had been on the bedside table after meeting with Aubrey last night. This morning when dressing, he'd automatically slipped the holster onto his belt. Like pulling on a pair of boots, it had been part of his daily routine for years.

"Habit, I guess." Henry took the gun and holster off and stashed it under the passenger seat. "I met Aubrey at that old corral by the ridge road last night. He wanted to show me something."

"So that's where you rushed off to."

"This stays between us, Vernon." Henry told him about Aubrey's past. "I don't want anything getting back to his cousins, or the police. He's been riding the McLean's horses up by that old corral. Aubrey said he'd seen some cattle there, Bar T cattle, and now he thinks a few are missing. For Aubrey's sake, I'd hate to see him get out of the frying pan

39

and into the fire."

"I see what you mean," Vernon said.

"It gets worse. I saw someone else. I suspect it was one of the McLean boys."

"Does Aubrey know?"

Henry shook his head. "I'm not sure I'll tell him."

"What other options you got?"

Henry shrugged.

Vernon ambled toward the shore. Henry followed, looking out over the lake. Sunshine had transformed the layer of floating mist to gold. The deep green water provided a stunning contrast to the sun's creation. Nature's alchemist.

"You've changed a lot over the years." Vernon spoke over his shoulder as he checked the drag on his fishing reel. "You've got a confidence about you I've never noticed before. That college education made you more sophisticated, maybe, but something else has changed. Grown into a good man, I guess. The west must be good for you."

"I don't think it's got anything to do with where I live. Confidence is something that comes with age. Like wisdom." Henry put on a mischievous smile. "Which means you ought to have a heck of a lot more confidence and wisdom than me."

Vernon chuckled. "Boy, have I missed you! I really wish you'd come back here to stay."

"I hate to admit it, but being here has made me more than a little homesick."

Henry sensed rather than saw Vernon's hopeful expression. That wasn't something he was ready to discuss. Besides, his attention was drawn to a rocky outcropping with overhanging branches and an inviting pool of water beneath. A moss-covered stump stuck out of the lake about four feet from the bank. It leaned away from shore at an angle that exposed a tangle of roots above and below the surface.

"Why hasn't Rory told me about his cancer?" Henry chose a spinner from the tackle box.

Vernon glanced up from his reel. "He will. In his own time."

Henry cast, dropping the line accurately into the calm water beyond the overhanging branch. He trolled between the branch and the stump. Almost immediately his line went taught. Setting the hook, he grinned at Vernon, who was digging in the tackle box.

"Have you got my yellow spinner?" Vernon asked. "The one with black spots?"

"I've got a fish," Henry replied. "And you'd better hurry and get your line in the water if you're going to keep up."

He landed the smallmouth bass then released it, feeling relaxed for the first time since arriving in Parsons Gap. Fishing had always been good therapy. He cast again, mesmerized by the concentric waves on the smooth surface of the lake until he felt the little rush of anticipation when a fish struck. Aside from the occasional splash of a fish fighting the line, the plunk of a lure into the water was the only sound in the still morning.

They fished until the heat of the late-morning sun persuaded the fish to seek cooler, deeper water. For a few moments Henry stood on the bank, staring out at the lake. He savored the fresh air in his lungs and the gentle sound of water lapping against the shore. Reluctantly he turned and walked toward Vernon, who was fishing a few yards from the parking lot. Vernon began to reel in his line as Henry approached.

Vernon checked his watch and swore. "I promised Della I'd help with some of the wedding errands and I'm about to be late. Good thing we didn't keep any fish. You'd have been stuck cleaning them all."

"That was probably your plan all along." Henry placed his rod in the back of the truck. "If we'd kept them, everyone would know who'd caught the biggest fish."

"Hey, without evidence your claims are unsubstantiated."

Henry rolled his eyes and climbed into the truck.

Vernon dropped him off at the cabin and left in a cloud of dust. Henry checked the kitchen clock. It wasn't quite noon. He'd promised Aubrey he would check the cattle in the daylight, so he packed a couple of a peanut butter and jelly sandwiches and drove to Parsons Hollow Road. He parked the pickup in a pullout, wishing he'd remembered to grab the pistol from Vernon's truck. Grabbing binoculars and sandwiches, he settled among the rocks near the cattle. He scanned the area while he ate, watching until he was sure no one was around.

He couldn't account for all the cattle from this vantage point. Finding the trail he'd used the night before, he descended toward the oak. The tree was even more massive in daylight. He glanced up at the sprawling limbs as he approached, anticipating the coolness in their shade.

Henry rounded the last cluster of boulders and scanned the corral. A spot of unnatural color caught his eye. Bright-blue cloth poked from behind an overturned watering trough near the middle of the corral. Henry walked along the fence until he could see what was there.

The cloth was part of a blue-checked shirt. A man was lying face down in the dust, a dark splotch on the back of his head. Beside him was a cowboy hat.

Aubrey Miller's hat.

CHAPTER 6

Henry jumped a fence rail and sprinted the final five yards to the trough. He fell to his knees and reached out, seeking a carotid pulse. The skin was cold to his touch, the muscles stiff. He slowly withdrew his fingers, feeling his stomach starting to churn. So far he had avoided looking at the face. Swallowing the lump in his throat, he examined the wound.

The hair was matted with blood and specks of bone. The blow to the head had obviously taken the man's life. He doubted the man knew what hit him. Henry forced himself to look at the face, though he already knew what he'd see. The curly hair spilling over the collar was easily recognizable.

It was Aubrey all right.

Several things whirled through Henry's mind as he knelt beside Aubrey. Disbelief, helplessness, pain, grief, anger. Each one circled around him, disappearing and reappearing again and again until he found amongst them a thread of reason. Grabbing at it, he pulled himself out of the eddy of emotions. He clenched his jaw and closed his heart to everything but the anger.

It left him cold inside. The anger helped to distance himself from the pain and loss he knew would eventually catch up with him. His mind focused. He had a purpose. He stared at the lifeless shell that had been his friend and promised to find the person responsible.

The answer had to be here. All he had to do was look.

Muddy Waters

The killer had to leave a trail, and reading tracks was something he knew how to do. He got to his feet and studied the ground around the body. Henry disliked the word body, but he had to stay objective. Blood had seeped into the soil in two separate areas. One under the head, another smaller spot several inches away. The body had been moved. Tracks here were scuffed and unclear, but obviously the body was rolled over to face down. Why?

The wound looked linear. He saw no dirt, bark, or splintered wood in the wound. Something heavy, likely metal, had been used. Henry scanned the corral. Nothing fitting that description was in sight. Maybe he'd find something once he tracked the killer.

Henry catalogued the surrounding area in his memory. Dried clumps of grass edged the corral. A few patches where the soil coloration varied slightly near the center. This was curious. He'd have to check that later. On the south side of the corral the split-wood rails hung in various states of disrepair. A loose stack of boards littered the ground near a dilapidated loading chute. He walked over and examined them. They didn't appear disturbed.

Beyond the loading chute, a small meadow was bordered by a clump of trees. The trees marked a bend in the rutted dirt road. Running parallel to the dirt road was a well-used horse trail. The north side of the corral was close to a hillside littered with fallen rocks. Between the fence and the rocks, a narrow game trail led into a stand of mixed hardwoods where rippling sunlight indicated water, likely a creek.

Turning, Henry returned to focus on the area around the body. Two sets of tracks, other than Aubrey's, were clear. One set had been made after the first, though both looked to be several hours old. He backtracked, noting the depth of the track as well as the long stride and large shoe size. These tracks led back toward the oak tree, where

Henry had met Aubrey last night. They originated from the other side of the dirt road, where he and Aubrey had seen the cattle. Henry had a good idea who the man might be.

Why had Aubrey returned to the corral? Had he seen something, or had his cousin lured him back? Was it about the missing cattle? An argument that got out of hand? What about the girl Aubrey had intended to meet? Could they have fought? He scratched his head and stared thoughtfully at the corral. He decided to concentrate on the first set of tracks.

These tracks were made by hiking boots. Henry backtracked along the edge of the corral and into the narrow space between rocks and wooden rails. Numerous animals had used the trail since, making it difficult to find a clear track. The trail ahead was confined, and unless a person climbed the fence or the steep hillside, the only way out was across the creek. Henry went directly to the creek and scanned the bank. He spotted a partial footprint in the muck, then a faint scuff on a moss-covered rock across the creek.

There was little evidence through an area of flat rock until he came to a patch of grass. Here he found a clear boot track. He pulled a small notebook out of his pocket to make a quick sketch and scribble a few notes. The trail led up a steep slope toward the road, ending at a pull-off. Tire tracks were obvious in the soft soil. After examining the imprints of the tires, Henry made another sketch. He glanced at the sun, realizing a couple of hours had passed. Making a few more notes on his general observations, he retraced his steps toward the corral.

Henry crossed downstream from the tracks and wound his way through the trees. Emerging from the trees, he looked toward the corral and stopped. The police were milling around the corral. The body had been discovered, it was now impossible to study tracks. Henry stepped back, hoping to remain undetected in the deep shade of the pine trees. He weighed the advantages of making his presence known versus fading quietly into the woods.

A blue jay squawked. Slow footsteps crunched loose rock on the ledge above him and Henry's hand moved involuntarily to where his pistol should have been. A man stood near the edge of the rocks, his back to Henry, attention on the activity in the corral. The man wasn't wearing a uniform, but a holstered automatic pistol rested on his right hip. Henry could hear him discussing the arrival of the coroner over a cell phone. As Henry decided the woods were the better option, the man turned and stared right at him.

Henry immediately recognized Louis Hannahan. Years ago, he'd been a sheriff's deputy in a drab uniform. Now he was the picture of authority and professionalism in crisp khakis, white shirt and tie. A badge was attached to his belt in a leather holder. Apparently he'd moved up a considerable number of rungs on the promotion ladder.

"Hello, Henry." Hannahan flipped his phone shut with one hand. "What's been keeping you so busy in those woods?"

CHAPTER 7

Detective Louis Hannahan had watched the man in the woods for several minutes before realizing it was Henry Smith. At first he'd thought it was the elder Smith. The two men shared the same wiry build, as well as several mannerisms. Not deliberately, he was certain. Then Louis caught a glimpse of a face too young to be Rory. He recalled hearing Henry was in town for the wedding.

Henry had been scribbling in a pocket-sized notebook as he studied the banks of the creek. Louis watched, realizing that Henry was tracking something. Or someone. He had decided to call a deputy to intercept when Henry turned to walk back toward the corral. Louis lowered the binoculars and waited. He expected to startle Henry from above, but he had to answer that cell phone call. Now he hoped to make the best of it.

"Hello, Mr. Hannahan," Henry answered in the same soft-spoken voice Louis remembered.

"Mind telling me what you're doing out here?" His own initial examination of the area revealed the tracks of four people, including the victim. One set appeared much fresher than the others. Henry's no doubt.

Henry shrugged. "That old corral is on Bar T land. I haven't been home in a long time, so I was having a look around."

Hannahan studied him while he waited to see if Henry would say anything else. Henry didn't seem nervous or apprehensive. If he was the killer, he was certainly playing

47

it cool.

"I'm especially interested in what you did at the corral. When you arrived."

"When I arrived," Henry repeated the words slowly. His gaze didn't leave Hannahan's face. "I saw a man lying in the corral and I checked to see if he might still be alive."

"You recognized him?"

Henry nodded.

Louis watched for any sort of reaction. Not even a twitch. "How were things between you and Miller?"

"I didn't kill him, if that's what you're asking."

"I'm not asking."

Henry took a deep breath. "We've remained good friends."

Louis nodded. "What else?"

"I found some tracks. The rest, I'm sure, you know."

"I might know what you were doing," Louis said. "I don't know what you found."

Henry rubbed his jaw. "How about I show you."

"All right. Meet me at the corral, down by the big oak tree."

Louis walked along the road, recalling what he knew about Henry. He had known the Smith family since his first year as a deputy sheriff. Parsons Gap had been just a small community then, before the influx of tourists and seasonal residents. The two families had attended the same church. The wives had belonged to the local art league. Louis had been the one sent to break the news when Victoria, Rory's first wife and Henry's mother, had been killed in an automobile accident.

Common history had not ended there. Their children had grown up together. Aubrey Miller had been present, too. In fact, Aubrey, Henry, and his oldest daughter had been inseparable. They went to all the sporting events the boys competed in during high school. Then Carlie and

Henry had begun dating. His wife had always imagined the two of them would end up getting married. The fact that they were young didn't really bother Louis because he'd always liked Henry. He had been a good kid, always polite and respectful.

Now Louis wondered what sort of man Henry Smith had become.

Henry was waiting for him under the oak tree, leaning against a fence post outside the police tape boundary. Deputy Bobby Monroe hovered behind him, his actions revealing his annoyance with a civilian so close to the crime scene. Henry wasn't showing any interest in the investigation going on behind him. Louis sensed something else was on his mind, something that smoldered inside him.

"What are you doing with yourself these days?" Louis took in Henry's cowboy hat, faded Levi's and cowboy boots. The low-heeled boots caught his attention. He had a hunch about one of those older sets of tracks.

"I work as a range manager for an association of cattle ranchers in Colorado and Utah." Henry rubbed the back of his neck as if it ached.

"Is that some sort of a cattle herding job?"

"It's more like a range detective. Using the word manager makes it easier for the public to swallow. The ranchers don't care what the title is as long as the job gets done."

"So you're a law enforcement officer, also trained in tracking?"

Henry nodded. "Graduated from the state police academy, and received a special commission."

"Interesting." Louis pointed at the crime scene. "What have you found?"

"Three people were here last night. Obviously, one was Aubrey Miller." He was willing enough to share his findings. "One came from those pines. The other from the west."

"And Aubrey? Where did he come from?"

"Up the lane from that small lake, as near as I can tell. I hadn't gotten that far."

Louis studied Henry for a moment. "Could either of the other two be the killer?"

Henry shrugged. "I'll need a little more information. I take it he was killed here, not somewhere else? What's the approximate time of death?"

Given the apparent history between Henry and Aubrey, Louis was surprised at Henry's detachment. He glanced at Deputy Monroe, giving him a slight nod to proceed.

"The coroner's initial findings are that he was killed here." Monroe read from his notepad in a monotone voice. "One blow to the head. Death was pretty much instantaneous. The body was moved, rolled over. Time of death is estimated sometime between ten and midnight."

Louis caught a slight reaction from Henry when Monroe gave the time of death. He thanked Monroe and turned to Henry.

"Let's take a look at what you've found."

Henry walked toward the corral with Louis and Monroe flanking him. He waved a hand toward the pine trees as they walked. In simple terms, he explained the trail coming from the pines was made a little later than the other set. He called them Trail One and Trail Two, and pointed to areas where Trail Two stepped on Trail One.

"There's another set," Louis said. "I saw tracks under the oak tree when I arrived here. We'll call those Trail Three. They led toward those pines, right beside Miller's tracks."

"Are they the same as the first ones?" Monroe asked. "I mean Trail One."

"I don't think so." Louis' gaze rested on Henry. "Of course, I'm not much of a hand at tracking. Maybe you could have a look at them for us."

"I can, but it's not necessary," Henry said. "They're mine."

Louis suppressed a self-satisfied smile. He'd been right about those boots. "Go on."

"Aubrey called me last night. Said he wanted to show me something. I met him here." Henry paused, as if gathering his thoughts. "He was worried about possible cattle theft."

"Theft of cattle?" Monroe frowned. "Why you and not the police?"

"It's what I do for a living."

"What time was this?" Louis asked.

"Nine thirty or so," Henry said. "He rode a horse up that lane and met me here. We had a look at the cattle, then he left. Said he had a date."

"What did you do then?"

"Drove to Uncle Vernon's cabin and went to bed."

"Was Vernon home?"

"No."

Henry's lack of an alibi didn't escape him. "How about these other tracks?"

"There's a lot of information here." Henry walked a short distance beside the tracks before he stopped. He fished a pair of glasses from his shirt pocket and slipped them on. "From the depth of the imprint, I'd say this guy weighed over 200 pounds."

"How can you tell just by looking?" Louis asked.

Henry stood and made a print next to the track he'd identified. "I weigh about 150, okay? Look at my print compared to this one. See the difference in the depth?"

"I think so," Louis said.

"Deeper means he weighs more."

"That's an obvious conclusion isn't it?" Monroe asked.

"Sure it is," Henry agreed. "After a while, you get to where you can judge the weight without comparisons. This guy has a long stride, so he's got long legs. That probably means he's tall. He strikes the heel on the outside first when he walks and his straddle is a little wide. Could be he's a bit bow-legged. The cowboy boots he wore look pretty new. There's a definable tread and a visible identifying mark here on the heel." Henry pointed at the crest surrounding the letters N.

Louis saw it clearly. "Nocona."

"Doesn't take you long to pick up on things." Henry chuckled. "Reading sign already."

Monroe snorted and rolled his eyes. Louis threw the deputy a stern glance. He found himself an eager student now, studying every crushed blade of grass, dislodged pebble, and broken twig that Henry showed him. They backtracked slowly, for nearly a quarter of a mile, until Henry found a place behind a stand of young pines littered with cigarette butts. Through the trees, Louis could see the crime scene. The coroner was removing the body and it was obvious Henry was making an effort to not notice.

"Can you place anyone here at a specific time?" The question was meant more as a distraction than something Louis expected Henry to know.

"Most likely before Aubrey was killed." Henry briefly explained age determination of tracks. "From the looks of things, this guy was probably here a long time. Impatient fellow, too. Lots of moving and shuffling around here. Heavy smoker." Henry indicated several cigarette butts littering the area. "A Marlboro man."

"How can you be so sure it's a man?" Monroe asked.

"Lots of things. Shoe size, weight. And the fact he urinated on this tree from over here." He indicated a set of tracks and a residue on a small oak tree, about two feet above the ground. "Hit the tree here. Most women can't do that."

"You saying one could?"

"I wouldn't want to meet her," Henry said.

"Looks like we need to get the crime scene people over here." Louis caught Monroe's attention and spread the thumb and little finger of his right hand, putting it near his ear like a telephone. Monroe nodded, wandered a few feet away and used his cell phone. Louis noticed another set of tracks. "How about these?"

Henry examined the tracks. "They look to be a day or so older, but very similar. Less definition, but it looks like this one may have been here more than once. See the partial Nocona imprint? That's a good observation, Louis." He waved a hand at the rough road leading down the slope. "How far to the lake?"

"Maybe half a mile or so. You can almost see the edge of the lake from here."

"Then I doubt he walked up from below. Those boots he wore weren't meant for hiking." Henry glanced around. "I'd guess there was a vehicle on the road."

As they talked, they returned to the oak. Louis had been examining the ground as they walked. Something bothered him about those tracks. Until the trail reached the pine needles,

he'd clearly seen the tracks made by Henry and Aubrey going to and from the cattle. In a few places, the Nocona tracks overlapped those made by Aubrey and Henry near the cattle.

"The man by the cattle, your Marlboro smoker. From the age of the tracks, do you think he may have been around when you met Aubrey?"

Henry turned to Louis, his face expressionless. He took off his hat and ran his fingers through his hair. "It's possible."

"Let's go take a look at those cows while we're here."

Louis pondered those tracks as they walked across the road and toward the pines. They certainly looked more recent, based on what he'd learned. If this cigarette smoker had been around during the same time frame, smoking and pacing, Henry would have known it. Louis had been observing Henry in action and figured he was too sharp to miss something like that. Which meant Henry wasn't telling him everything.

The path they followed descended slightly, ending in an open area littered with beer cans and fast-food containers. Most of the cows had stopped grazing to stare at them.

Henry pointed ahead, toward the edge of the clearing. "There's a salt block and a few places where grain has been left. I haven't had a chance to ask anyone at the ranch about it."

"Let me know if anyone at the Bar T is responsible." Louis looked around. "Now, where are we with Trail Two?"

Henry pointed to the rocks between the road and the corral. Louis and Monroe followed as Henry led them along the edge of the corral in the narrow space between rocks and wooden rails.

"All those recent animal tracks made finding a clear track difficult."

Louis glanced at the narrow path. Unless a person climbed the rickety fence or the rocks, the only way out was near the creek. The creek was where Louis had first observed Henry. Had he reached the same conclusion? Henry led them to the creek's edge, where he pointed out a partial footprint in the muck. He walked downstream a few paces before crossing the creek. On the opposite bank, he showed them another partial track. They walked uphill and across a large area covered with rocks. Henry paused to indicate a patch of grass with a single boot track.

"How did you follow the trail across the rocks?" Louis examined the smooth rock but saw nothing to hint at a trail.

"Small rocks can be overturned or unsettled from their original place. If the person or animal steps in soft soil before crossing rocks, there's typically a residue from the shoes or paws on the rocks. Sometimes there's a scrape from a claw or shoe. Sometimes, depending on the time of day or occurrence of recent rainfall or dew, the moisture or dust naturally covering the rock is disturbed. Any man or animal that moves across the ground is going to leave evidence. If you know what to look for, you'll find it."

Louis smiled. He was beginning to appreciate the amount and quality of information a good tracker could reveal.

They followed Henry up a short, steep slope which brought them out of the trees near the road. They stopped in a pull-off, where he pointed out an obvious tire track in the soft soil. Louis told Monroe to request the crime scene team.

"This has all been very enlightening, Henry. I do have one more question." Louis had more than one question in mind, but he was only willing to share one at present. "What are the chances this Marlboro guy saw anything?"

Henry shoved his hands in his pockets. "Tracks can't tell you everything."

CHAPTER 8

Henry returned to the large oak while Louis and Monroe met with a couple of deputies near the corral. The cool shade was welcoming, but he was anxious to get away from the murder scene as quickly as possible. Succumbing to the grief was his biggest fear right now. That brain-numbing condition tended to freeze one's analytical thoughts, and the only antidote he knew was to keep his mind busy. Agreeing to track for the police had given him insight. He needed to mull over his notes and piece some details together.

He felt relieved when Louis approached.

"Why didn't you call the police when you found the body?" Louis asked

Henry knew the question was coming but still wasn't ready for it. "I felt it was important to follow the trail while it was relatively fresh. Where I work, well, I guess you could say it was habit."

Monroe joined them. "Or maybe you took time to hide the murder weapon."

The realization he was a suspect hit him like a bucket of icy water. Henry bit back his clichéd declarations of innocence. Louis had played him. Maybe to get information from his tracking, or maybe as a test of his honesty. No doubt Louis knew whose footprints were by the oak long before Henry had claimed them.

"Is that your beat-up truck parked on the road?" Monroe asked.

"It's my truck."

Henry bristled at the deputy's description of his cherished 1965 Chevy. Maybe Monroe would eventually grow tired of baiting him if ignored. Besides, some cooperation now would be the path of least resistance. Henry wouldn't be able to find Aubrey's killer if he was in jail.

"Odd place to park, isn't it?" Monroe either smiled or smirked, Henry wasn't sure.

Louis left them when his cell phone rang.

"The crime scene team is going to take a look at it," Monroe said. "Detective Hannahan will drive you to the Bar T Ranch. I'm sure he'll want to talk with you again."

"I've answered a lot of questions already."

"Murder investigations are a lot different than chasing stolen sheep."

Henry's tolerance was wearing thin. He smiled, which seemed to irritate Monroe more than any caustic remark. He found mild satisfaction in that as he watched Louis return.

"Check his background." Louis was speaking into his cell phone. "I want to know everything about the incident. I've got a feeling it's connected."

Henry leaned against the oak as he listened, like he did while waiting for Aubrey last night. He recalled the sound of hoof beats and frowned. He'd seen no horse tracks at the murder scene, or near the body. What happened to the horse? Had Aubrey put the horse up, then returned? Had his cousin taken the horse, or had someone else?

"What did you say he was arrested for?" Louis glanced at Henry, his eyebrows raised. "Get me a copy of that report... Right... Thanks."

Louis closed the phone and turned to Henry. "You arrested Aubrey Miller for cattle theft in Colorado, and now there's cattle theft here."

"Aubrey wasn't involved in rustling here."

"What makes you so sure?"

If Aubrey felt he owed his cousins enough to keep the police out of it, Henry would honor that request. He couldn't share what he'd overheard last night.

"A hunch." Henry blurted the first thing that came to mind. It sounded idiotic, so he added, "Among other things."

Monroe didn't miss the opportunity. "A hunch Miller had figured out how to make a few extra dollars by dusting off his old habits?"

Louis nodded in agreement. "He had the perfect job to do it."

"That's true enough," Henry said. "But it doesn't fit. He'd need something to haul the cattle. And a truck to pull it. Besides, Aubrey wasn't stupid. He wouldn't have asked me to meet him out here to look into missing cattle if he was guilty. He knew I'd find the truth."

"The truth that he had a partner, and the partner took the truck and trailer." Monroe produced another self-satisfied smile.

"I agree with Monroe," Louis said. "Someone else could be involved. Maybe that person killed him because Miller tried to back out."

"I don't agree." Henry waved toward the rutted lane. "There aren't vehicle tracks to support that. No cattle tracks going up the slope to the road. Besides, Aubrey wouldn't have considered it. He was scared straight after his brush with the law in Colorado."

Monroe let out an obnoxious guffaw. "Yeah, scared straight. That happens with criminals all the time."

Louis was interrupted by another call on his cell phone. It was brief. After hanging up, he sent Monroe on an errand to the crime scene team. Once he was gone, Louis wheeled, his anger emphasized by his finger nearly poking Henry's chest. "You've been holding out. I don't like that. At all. Now tell me about Miller's arrest."

Henry slipped his hands into his pockets. "I guess you could say he was caught red-handed."

"By you."

"By me."

"Why is it he didn't get any jail time? I would think that sort of theft is pretty serious business out west. We're talking livelihoods, aren't we?"

"There's more to the story than what is in the report." Henry related a very condensed version of the incident. A death at his hands was not something he wanted known, especially if his family might hear about it. "Aubrey Miller saved my life."

Louis glared at Henry. "I've heard rumors about cattle theft around town. So maybe Miller wasn't stealing cattle. Maybe his cousins were. How far would they go to keep it quiet? There may not be an honest bone among that bunch. That's why I find it difficult to believe cattle theft isn't at the root of this. Take it away, and who else had motive?"

"Isn't that what investigating is meant to discover?"

Louis narrowed his eyes. "I notice there's no 'we' in what you said, and that's a good thing. I don't want you involved in this."

Henry considered voicing an objection, but thought better of it. What Louis didn't know wouldn't hurt him.

CHAPTER 9

"**A**ubrey Miller dead?" Sally Ann repeated. Eyes wide, her hand moved to the base of her throat. "How can that be?"

Louis knew her question was not directed at Vernon, who had announced the news. It wasn't really addressed to anyone. It was a reaction he'd seen too many times. He stood inside the main door at the Bar T Ranch, feeling like an intruder. Following the delivery of bad news, he was often acutely aware of his position as an outsider witnessing what should have been a private emotional upheaval. He also knew the importance of observing reactions.

Sally Ann stared out a window. After a few minutes, she turned, eyeing Vernon as if suddenly realizing he was in the room. Louis shifted his feet and glanced out the screen door.

"Why are the police here?" She asked.

"Because it seems he was murdered on the ranch." Vernon stood calmly, arms folded over his chest.

"Who was murdered on the ranch?" Rory Smith appeared at the doorway of the living room. Vernon repeated the news.

"Henry knew that boy, didn't he?"

"Of course, Henry knew him," Sally Ann snapped at her husband. She took a deep breath, then spoke in a calmer voice. "They grew up together. They left for college together. Where's your head?"

Vernon frowned at his brother.

"Go ahead and say it, damn it." Rory scowled at Vernon.

"Say what?" Vernon spread his hands.

"Whatever it is you're busting to say."

Anger was obvious in Vernon's voice. "Why don't you talk to Henry? Don't you think fifteen years is long enough for you two stubborn idiots not to have had one meaningful conversation?"

Rory let out a long sigh. "Maybe I don't know what to say."

"How about 'Welcome home, Henry' for a start?"

Louis stepped back as Vernon brushed past, slamming the screen door as he stomped outside. Louis cleared his throat and broke the uncomfortable silence. "I'm sorry to interrupt. I'm afraid I need to ask some questions."

Both Sally Ann and Rory turned to stare at him, as if just realizing he was present.

"Did either of you see or hear anything last night? Lights of a vehicle anywhere near the old corral?" As the crow flies, Louis knew the corral wasn't really all that far from the house. The road above the corral could easily be seen from the side porch.

Sally Ann and Rory glanced at each other briefly before shaking their heads in unison.

"You had folks over for supper last night, I understand. Who all was here?"

Sally Ann slowly recited the names.

"What time did they leave?" Louis knew a heavily used horse trail led from their barn past that corral.

"Oh, Henry left first, at about eight-thirty or nine." Sally Ann paused. A worried look crossed her face. "After a telephone call from Aubrey."

Louis told her he knew about the call and waited for her to continue.

"Jimmy Lee and Vernon left a short time later, around nine thirty or so. Rory and I stayed here, of course."

"Right," Louis said. "There are six head of Bar T cattle near that old corral. Looks like they've been getting grain on occasion. Either of you know anything about them?"

Rory shook his head. "Might ask Jimmy Lee. Sometimes he and the wranglers do a little cattle herding with the more enthusiastic guests. They feed some to keep them close."

"You know where Jimmy Lee went?"

"I thought he went to the barn," Sally Ann offered.

"He drove away right after I told him about Miller's death."

"You don't think he had anything to do with it, do you?" Sally Ann's gaze flitted about the room like a trapped bird.

Louis considered telling a lie, but knew Sally Ann would see right through it. "I'm not counting anyone out at this point."

He thanked them and stepped outside. He saw Vernon and Henry near the barn, leaning on the top rail of the fence. Their backs were to him, and he caught a sporadic murmur of conversation. Vernon occasionally pointed toward the horses feeding at the hay rack, or perhaps beyond, toward the corral where Aubrey Miller's body had been found. Louis believed he'd approached quietly, but Henry spotted him before he'd gotten within ten yards.

"How long will your people need my truck?" Henry jerked his thumb at Vernon. "He's offered the use of one of the ranch vehicles."

"I'm guessing a few days." Louis thought Henry looked more drained than he had earlier. Perhaps the reality of Miller's death was starting to hit him. "I've got a few more questions for you, but I need to speak to Vernon first."

Louis waved Vernon into the house. Henry nodded and said he'd wait outside.

Before going inside, Vernon paused to put a hand on Henry's shoulder. It was a gesture that didn't need words, and it made him realize Vernon was probably more of a father to Henry than Rory would ever be. It saddened him in a way he found difficult to define. Long ago he'd only gotten a glimpse of how rocky things were after the death of Henry's mother. The situation wasn't a topic of discussion, though he knew it wasn't good.

Louis followed Vernon into the great room where he asked Vernon the same questions he'd asked Rory and Sally Ann. He received similar answers.

"What about when you left here last night? See anything on the way home?"

"I went the other way." Vernon gave him a sly grin. "Toward Della's place."

"Right." Louis scribbled in his notebook to check with Della on the time Vernon arrived. "I'll be leaving after I have a word with Henry. If you see Jimmy Lee, please tell him I want to see him. And I don't mean when he finds time."

"Sure thing." Vernon retreated into the living room. Louis paused inside the screen door and glanced outside. Henry was leaning against the house, gazing toward the mountains. Louis looked toward them, too. Three vultures circled slowly above a recently mown hay field, and he wondered if Henry was contemplating the mountains or the vultures.

A vehicle approached, and Louis' gaze shifted to the shiny black Ford pickup pulling to a stop in the driveway. The windows were deeply tinted and across the top of the rear window were the words, "Bad Ass Boys Drive Bad Ass Toys" in red lettering. Jimmy Lee climbed out and ambled toward the house. His steps slowed as he approached the door, where Henry stood. Louis took a step back from the screen door, where he'd be unseen but still able to hear.

Louis saw Jimmy Lee's hand reach for the door.

"Hey," Henry mumbled the southern version of hello. "Vernon's looking for you. He was worried, and he'll be glad you're back."

"Don't go thinking we're gonna play happy family." The hand dropped from the door handle. "That ain't how it is. You been away a long time. Things have changed, so don't be planning on anything permanent here."

"I really haven't given it much thought."

"Maybe we should have us a little talk about it, before you do any thinking." Jimmy Lee slapped a fist into his palm. "I'd like to have a say-so."

"You're joking, right?"

"Joking? I've worked my ass off here for Rory, and now you show up to try and take it all away. I ain't giving it up without a fight."

"What makes you think I want anything from the Old Bastard?"

"You gonna try and tell me different?" Jimmy Lee was practically snarling.

Henry's voice was subdued. "I don't believe I've told you anything yet."

"Remember this, Mister Colorado Big Shot." All Louis could see was the disembodied hand, menacingly shaking a finger. "You ain't never been in a fight 'til you tangle with a Carolina mountain boy."

Henry's voice remained quiet, but Louis picked up a sudden hardness in his words. "Don't push it, Jimmy Lee. This isn't the time or the place."

"Why's that? Because your friend went and got himself killed?" Jimmy Lee spat near Henry's boots. "Alva Jean took quite a shine to him. She was my girl 'til he showed up. Maybe she'll come back to me now he's out of the picture." Jimmy Lee added, "I'm not sorry he's dead."

Figuring Henry was half second away from going for Jimmy Lee's throat, Louis pushed open the screen door and stepped outside. He spoke in a voice that sounded much calmer than he felt. "Did you want him out of the picture enough to kill him, Jimmy Lee?"

A look of surprise on his face, Jimmy Lee stumbled backward. "Didn't mean it that way."

"Not a very smart thing to say during a murder investigation." Louis glared at Jimmy Lee long enough to make him fidget.

"Will you excuse us, Jimmy Lee?" Louis said. "I need to talk to Henry. But don't go far. I need to talk to you about a few things, too. Including that fight you started with Aubrey outside the Watering Hole Saloon the other night."

Jimmy Lee turned on his heel and stalked into the house, slamming the screen door.

"That boy's always had quite a chip on his shoulder," Louis said. "I keep hoping he'll outgrow it."

Louis suggested they move to the front of the house where the large porch provided shade, and some privacy. Henry walked ahead and settled into a rocking chair. Louis stopped near the steps and gazed across the valley. His mind was no longer focused on the investigation. All he could think about was his youngest daughter with Aubrey Miller, and he grew angrier.

He tried thinking about the Bar T Ranch instead. Sally Ann and Rory had changed the place. It was a delightful change. The new wrap-around porch caught cooling breezes, no matter which direction they blew. A quiet place to gather one's thoughts. He took a few deep breaths, something his wife recommended he try. The bunched muscles in his shoulders slowly relaxed and he turned his mind turned back toward murder.

He spoke without turning around. "Tell me, Henry. What brought you back?"

Nearly a minute passed before Henry answered. "I thought it was Vernon's wedding. Now I'm not so sure about anything."

"I don't believe in coincidences. Sometimes a person

feels pulled in some direction and ends up being in a certain place at a certain time without really knowing why." Louis put his hands in his pockets and stared across the valley. "Sometimes fate plays a hand and things end up in an unexpected way. For instance, about thirty-five years ago I came to North Carolina on a fishing trip with some friends. Met the future Mrs. Hannahan the second day I was in town."

"Some people have better luck than others."

"Like dating a much younger woman, for instance?" Louis finally looked at Henry. "How long had Aubrey been seeing Alva Jean?"

Henry's eyebrows rose. "You didn't know?"

"If I had, I would've been in the running for prime suspect."

CHAPTER 10

Alva Jean was absently wiping the countertop when Henry entered the Corner Café a few hours later. She looked up with red-rimmed eyes and offered an unconvincing smile as she handed him a menu. He was surprised to see her here. No doubt she was at work hoping her father wouldn't figure out she'd been seeing Aubrey. Understandable, after witnessing his reaction to the news of their relationship.

Glancing around, Henry didn't see Louis, who must have gotten sidetracked or he'd already be here looking for answers. He spotted Jimmy Lee and a couple of his friends in a booth and swore under his breath. Being questioned by the police wasn't the best way to end the day. Clashing with his step-brother would make it much worse.

Henry had hoped to relax and enjoy the blue-plate special. Since the cupboards were bare at Vernon's cabin, he decided a quick sandwich would be a better choice. He moved along the counter to an end seat where he could keep an eye on Jimmy Lee.

"I've always wondered how she makes this job look so easy," Alva Jean said as she placed a glass of iced tea on the counter.

He looked up from the menu and followed her gaze. Della Kendall, his uncle's fiancé, moved among the patrons at the Corner Café, wearing a friendly smile and patting her hair with one hand while refilling coffee mugs with the carafe she carried in the other.

69

Alva Jean smiled. "She's that cheerful even when the café is slap full and everybody's hollering at once for a bottle of ketchup."

She slipped napkin-wrapped silverware beside his iced tea. "I asked her once. She laughed and said it's just years of experience. I figure it's patience, but dang, she must have the patience of a saint. You know it took four years to wear Vernon down? They think it's a big secret he finally proposed, but half the town knew the next day."

Henry realized she was rambling, but if it made her feel better he was willing to listen. Ordering supper could wait. He had a few questions of his own that begged for answers. Had she met Aubrey the night he was killed? Had she seen anyone else? He'd not had a chance to examine the tracks around the body, and the arrival of police at the scene had spoiled a second look.

"You know, Vernon isn't bad looking for an older man." She wiped the counter for the third time. "I used to think turning twenty-two a few months ago made me positively ancient. Then I met Aubrey. All of a sudden, thirty-five wasn't that old. Not that any of that matters anymore."

Alva Jean wiped tears from her eyes.

Henry handed her a napkin. "Look, I really don't think you should be working. Your parents aren't going to kill you. I think they'll understand."

Behind her, the cook cleared his throat as he placed three plates on her tray. Alva Jean checked the order with the pad she pulled from her apron pocket. "Where's my fries?"

"They're coming."

"So is Christmas."

The cook looked up from the grill and wagged a pudgy finger at her. "I'm glad to see you smile," he said. "Even if it's just a little one. Do like the man says. Go home. Be with your family."

He handed her a plate heaped with fries. She wedged it onto the tray and moved through the café. Henry watched her, comparing her shoe size to the boot prints from the corral. Those hiking boots could just as easily belong to a woman. Alva Jean emptied the tray with practiced efficiency, grabbed ketchup from a nearby table and refilled coffee cups with a smile that looked a lot like Della's.

"Don't tell me you're watching her ass."

Henry turned sharply as Vernon took a seat next to him.

"I looked for you at the cabin," Vernon said. He put his hand on Henry's shoulder and lowered his voice. "I know you and Aubrey went way back, and I'm sorry."

Henry silently nodded his thanks.

"Some woman dropped this off at the cabin for you." Vernon slid a manila envelope to him. "It's stamped National Park Service, Blue Ridge Parkway."

"You open it?"

"Well, it wasn't sealed."

"Did she say anything?"

Vernon nodded. "She recommended the botany job. Said you'd be assigned to a crew, but technically you'd be working for her. There's a note inside."

Henry stared at the stamp a moment before opening the envelope. Ignoring the anticipation on his uncle's face, he read the note. *Best bet is bio-tech job, invasive plant crew/botany. Don't think too long. Job closing date is in three days. Call me if you decide to go for it. I can give you a few pointers on federal hiring process.*

"So?" Vernon asked. "Who's that from?"

"Someone I know from Colorado." Henry closed the envelope. "This was her idea, not mine. She's been here a few years now."

Alva Jean refilled Henry's tea. "What can I get you, Vernon?"

He ordered coffee.

71

"Della said to tell you she's taking a smoke break around back."

"But she doesn't smoke," Vernon said.

"Duh." Alva Jean winked as she pointed toward the side door. Grinning, Vernon jumped off the stool and headed for the side door.

"This is one of those Saturdays that we got swamped by tourists." Alva Jean glanced around the café and sighed. "They've thinned out, thank the Lord. Mostly it's just locals that come here, but Saturdays are unpredictable. Every Sunday it's the same, though. The mornings are busiest. Saturday night partiers in various states of sobriety followed by the church-goers dressed in their Sunday best."

The cook rang the kitchen bell. Alva Jean retrieved the order, then carried it to Jimmy Lee's booth. Henry thought the other two might be wranglers from the Bar T. The table had been rowdy and obnoxious since Henry had entered the café. He'd been disregarding their louder comments when the clatter of dishes and silverware had failed to drown them.

"What's gotten into you boys?" Alva Jean asked the red-headed one. "You taking your Friday night right on into Saturday night?"

"Ain't nothing wrong with that." Jimmy Lee slipped a pint bottle from his jacket pocket.

Henry doubted either of the companions were old enough to legally drink alcohol.

"I'm not saying Friday night wasn't epic," Jimmy Lee said. "We been hurting all day, for sure. Everything was fine last night until Uncle Vernon showed up and, well, you know he's a whiskey man... I ain't never mixing my alcohol again."

"Not the first time I've heard that one," Alva Jean said.

"Yeah, well, this time I mean it. I had to bust out a little hair of the dog this morning, just to ease the pain. Next thing I know, it's almost Saturday night."

His friends laughed as he waved the empty bottle at her.

"A little hair? That's more like the whole dog." Alva Jean flashed Henry a wicked smile. "Maybe there's something on your mind. Worried your brother is going to move back here?"

"That's step-brother. He ain't staying if I got anything to say about it." Jimmy Lee slapped the table for emphasis. "I've got a good mind to kick his ass all the way back to Colorado right now."

"From what I hear, his ass might not be so easy to kick."

"You mean that story about him being some big, bad range detective? It's bullshit."

"Vernon's the one that said it."

Jimmy Lee said something derogatory as he brushed a loose strand of hair behind his ear. He preened his ponytail and leered at Alva Jean.

She gave him a "dream on" look.

Jimmy Lee's gaze was steady at breast level. His eyes traveled from there to her hips, like he was mentally undressing her. It really annoyed Henry.

"Since your man ain't gonna be around no more, you ought to think about calling me sometime."

"Why don't you just hold your breath 'til I do?"

His buddies laughed loudly. Alva Jean grabbed the serving tray and whirled, narrowly missing Jimmy Lee's head as she marched toward the counter. The jangle of the cowbell above the door drew Henry's attention. Louis Hannahan stood there, his concern obvious when his gaze settled on his daughter.

Alva Jean placed her tray on the counter when she saw him. "Oh, God."

Henry touched her arm. "It's okay, he knows."

"He does?" Tears began to spill.

He nodded, and she ran into her father's waiting arms.

Muddy Waters

Henry turned away from the emotional scene not because it embarrassed him, but because he feared he might cry, too. He got to his feet and eased toward the door. Before he could get outside, two men and a woman crowded through, pushing him aside with insincere apologies.

The McLean brothers were easy to recognize, given Aubrey's description. Powerfully-built and frequently ill-tempered, he'd said people tended to cross the street to avoid them. While the three siblings were similar in appearance, Henry recognized the youngest brother immediately.

He'd seen those features in the glow of a lighter.

CHAPTER 11

Realizing he'd forgotten the envelope, Henry stopped on the sidewalk outside the café. He stepped aside as Louis escorted his daughter toward a black Chevy Suburban. When Henry re-entered the restaurant, his attention was drawn to Jimmy Lee's table. Vernon was there, angrily drumming the table with two fingers as he spoke.

"Dammit, Jimmy Lee, show some class," Vernon said. "If your mamma knew you treated women like that she'd skin you alive."

"Like what?"

"Like they're inanimate objects, that's what. You look at women like a thirsty man looks at a cold beer. When all you want is a long drink, women are quick to figure it out."

"You should talk," Jimmy Lee countered. "You've had your share of long drinks."

"Still treated them with respect. You ever notice my exes will speak to me? Can't say the same about yours."

"Alva Jean ain't one of my exes."

"Maybe that's why she still talks to you." Vernon shook his head. "At least until she hears you've been lying to folks, saying she is an ex."

Vernon turned and walked out the door.

Henry suppressed a grin as he moved toward the envelope on the counter, threading his way through a small group of people waiting for a table. As he passed the McLeans, he bumped into the younger brother, whose hand clamped onto Henry's arm like a vise.

"You got a problem?"

People stepped back from the area immediately around them. A sudden silence fell in the café. No one spoke. Not even a dish clanked. Henry glanced at the sneering face, surprised by the open hostility. The smell of stale cigarette smoke and tequila was heavy in the air between them. From the noticeable sway in the man's body, he was still intoxicated.

"I'll say he's got a problem," a voice said from behind the man. "He was stupid enough to come back to this podunk town."

Henry grinned as Hugh McLean pushed his brother aside.

"Henry Smith, I'll be damned." Hugh offered his hand. "You remember my little brother, Beau?"

"He's grown a bit." Henry shook hands first with Hugh, then Beau.

Hugh then introduced his sister. Odessa's grip was as firm as that of her brothers.

"This dude," Hugh said, pointing a thick finger at Henry. "Pitched a no-hitter that won us the conference championship our senior year. Then he gave up a baseball scholarship at Appalachian State to go out west."

The other two McLeans traded glances, faces expressionless. Neither of them seemed interested in baseball, championships, or polite conversation.

Henry smiled. "I guess I took that 'go west, young man' a little too literally."

His reference to their high school American history class flew over Hugh's head.

"I'm sorry about your cousin."

Hugh nodded, his eyes not meeting Henry's. "I'm sorry, too. Y'all were close, I know. We're in town to take care of arrangements. Seems like we just did that same thing for

Dad. It ain't been easy since he passed last year. We've been doing our best to keep the family business going and Aubrey was a great help. I don't mind telling you he's going to be sorely missed."

"Yeah." Henry noticed the hum of normal activity in the café had resumed.

A waitress carrying an armful of menus came to show the McLeans to a table.

Hugh lingered. "Maybe we can get together while you're in town and have a few cold ones."

"I'd like that," Henry said. "Y'all enjoy your breakfast."

He watched the three of them squeeze into a booth near Jimmy Lee and his buddies. The two wranglers fidgeted and exchanged glances before jumping to their feet. One of them nudged Jimmy Lee toward the door.

"Too bad," Jimmy Lee said. He glared at Henry as he went through the door. "I thought sure we were in for a good ass-kicking. Ain't nothing like dinner and a show. Not that the show would have lasted long. Beau would have tied that so-called cowboy's ass into a pretzel in short order."

"You're making friends fast." Della appeared beside him.

Henry grabbed the envelope off the counter. "I forgot to pay for my tea."

"Why don't you stay and eat," Della said, handing him a menu. "Looks like you could use a good meal."

Rather than argue, he settled onto a stool at the counter. Della returned with a fresh glass of tea and a menu. Fishing his wire-rimmed eyeglasses out of his shirt pocket, he slipped them on and read the menu. After he ordered a sandwich, Della leaned toward him.

"You know Vernon thinks the world of you." She tapped the envelope. "We're both hoping you'll stay."

"To be honest, I really haven't thought much about it."

"I imagine things aren't the clearest right now. Give it

time," Della said. "This is a good place to settle down."

"That's the same thing Aubrey tried to tell me."

"Your friend Aubrey had lots of nice things to say about everything and everybody. Even his uncouth cousins. Even you. I sure don't know why anyone would want him dead."

"I keep asking myself that, too." Henry shook his head. "Can you remember Alva Jean saying anything that would help find who killed him? Or something that happened when they were together?"

"There was that fight he got into with Jimmy Lee a few days ago."

"What was it about?"

"Alva Jean, of course."

Henry raised his eyebrows in question.

"I don't know what set him off." Della patted her hair, which was styled atop her head and lacquered with hairspray. "She did say Jimmy Lee was dumb as a post in high school and nothing's changed. What's worse is he thinks he's smart. She asked him once about that General Custer look he's into, with the long hair and beard and all. You know what he said? He didn't even know who Custer was, bless his heart."

Henry couldn't quite conceal a snicker. Della picked up the coffeepot and made the rounds. She returned a few minutes later to refill his tea.

"Do you know if Alva Jean met Aubrey last night?"

Della frowned. "Funny you should ask. That just added to her troubles when she heard the news. One of the other girls called in, so Alva Jean had to stay until closing. She missed their date."

Henry considered this. Had he planned to meet another young lady last night? After the way Aubrey behaved at the café the other morning, he doubted it could have been anyone but Alva Jean. So where was the horse? It belonged to the McLeans, and Aubrey said his cousins kept their horses in the barn by the lake. Since he'd ridden to the old corral frequently, it must be close.

"Aubrey always called you Whispering Smith." Della placed his order on the counter in front of him. "What's that about?"

"Just a nickname." Henry wondered again what Aubrey had said. "The Smith part is obvious. Years ago, someone thought I looked like a character by the name of Whispering Smith in an old western movie. The nickname stuck."

Della looked at him, her expression blank.

"Alan Ladd was in it," Henry said. "The movie."

"Alan Ladd? I remember him, though not that particular movie. *Shane* is the only western I remember."

"Similar character."

Della studied him for a moment. "You do favor him, I suppose. That nickname probably isn't just based on looks, not from what I've heard, anyway." She pointed at his eyeglasses and smiled. "And that mild-mannered professor look doesn't fit at all."

"What do you mean?"

"Well, aren't you some sort of a cowboy detective who chases down cattle thieves and gets into wild gunfights?"

"I think Aubrey told some tall tales." Henry tried to laugh it off.

"He was quite the story-teller all right." Della moved toward the door to greet a pair of newcomers. She showed them to a table and returned.

Looking across the counter at Henry, she asked, "Is it true they still have cattle rustlers out west?"

"Not just out west." He decided not to bore her with statistics and details. "Lots of places have that sort of trouble. Where I live, it sometimes seems things haven't changed much in the last hundred years or so."

"Are you talking attitudes, economics or life in general?"

"All three." Henry looked at her in a different light. He wasn't sure what he'd expected, but realized he had stereotyped her. It wasn't often he underestimated people. "Why don't you tell me about the attitudes and economics of Parsons Gap. I've been away awhile."

"Sure thing, honey." Della refilled his tea. "You wait right there."

She wasn't gone long.

"I'm sure you've noticed things changed around here since the tourist business hit town." She spoke as she hung another order ticket for the cook. "More shops, more restaurants, and more traffic. At heart, Parsons Gap is still the same old dull, unexciting little town. News still spreads fast 'round here, and secrets even faster." She added with a smile, "In fact, folks here probably knew you were coming home before you did."

He laughed. "Doesn't sound like I've missed much."

"Your folks made a smart move turning their place into a riding stable and guest ranch. That's my opinion, anyway. Most thought they were crazy until tourism hit these mountains. Now those same people are wishing they'd thought of it first."

Della left to check her other customers. Henry heard the cowbell jangle. Louis entered and took a seat on the other side of Henry.

"How's Alva Jean?"

"She's with her mother now." Louis glanced at the floor, a sadness in his voice. "She's a strong-willed young lady. She'll get through this all right. It'll take some time, of course."

Louis asked for coffee, then turned back to Henry. "Have you seen Carlie yet?"

Henry shook his head, feeling a lump rise in his throat.

"You should." Louis sipped his coffee. "I imagine she'll be glad to see you."

"How long has she been back in Parsons Gap?"

"Almost five years. She stayed in Greenville a while after her divorce, but finally decided to come home and open her own practice."

"I heard she's a doctor."

"Yeah. A veterinarian."

Henry stared at the ice in his glass. "Divorce? I take it she ended up marrying Tommy Blevins then?"

"Tommy Blevins? Where on earth did you get that idea?"

"Just before I left town, Carlie told me..." Henry paused, confused.

"She married a Mitchell County boy," Louis said. "About four or five years after you left for college."

Back then, he had been on the verge of marrying Carlie. She had turned out the lights on what he'd considered a bright future by saying she'd been seeing Tommy on the side, and that he'd proposed. After that, Henry couldn't wait to get away from Parsons Gap.

So why was he having difficulty telling himself none of it really mattered?

CHAPTER 12

"**S**aw Henry Smith in town today." Louis hoped to sound casual. He crossed his ankles on the footrest of the recliner and glanced over the newspaper at his eldest daughter. She was seated on the sofa with a magazine, sharing the lamplight. "He's helping with an investigation, in fact."

Carlie curled her bare feet beneath her, turned a page in the magazine, and answered without looking at him. "I heard he was in town."

Her feigned disinterest wasn't fooling him. He reached down and scratched the ears of the Australian shepherd sleeping beside his chair. "He hasn't changed all that much, really. Of course, he looks a little older, like the rest of us."

A few quiet minutes passed.

"He asked me about you and Tommy Blevins."

"What about Tommy?" The strain in her voice was conspicuous. The magazine slipped from her hands and clattered to the floor. It woke the dog, who lifted his head, ears pricked.

"Henry asked me if you'd married him," Louis said. "I was a little confused. I didn't even know you'd dated Tommy."

"What did you tell him?"

"Just that you hadn't married Tommy. Why?"

"No reason." Carlie retrieved the magazine. She placed it beside her on the sofa. "Does 'helping' mean he's a suspect in whatever you're investigating?"

"Would it matter if he was?"

There was no response. A few minutes later, Carlie

abruptly announced she was going home to bed and left the room. Her house was practically in the back yard, though she and her son spent much of their time here, something Louis never wanted to take for granted.

Louis sighed and folded the newspaper. "More to that story than meets the eye, don't you think, Quirt?" He spoke to the dog, whose ears twitched at the mention of his name. Quirt didn't bother to lift his head, and Louis figured he ought to be disturbed that the dog was growing used to this type of conversation. He continued anyway.

"I don't know about this Mr. Smith and his reluctance to tell me what he knows. I doubt threatening him with jail for obstruction will get me anywhere. You got any ideas?"

Quirt placed a paw over his eye and went back to sleep.

"I suppose it's true, what they say. It's easier to catch flies with honey." He reached for the remote, flipped through the television channels to see if he might catch an old movie. Nothing looked interesting, so he switched back to the headline news channel. Quirt lifted his head when the back door opened. They both recognized the familiar shuffle of his youngest daughter's feet as she approached the den.

"How's A.J. this evening?"

She leaned over the back of the recliner to kiss his cheek. "I don't know how you manage to hear anything over that television." Alva Jean flopped onto the sofa. "I'm not feeling too bad. I met up with a couple of friends and went out for a beer."

"Just one?"

"Yes, Daddy. I do pay attention to some of your lectures." She leafed through the pages of Carlie's magazine. "Journal of the American Veterinary Medical Association. Sounds like a big fat sleeping pill."

"Apparently so. It worked for Carlie."

Alva Jean smiled at him.

"Anything exciting happen today?" Louis was glad to see her smiling again.

"Well, Jimmy Lee asked me out again." She sighed. "For the twenty-seventh time."

"What'd you say?"

"No, of course."

"You're not getting any younger. He's from a good family, as I'm sure you're aware. You might want to consider his offer."

"Sure thing, Daddy, a girl's got to have a plan for her future." She rolled her eyes and giggled. "What about someone else from the same good family? I met Henry Smith the other day. He's nothing like Jimmy Lee. Very polite, plus he's quiet and well-mannered. No wedding ring, either. So maybe I'll ask him out."

"I forget girls ask boys out these days." Not long ago she would have been complaining that all the guys she met were too old. That was before she'd met Aubrey Miller. Louis didn't want to be as understanding as his wife insisted he should be where his daughters were concerned, though he knew she was right. The simple truth was Alva Jean had lost someone she loved. The fact that it was Aubrey shouldn't matter, but it did. Their relationship bothered him almost as much as her not telling him they were seeing each other.

That was something he could discuss with her another time, if ever. Tonight he needed to ask about their rendezvous the night Miller was killed. Emotions were still raw, and he tried to figure out how to phrase the question.

"You should know Carlie used to date Henry Smith in high school." Louis watched her closely. Perhaps she knew something about what Carlie wasn't willing to discuss.

"So, what happened?" Alva Jean asked. "Must have been something pretty awful. I mean, ever since I told Carlie that Vernon's nephew was coming back to town for the wedding, she's been in a terrible sulk. Now I know why."

"Carlie hasn't been inclined to discuss the subject."

Whatever happened between them was something Carlie kept to herself. She had been ill-tempered for months after

Henry left for college. Despite a discrete investigation, Louis never found out the details. Even his wife had been in the dark.

"Sounds like an intriguing mystery for you to solve, Daddy."

Louis chuckled. If she only knew.

"What made him choose a college so far away?"

"He was offered a full scholarship. That's something too good to turn down."

"I don't know if I could move that far from home, even for a free ride."

"You'd better."

"You're so practical, Daddy. I often wonder how you and Momma ever got together. Artists aren't always practical people."

"Your mother learned practical from me."

"Sure she did." Alva Jean rolled her eyes again. "What sort of scholarship did Henry get?"

"Baseball, I think, but I heard he really wanted to go there for the roping team."

"Roping? He sounds like quite the cowboy. No wonder you liked him."

"Who told you I liked him?"

"Momma, of course." Alva Jean laughed. "Only I didn't realize she was talking about Henry Smith until now. I told her about this cowboy I'd met from Colorado. She told me about an old boyfriend of Carlie's that moved out west and became a cowboy. Turns out they're best friends. Or were."

Louis thought she was on the verge of tears.

Alva Jean sighed and rubbed her eyes. "I'm tired, Daddy. I think I'll go to bed."

"Before you go, there's something we need to talk about." Louis turned off the television, wishing his wife was still awake to help with the mess he was about to make.

CHAPTER 13

Morning sunlight slanted through the surrounding trees, transforming the dew on the pasture into sparkling diamonds of light. Steam rose from the rusted metal roof of the McLean's wooden barn. Three horses grazed nearby, tails swishing at flies. Henry recognized the bay mare Aubrey had ridden the night they met at the old corral. Two other horses, a buckskin gelding and a roan mare, cropped grass a few yards away. The buckskin lifted his head and ambled toward him, following Henry as he walked parallel to the fence.

The buckskin scratched his neck on the corner post and tossed his head. Henry reached out to rub the horse's cheek and nearly lost a chunk from his arm. Aubrey hadn't been joking when he said his cousin's horses were a little rough.

The door on this side of the barn was close to the fence. Henry kept a safe distance from the buckskin while he worked the latch. It wouldn't budge. Looking up, he realized the door had been nailed shut. He edged around the building toward the main doors, which he found chained and padlocked. At the rear of the barn, a recently added lean-to opened to the pasture. Looking through a dirt-crusted window, he discovered it was separated from the interior by a connected line of metal gates.

He checked the horses. They grazed contentedly some distance away. Pulling on a pair of leather work gloves, he climbed the pasture fence and quickly crossed the lean-to. He mounted the makeshift barrier and leapt onto the barn floor. Without touching anything, he scrutinized the interior. If Louis still considered him a suspect, he didn't want to leave fingerprints.

Three clean, well-used saddles rested on new saw horses in the tack area. Saddle blankets were underneath. One saddle had a bridle draped over the horn. Two more bridles hung from hooks driven into a crossbeam. Empty grain bags and burlap sacks were carefully stacked in separate piles beside a large plastic barrel with a lid. Two shovels and a pitch fork leaned against the wall near an empty wheelbarrow with a mud-crusted tire.

Near the saddles, a cork bulletin board was fixed to the wall. Three photographs and a yellowed slip of paper were pinned with horseshoe nails. The note listed the amount of grain to feed each horse. From one photo, Aubrey and Alva Jean smiled happily at him. It looked like it had been taken in the hay loft. In another, Odessa sat on the tailgate of a black pickup with red lettering in the rear window. The third snapshot was older, portraying much younger versions of the McLean brothers with a boy of around seven or eight years of age.

He glanced around the barn again, recognizing signs of Aubrey's compulsive tidiness. Henry's shed had looked like this when he and Aubrey were roommates, before they'd drifted apart. Once Aubrey began dating a girl from the Conner clan, a wedge was slowly driven between old friendships. Especially those involving range detectives.

The hard-packed dirt floor and scattered straw meant little chance of finding useful tracks. He scanned the interior again, willing something to jump out and shed light on Aubrey's last ride. Specifically, had he brought the bay mare back, or had someone else? When Henry's gaze fell on the bridle draped over a saddle horn rather than hanging beside the others, he knew the answer.

The sound of an engine drew him to the nearest

window. A silver Dodge pickup with a matching topper was pulling to a stop outside the barn, Odessa at the wheel. Henry spun around, ready to run. The horses were eagerly trotting into the lean-to, with the buckskin closest to his escape route. Ears back, the gelding watched him. Whether the horse expected a scoop of grain or anticipated a chance to bite was anyone's guess. Henry's only option was the loft. He scrambled up the ladder as the chain rattled on the main door. Few bales remained. The only area offering any sort of concealment was a shadowy corner. He darted toward it.

The door squealed on the box rail. One of the horses nickered and Odessa cooed in response. Henry remained still. He heard rustling below, near the tack area. An odd chuckle followed by crumpling paper, then the rattle of the grain bin. Scoops of grain pouring into a bucket, footsteps crossing toward the lean-to. Odessa murmured to the horses as grain was dumped into a wooden trough. More rustling below, then a footstep on the ladder to the hay loft.

Henry's heartbeat quickened. If she spotted him, how would he explain his presence? He'd be worse off if she reported him to the police.

"Damn, I forgot the apples in the truck." Odessa's normal voice rasped like that of a long-time smoker. "Aubrey told me y'all love apples, and to be sure I brung 'em."

Footsteps retreated. Henry weighed his chances of remaining hidden, decided they were slim, and jumped for the ladder. He half-climbed, half-slid down it, missing several rungs. The floor came up fast and hard. His last-second tuck and roll barely softened the landing. The Dodge's door slammed. In two stumbling strides he made the barrier at the lean-to. The buckskin was watching, but Henry didn't hesitate. He vaulted the gates and hit the ground running. The pasture fence was close, but as he clambered over it, the buckskin sunk his teeth into Henry's left shoulder.

Leveraging himself over the fence, Henry sprawled onto the ground with a loud grunt. He scrambled on all fours into the dew-drenched undergrowth for cover. Cautiously, he turned and peered out. Odessa was not in sight.

The buckskin threw his head triumphantly, a piece of

Henry's denim jacket in his teeth.

CHAPTER 14

Henry left the pharmacy and was turning the borrowed Bar T truck onto High Street when Louis flagged him down. He pulled to a stop next to the unmarked Tahoe.

Louis leaned in the open passenger window. "Interested in a late lunch? I'm not fond of eating alone and thought if you weren't busy, you might join me."

The business-like manner made Henry doubt he had an option. "I could eat."

He parked the truck in the space ahead of the Tahoe. Maybe the meeting would provide an update on the investigation, or an inadvertent scrap of information that suddenly made everything fall into place.

The throbbing in Henry's shoulder hadn't eased. Though the buckskin hadn't ripped away any flesh, the bite had broken the skin and left a good-sized bruise. The wound oozed a little, so Henry had grabbed a clean shirt after applying a makeshift bandage at the cabin. The pharmacy stop had been for better bandage material and a bottle of ibuprofen. Henry had downed a few already, so there was nothing else to be done.

"I do some of my best thinking over an ice-cold root beer." Louis pointed toward the double doors of the Parsons Gap Brewery. "This place serves exceptional micro-brewed root beer. The wings aren't bad either. I almost feel guilty coming to the tourist part of town."

"I can think of worse places to be caught."

Louis gave him a sideways glance. "The Watering Hole

Muddy Waters

Saloon has better wings, but their root beer is bottled stuff. It's the same root beer, but it doesn't equal what you get at the source. And, of course, the atmosphere is very different."

"Root beer?"

"I'm on duty," Louis said. "And you're driving."

"Sounds like I'd better try the root beer." Henry followed Louis through an ornately carved door. Parsons Gap Brewery was spelled out in gold letters in the transom window. The interior was cool, dimly lit, and empty. Two women in office attire were seated at a back table, and a young man stacked glasses behind the bar. The muffled clatter of dishes in the kitchen indicated the presence of others.

The barman greeted them with a friendly smile and welcomed Louis by name. As Louis introduced the bartender, he put a heavy hand on Henry's wounded shoulder. Henry winced and bit the inside of his lower lip to stop a groan of pain. He managed a smile as he shook the offered hand.

Louis ordered two root beers. "How's your mother?"

"She's out of the hospital now." The barman spoke as he filled the mugs. "The doctors think she'll do well on medication and diet changes, as long as she takes it easy for a while."

"That might be a challenge. It's garden season, and I know she'll be itching to get out and work the vegetable patch."

"That's why my sister and I are ganging up on her." The barman placed the mugs on the bar. "I help out in the mornings, before I come to work. Then she takes care of things in the evenings. Between the two of us, we'll keep Momma in line."

"She's lucky to have you two."

"Thanks, Mr. Hannahan." The young man smiled.

"Haven't seen you around much lately. I guess this murder keeps you busy. It's a shame. I didn't know Aubrey Miller well, but I liked him. Don't care for his cousins much, but I imagine a lot of folks around here feel the same."

"You'll get no argument from me."

"You know, I'd always thought Parsons Gap was a quiet little town. Momma told me this isn't the first time there's been a murder around here. Said it was years ago, before you were even a deputy. That feller was never caught. I hope you get this one."

Louis nodded and moved toward a nearby table, a mug in each hand. Henry picked up two menus and followed. He swapped a menu for one of the mugs, then put on his glasses to browse the lunch selection. Louis recommended the wings. Henry agreed.

The barman, who had obviously heard the conversation, held up one finger. "Dozen?"

Louis flashed two fingers. The barman nodded and disappeared into the kitchen.

"I've known his mother for years. We're close in age. She had a heart attack last month. No warning. Nothing. Makes you think about your own mortality. It's sure made me appreciate some things I'd been taking for granted."

Henry wasn't mentally prepared for deep conversation involving mortality. Instead of making an inappropriate comment to lighten the mood, he tried the root beer. It was better than promised.

"I think there was progress made yesterday." Louis paused to sip his root beer. "I've got a feeling things will begin to fall into place before long. My wife thinks I'm very intuitive. She says it's a good trait for a detective to have. I'll be the first to admit I don't always feel intuitive, though I do have my moments."

Henry absently made watery circles on the table with the mug.

"Take the other day, for instance," Louis said. "I may not know much about tracking, but I know I saw a few of your footprints on top of the cigarette smoker's tracks. I also saw some of his boot prints over yours. That means the two of you were there around the same time. As you can imagine, I can't help but wonder why it is you've said nothing about this man."

Henry shifted in his chair. So much for hoping the conversation might lead to missing pieces of a puzzle. He looked up from the water rings. "I'm not looking to exact justice on my own, if that's what's on your mind."

Louis flashed an unfriendly smile. "I'll admit it is."

Henry stared at the chestnut-colored liquid in his glass. "It has to do with a promise I made to Aubrey. I gave him my word. Besides, I'd hate to see a particular subject of his past come to the foreground when it's not relevant."

"You don't believe cattle theft has anything to do with his death." Louis leaned back in his chair and made a steeple with his fingers. "I'm the investigating officer, and that's something I determine. It's easier when I have all the facts."

Henry said nothing.

"Did you know Jimmy Lee had already reported the cattle missing? Maybe it scared Aubrey, and he wanted out. Then Aubrey's accomplice wanted to keep him quiet because he'd threatened to go to the police."

"Aubrey wasn't out to get anyone arrested," Henry said. "That's why he called me. He simply didn't want to be blamed for the cattle thefts."

"Could be a clever misdirection."

"Aubrey wasn't that devious."

"Maybe his accomplice is," Louis said.

"In my experience, the leap from cattle theft to murder is usually a big one."

"That depends on what's at stake."

"They don't hang people for rustling anymore."

Louis appeared to concede the point. "What else aren't you telling me?"

Henry decided either his poker face needed work, or Louis was too perceptive. He took another sip of root beer. "Your intuition acting up again?"

"Look, Henry." Louis lowered his voice. "I've heard the same rumors you have. I've got a good idea who was out there. Why protect him?"

Protect wasn't the word Henry would have chosen. Postponing justice might fit the situation better. From what he'd seen, the McLeans weren't smart enough about the thefts to avoid being caught. Given time and enough rope, they'd hang themselves. While Aubrey's death may have thrown a wrench into their operation, he really didn't expect they'd stop for long. If Louis went public with the rustling, Aubrey's past would come up. Henry didn't want that. He hoped to convince Louis that in this particular situation, patience was a virtue.

"Aubrey asked me not to go to the police," Henry finally said.

Whatever Louis had been about to say was interrupted when an enormous platter of wings was brought to their table. Two smaller plates and a stack of paper napkins were placed beside the platter. Henry drained his glass of root beer and asked for another.

Waving his hand in invitation, Louis attacked the wings. "I expect you to eat at least half. Lord knows I don't need all these. I'll be miserable."

"I'd hate to see you suffer." Henry reached for a small plate and filled it.

The door of the brewery opened with a bright flash of sunlight. Once his eyes readjusted to the dimness, Henry was surprised to see Jimmy Lee with Odessa McLean. Even more surprising was Jimmy Lee's hand stuffed in the back pocket of Odessa's blue jeans. Engaged in intimate conversation, they seemed oblivious to their surroundings. Jimmy Lee quickly extracted his hand when his eyes fell on Henry and Louis. He nodded in greeting but didn't speak.

"I understand her brothers are very protective." Louis didn't offer further explanation, nor did Henry need any.

"I suppose he's old enough to know what he's doing," Henry replied.

The barman brought another round of root beer. Henry ate quietly, studying the abstract shapes and patterns made by the wing sauce on the empty platter. Most of the shapes resembled birds. Some were leaves. Rorschach wing sauce. He wondered what that said about his personality, or his emotional function. He laughed to himself and glanced at Louis, who was giving him that look again.

"You still haven't told me which McLean you saw."

"I'm not sure who I saw, McLean or otherwise." Henry wiped sauce off his cheek with a napkin. "It was dark. Besides, it's difficult to sneak up on a person. Especially as close as I'd have to be to positively identify someone in the dark."

"You expect me to believe that?"

Henry shrugged. He turned to watch Odessa feed the jukebox, then join Jimmy Lee at a table in the opposite end of the big room. Louis appeared to be waiting for an answer, his fingers drumming the table to the rhythm of an old country song.

"If the cattle thefts don't stop," Henry replied. "I'll be happy to revisit this."

Louis didn't hide his anger. "You know what perverting the course of justice means, right?"

Henry decided to throw Louis a bone. He leaned back in his chair. "The night I met Aubrey, he was riding one of the McLean's horses. They keep their horses at a place about a half mile south of the corral. That dirt road takes you near it. The mare is back in their pasture now. How did she get there? Cigarette man's tracks weren't on that road."

"Forget the horse for a minute," Louis said. "What makes you so sure this cigarette man didn't kill Aubrey?"

Henry recalled the overheard phone conversation. "Why kill your patsy?"

Louis studied him. "I hate to admit you're making sense."

Resisting the urge to smile, Henry reached for another wing.

"So, given your area of expertise," Louis began. He glanced at Odessa and lowered his voice. "Would an investigation of the slaughterhouse turn up anything useful on cattle theft?"

"Sometimes it can be difficult to prove." Henry wanted to discourage him without sounding obvious. He continued, "Especially in this part of the country, where brands aren't used much. There's paperwork on every animal slaughtered, and you'd have to follow up every seller. That could be anywhere from a few hundred to several thousand animals to check every month, depending on the size of their slaughter operation. It's most likely a legitimate seller including a stolen steer now and then, and there's always the possibility that solid evidence might never be found. If the McLeans raise cattle of their own, it could be even more difficult."

Louis drained his root beer. He set down the empty mug with a thud. "That's what you do out west? Track down paperwork?"

"Well, the Department of Agriculture people usually get involved with the paperwork side. Ranchers use brands, and sometimes brands are altered. Or a bill of sale forged. Sometimes things are discovered after the fact. The rancher is still out the time and money invested in that animal. I guess you could say my specialty, for the most part, is loss prevention."

"Loss prevention," Louis repeated. He smiled, and this time it was friendlier. "Tell me what you would do in a situation like the one here, for instance."

"That depends."

"On?"

"There are different factors involved. Location, access, evidence found." Henry wiped his fingers with a napkin. "Might warn the thieves to stop while they're ahead. If they didn't, I could get lucky, catch them in the act, or make them think I had enough evidence to nail them. A lot of it is preference."

"What do you mean?"

"My preference depends each situation." Henry finished the last of his root beer. "Let's suppose Mr. Thief is suspected of rustling cattle. He's small-time and doesn't steal often. Might make it difficult to catch him in the act. Rather than let him keep stealing, I scare him. Let him believe I could put him in jail. I'd say things would stay strictly between us, as long as he stays out of trouble."

"Go on," Louis said.

"It's sort of a bluff, and it doesn't always work. If it does, there are some positive outcomes. For one, Mr. Thief's extracurricular activities stop. But suppose he knows someone more active. Mr. Thief doesn't want to get blamed for things he didn't do, so now he's an informant. It's a win-win situation, though it's not always pretty."

"Why isn't it pretty?" Louis reached for the last wing on the platter.

"It's still blackmail."

Louis shrugged. "I guess it could be said there's no harm in a little innocent blackmail if it keeps a few criminals closer to the straight and narrow."

CHAPTER 15

Hugh McLean was in the U.S. Department of Agriculture office at the slaughter plant, discussing export certificates with the veterinary officer, when his secretary found him. They were both startled by Janice flinging open the office door without knocking.

"Hugh, there's a fellow here to see you." Her fingers danced on the door jamb.

"Did I forget an appointment?" Hugh asked, frowning.

"Not that I know." Janice said, "Of course, it wouldn't be the first time one wasn't written down."

Hugh forced a smile. Older secretaries always began acting like his mother after a few months. Unfortunately, the younger ones were too distracting for his brother. He'd learned to put up with the motherly types.

"Well, he'll just have to wait." Hugh still had a few questions about beef exports he wanted clarified. It was almost quitting time and he was ready to go home. On top of that, he didn't feel like being bothered. There was too much going on in his head, especially with his cousin's murder. Thank God for that bottle of whiskey he'd found in his father's desk drawer.

Hugh had wanted to shut down the whole operation because of Aubrey's death, but Beau suggested closing the meat market and only running the slaughter facility. It made sense. If they had a decent-sized holding pen for cattle not processed that day, it would have been different. Like Beau pointed out, they had plenty of storage space in the cooler.

"I think you'll want to see him as soon as possible." Janice threw a quick glance at the veterinarian.

Hugh moved toward the door, thinking maybe Janice would do after all. She had sense enough not to discuss private business in front of the USDA inspector.

"I'll talk to you later, Doc."

Once outside the office, Hugh turned to Janice. "Who is it and what does he want?"

"I don't know who he is. He certainly knows his way around a slaughter plant. He's had a look around and now he wants to talk to you."

"Is he some sort of inspector?"

Janice shrugged. "Didn't say."

Hugh scowled and followed her to the facility office. He paused to look through the glass door at his visitor. The man had his back to them, one hand clasping a cowboy hat as he stood in front of a yellowed poster of common cattle breeds. When Janice opened the door, Henry Smith turned and acknowledged Hugh with a slight nod of his head.

The metal office door clanged shut behind Hugh, making him jump. Janice stepped around him and went to her desk, where she fidgeted with a stack of papers. Hugh gathered his thoughts as he crossed the room. He'd heard enough from Aubrey to know what Smith did for a living. What else could've brought him here? Aubrey had to go and show him those damned cattle.

"What can I do for you?" Hugh got right to business. The sooner Smith was gone the better.

"I stopped by to discuss something. If you don't mind, that is."

Hugh smiled and tried to appear agreeable. "Why should I mind?"

"Do you have an office? It might be better if we talk there."

"Sure thing." Hugh showed him into a small office. He closed the door, ignoring Janice's worried expression. He offered a chair to his guest as he settled behind the desk. Smith ignored the chair and leaned against the doorframe, hands motionless on the brim of his hat.

Hugh waited for what seemed like an hour before Smith spoke.

"Aubrey was a good man."

Hugh nodded. "We're sure going to miss him and his sense of humor around here."

Smith's face was unreadable. "You knew about his history of cattle theft?"

"We all knew about it." Hugh was suddenly wary. He shifted in his chair. "He told us up front. Why you asking?"

"The night Aubrey was murdered, he showed me some cattle near a corral off Parsons Hollow Road. He felt the circumstances were suspicious."

"So?"

Smith smiled. Hugh was uncomfortably reminded of the snarl of a wolf, right before it lunged for the kill.

"Some things may be different in this part of the country, but suspicious circumstances involving livestock are something I'd recognize anywhere."

Hugh forced himself to remain motionless behind the desk. Better to stay calm.

"Seems Aubrey heard rumors his cousins may be involved," Smith said. "Obviously, he was concerned the blame would fall on him if those rumors turned out to be true."

"Surely, you ain't suggesting—"

Smith's smile faded. "Maybe you have another explanation for your brother's keen interest in those cattle by the corral."

"You've got no right coming here, accusing me of stealing cattle." Hugh rose from his chair, expecting to intimidate Smith.

Smith didn't flinch. In fact, he appeared to ignore Hugh altogether. He did sense a subtle change in Smith's posture. Remembering Aubrey's stories, Hugh took a closer look at the man. All he saw was a wiry, little twerp, not even six foot tall. How could this be the sort of man others feared?

Well, they were only stories, after all.

Right now, he wanted nothing more than to grab Smith and squash him like a fly. Their high school friendship had become history as far as Hugh was concerned. He didn't want trouble at work, though. This was something Beau could take care of later, away from work. Hugh smiled thinking about it.

Beau would consider it a special treat.

"You may have gotten away with certain things in the past. Don't make the mistake of thinking you will in the future." Smith's soft-spoken voice didn't even sound threatening, which infuriated Hugh even more. Was this how he'd gotten the nickname of Whispering Smith?

"You got no authority here," Hugh said.

His brother would enjoy making Smith pay for this, far more than calling the police on him at that corral. After Beau was finished with him, he'd be known as Whimpering Smith. Hugh found his own joke funny and coughed to hide his laugh.

"You misunderstand me." Smith's gaze made Hugh uncomfortable. "Authority doesn't come into it. This is personal, which could be more serious for you. One thing Aubrey made clear to me was he didn't want the law involved. I'm willing to honor his wishes, but only to a point. I came here to offer advice. Take it, and there won't be anything more to worry about. Nothing should happen to prove rumors about cattle theft are true."

Hugh struggled to keep his cool.

Smith paused as he reached for the door. "Pass on to

Beau that he doesn't know his way around the woods as well as he thinks he does."

Smith left the office, closing the door behind him. Hugh uttered several words he hoped Janice couldn't hear. Yanking open the bottom drawer of his desk, he grabbed the bottle of whiskey and the dirty glass beside it. He poured a generous shot with trembling hands.

"Damn it to hell." He gulped it, wishing the bottle wasn't empty.

CHAPTER 16

Henry sat on the unlit front porch of Vernon's cabin, absently tapping the manila envelope against the chair. His thoughts were on the jobs, and the message Vernon had relayed. The hint of something below the surface of the position descriptions intrigued him. Perhaps, like Aubrey had suggested, he should consider a new line of work.

He gazed across the valley, where the Blue Ridge Mountains were steeped in blues and pinks as the sun faded. There were some things he missed about this part of the country. Sunsets like the one he was witnessing. Fishing with his uncle. The smell of freshly mown hay. Green-clad mountains shrouded in early morning mist. Even the sounds of insects. They were beginning their evening serenades, while the summer sky held its breath somewhere between dusk and twilight.

Gingerly rubbing his sore shoulder, he reflected on the past. Any happy remembrances were bleached by unhappy ones. They started with the loss of his mother. After that, it was unending arguments with his father up to his first heartbreak. He escaped by accepting a scholarship at a small college in Colorado. Being home refreshed his memory of things he'd rather leave in the past.

Was he willing to move back to his home state? Making a career decision now was something he didn't trust himself to do. He also recognized that applying for a job and accepting employment were separate matters. Typically, the federal process was slow. He saw no harm in completing an application. A few months might bring a change in his thinking, especially if his father's illness progressed. That was another topic he didn't trust himself to contemplate tonight.

Henry stood and stretched, mindful of his wound. He'd been holed up in the cabin, reviewing his notes, since leaving the slaughterhouse. If his visit with Hugh served its purpose, future cattle rustling would be delayed for a few months. Perhaps long enough for Louis to find the killer without the need to publicly dredge up Aubrey's past.

Reviewing his observations from the crime scene had reminded him of the discolored spots in the soil. With an early start in the morning, he could take another look at the corral in angled sunlight, when shadows and indentations were easier to spot. He leaned against the porch railing and listened to the night sounds.

Increasing darkness brought a subtle change among the chirping insects, some had quieted while others were starting. On the highway, a vehicle slowed. Wondering if it might be Vernon, Henry looked for headlights. He saw none, and the engine sounds faded. He thought nothing of it until tires crunched gravel in the driveway.

The prickling sensation on his neck made him wish his pistol wasn't locked in Vernon's gun cabinet. His rifle was locked in the borrowed truck, which he'd parked around back. The keys hung on a peg by the back door, which was also locked. Opening the front door would make too much noise, and the nightlight in the kitchen would silhouette him in the doorway. He glanced toward the driveway. Who would be paying a secretive visit?

Deciding to discover the answer on his own terms, he assessed the terrain around the cabin. It was nestled on a hill, surrounded by small meadows on two sides, and forest in the rear. A strip of mixed hardwoods lined the opposite side of the curved driveway and partially hid the house from the road. Slipping off the porch and toward the trees, he kept below the crest of the slope to avoid being sky-lined.

It took several minutes to ease among the hardwoods until he was a few yards away from a dark-colored pickup stopped halfway up the drive. Movement at the front of the truck caught his attention. Two men were joined by a third, who approached from the direction of the cabin.

"Su camioneta no está aquí. No hay nadie en la casa." The man spoke in Spanish, a language Henry had acquired in Colorado. *His truck is not here. There's nobody home.*

"Ya vámonos de aquí," another said. *Let's get out of here.*

"Si Mauro, las historias. Ese hombre está loco," said the first. *Yes Mauro, the stories. This man is crazy.*

"No me quiero morir." The second man's voice wavered. *I don't want to die.*

The third man, a thickset man whom Henry guessed was Mauro, only grunted. He opened the driver's door and climbed into the pitch-black interior. The others jumped in the cab as the engine roared to life. Mauro backed slowly out of the driveway. Once on the highway, the headlights flicked on, but the truck was too far away for Henry to get any sort of description.

He remained among the trees for some time. When satisfied no one had stayed behind, he walked to the porch. Cautiously opening the door, he was greeted by his uncle's cat. Pancho's only interest was dinner as he meowed and rubbed against Henry's legs. He fed the cat, then went to the gun cabinet, where he examined a few of Vernon's hunting rifles before retrieving his pistol.

It wasn't difficult to figure out where the men had heard the stories. For once, Henry appreciated Aubrey's endless telling of those larger-than-life tales.

CHAPTER 17

Della patted the countertop in front of Henry, promising to return after taking orders from a table of five. In spite of her frenzied pace, it appeared to be a slow morning in the café. Only three tables were occupied. Other than a man in owlish glasses sitting a few seats away, the counter was empty. The man appeared buried in a newspaper, but Henry had looked up from the menu a couple of times and caught him staring.

Della returned, placing a glass of iced tea in front of Henry. "Sweet, right?"

"You bet." He scratched the stubble on his chin. He hadn't slept well, thanks to his mysterious visitors. His plan to stop at the old corral had been delayed by a police car parked on the road. He opted for breakfast in town, then he'd try the corral on the way home.

Della rapped the counter with her ink pen. "What can I get you, honey?"

Henry ordered a light breakfast and absently watched as she leaned across a narrow counter to hand the order to the cook. Her personality seemed to complement Vernon's, even his occasional crazy streaks. The apron tied around her waist accentuated her figure in that tight-fitting, blue dress she wore. She didn't possess the too-thin body most women seemed to desire these days, a trend he didn't favor. Aside from the fact she was twenty years his senior, he found her figure pleasing. He had unconsciously raised a speculative eyebrow before realizing she'd turned and caught his frank appraisal.

Henry felt his cheeks flush with embarrassment. His uncle's fiancé, no less.

Della patted her hair and smiled, making no mention of his bad manners. "I heard the memorial service will be held soon. Aubrey has family in the area, doesn't he? Besides his cousins, that is. Another uncle, I think. Not sure if that's on his mamma's or his daddy's side."

Henry focused on keeping his eyes above Della's neckline. She had a habit of patting the bottled-blonde hair piled atop her head when she talked, which seemed to be often this morning.

"The whole town will be there anyway," Della said. "Since it was murder and all. Everybody's been talking about it. Hasn't been anything happen like this around here for over twenty years."

"A murder?" Henry felt idiotic. She clearly didn't mean a funeral.

Della nodded.

"What happened?" He didn't really need to prompt her. She was launching into the story before he finished the question.

"I didn't live in Parsons Gap back then, but it was big news for miles around. There were two college folks staying out near the wash, digging around for fossils or rocks or something."

Henry had no idea where or what the wash was and didn't get a chance to ask.

"The man killed the woman, then skipped town," Della said. "Never found him. Probably left the country. An argument started it all, but not like you'd think. It was over a rock. People said they were bickering about it in town that day. It was years ago, and I don't remember the whole story. Of course, I was very young." She sighed and patted her hair, as if any could fall out of place with all that hairspray.

"Time sure flies, don't it?"

Della reached for an energy drink she'd stashed under the counter and took a long sip. Henry noticed the dark circles under her eyes that makeup didn't hide.

"This wedding is wearing me out." She paused briefly, which Henry imagined was only to catch her breath. "Even though it's going to be small, I've had lots of things to take care of lately. It's getting to Vernon, too. He'd just as soon fly to Las Vegas for the weekend."

"You two wouldn't do something crazy like that, would you?" Henry imagined them in Las Vegas, being pronounced man and wife by an Elvis impersonator.

Della smoothed her apron. "What's so crazy about getting married in Vegas?"

The man reading the newspaper politely cleared his throat and pointed at his coffee cup. Della grabbed the coffeepot, filled his cup, replaced the pot, and was back in front of Henry in one fluid motion.

Henry tried a new subject. "Do you know how long Alva Jean had been seeing Aubrey?"

"That Aubrey!" Della waggled her eyebrows and patted Henry's arm. "I don't think he was in town a day before he was after that girl. Saw her in here one morning and that was all she wrote. Alva Jean's a looker, isn't she?"

"Definitely." After being caught ogling Della, there was nothing else to lose.

"Hit it off right away. They made a date for later that night at the Watering Hole Saloon. They would get together about every night."

"Did Jimmy Lee go out with Alva Jean before that?"

Della laughed loudly. "Jimmy Lee is the only one ever thought that. She told me they went out once, in high school. That was enough for her. She wouldn't have a thing to do with him after that. For some reason, he seems to think he has special rights over her. She refers to him only as 'The Asshole' now. Excuse my French."

"Besides Jimmy Lee, did she ever mention anything about anyone being angry with Aubrey, or the fact they were dating?"

"Don't you sound just like Louis?" She didn't seem to care that he did, and continued without taking a breath. "Not that I'm aware. Any trouble in town usually has to do with the McLeans. They don't like much of anyone, but Aubrey was kin. That carries weight with them."

Henry agreed, recalling the conversation he'd overheard a few nights ago.

"Odessa seems to have taken a shine to you." Della eyed him speculatively. "I heard her talking to Hugh about it the other morning."

Henry shifted on the stool. "First time I met her she looked at me like she would a beef carcass, figuring out where to make the first cut."

Della winked. "Maybe that's the way she measures her men."

"She's not really my type."

"What is your type?" She leaned close. "I've got some single friends."

He looked at her, expressionless. "Have you seen Louis around this morning?"

If Della was disappointed he didn't jump at the offer, she didn't show it. "I imagine he's taking his grandson to the doctor. Lord knows, that boy is a handful. Broke his arm several weeks ago, riding a fancy new skateboard. Gets about whatever he wants from his granddaddy. Jack's a good kid, though. He's my cousin, in case you're wondering how I know all this."

"Louis is the grandfather of your cousin?" Henry wondered if everyone in Parsons Gap was somehow related. He'd forgotten that facet of small town life, what he used to jokingly call the Theory of Rural Relativity. He finished the tea, watching Della as her gaze swept over her customers. This time he made sure his eyes avoided her blue-clad curves.

Della refilled Henry's glass. "He's only nine, but bless his heart, he's quite the little con artist when he's of a mind. That's how Louis came to buy him that skateboard for Christmas. Always looking for some new excitement, that boy. Drives his mother crazy with worry, I'm sure."

"How is he your cousin?" Henry grabbed the opportunity to ask the question when she paused to catch her breath.

"I call him my cousin, but I guess he really isn't anymore. You know Carlie, Alva Jean's big sister? That's his mother. She's the veterinarian. Used to be married to my late husband's cousin, Brett." A bell rang in the kitchen. Della patted his arm again. "That'll be yours, I bet. Be right back."

Henry had assumed Louis' son was the one supplying grandchildren.

When Della returned, she was armed with an overloaded tray. She slid a large bowl of oatmeal and a trough of sliced fruit in front of Henry. She grabbed a pot of coffee and filled the newspaper reader's mug while expertly balancing the tray. Henry thought it best to stop watching her, so he looked out the window at passing vehicles.

"Speaking of." Della dipped her lacquered head toward the window.

Outside, an auburn-haired woman in green surgical scrubs climbed out of a Jeep Cherokee. She paused to check for traffic then hurried across the street and into the drug store.

"Some of the boys around here call her the 'Ice Princess' because she won't give them the time of day. I've even heard the rumor she bats for the other team." Della leaned close and lowered her voice to a whisper. "You know, a lesbian. I don't believe it at all, of course. Not that I'd blame her much if was true. Being married to Brett must have been hell."

He realized the woman was Carlie Hannahan. Della was watching him, so he managed a halfhearted smile.

"Brett wasn't much of a husband. Or a father, either," Della said. "Bless his heart."

"That bad, huh?"

"I think he was just too immature for all the responsibility. He used to drink a bit. He was never abusive, mind you. Louis would have killed him if he'd hurt a hair on his daughter's head. And I doubt they'd ever have found the body."

Henry had witnessed Louis' reaction to the relationship news about his daughter and had no problem imagining that was possible. The cowbell clanged, interrupting their conversation. Jimmy Lee paused in the doorway to scowl at the bell, as if that would stop the ringing. His gaze met Henry's and he sauntered to the counter, settling his lanky frame onto the next seat.

"Morning, Jimmy Lee." Della greeted as she poured him a cup of coffee.

Jimmy Lee nodded, but kept his eyes on Henry. "How about some news?"

"News about what?" Henry placed his spoon on the plate.

"That murder," Jimmy Lee said. "Your head was so far up Hannahan's ass the other day I figure you'd have the inside scoop, so to speak."

Vernon had been right about Jimmy Lee's persistence.

"Della, it's been a pleasure." His meal half-eaten, Henry rose, dropped money on the counter and left the café without another glance at Jimmy Lee.

CHAPTER 18

Henry strode out of the café and ran into a woman, nearly knocking her down. The bag she'd been carrying hit the sidewalk with a soft thud. He scrambled to pick it up for her, inadvertently bumping heads with the boy who had been walking beside her. Henry mumbled a quick apology, glancing up at the woman as she put a hand on the boy's shoulder. Realizing it was Carlie Hannahan, Henry pulled his Stetson low and avoided eye contact as he returned the bag. The sun was at his back. Maybe she wouldn't recognize him.

"Henry?" Surprise was evident in her voice.

He removed his hat and forced himself to look at her. "Hello, Carlie. Been a while."

"I'd heard you were in town." Her hand shaded her eyes against the morning sun.

Henry forced a smile. When she returned the smile, he was shocked to feel his heart thump in his chest. After all that had happened between them, and the time that had passed, he still found her inexplicably attractive. "I hope nothing is broken."

"What?"

"The bag." He pointed toward it. "I hope it's not broken."

"Oh, it's a plastic bottle. Don't worry." She glanced at the boy. "This is my son, Jack."

He offered his hand to the boy, who grinned and lifted his right arm, which was enclosed in a cast from above his elbow to below his wrist. Henry shook his left hand.

"Pleased to meet you, Mr. Henry."

Henry tried to think of something clever to say, but when he looked at Carlie his mind went blank. Shoving his hands in his pockets, he fought to ignore the odd pressure in his chest. She was even more beautiful than he remembered. Hazel eyes watched him from a face that was familiar yet new. Unlike Della, she wore very little make-up. Those loose-fitting scrubs did nothing to hide her athletic figure. This time he used peripheral vision, not wanting to get caught in the act again.

"I've got no right to ask," Carlie said. "But I'd really like a chance to talk with you. Right now, I'm late meeting Dad so Jack can get to an appointment." She glanced at her watch and fidgeted with her keys. "If it's okay to talk, I mean."

"Sure, it's okay." The words tumbled out. Why was he so agreeable?

She asked for his phone number. "I'll call you after work. I don't always know when that will be, but usually around 5:30."

Henry gave her Vernon's number at the cabin.

"Maybe we could go have a cup of coffee? Make that tea, okay? I'll call you later, when I have a better idea about my schedule."

He watched her climb into a red Jeep Cherokee, wondering what he'd just gotten himself into. Reopening old wounds wasn't in his plan. He was angry with himself for even being interested in what she might have to say. Things weren't working out right. He wanted to be angry, just not at himself. The matter of his unexpected attraction only made things worse. So did the fact she remembered he preferred tea.

"Excuse me, Mr. Smith?"

Henry spun around. The man in the owlish glasses

stood there, squinting in the sunlight.

"I'm Wayne Hewlett, with *The Messenger*. The local newspaper. Can I ask you a few questions?"

Henry frowned. "About what?"

"You're Whispering Smith, right?"

"I'm Henry Smith."

Hewlett pulled a notepad from his back pocket. "Can you tell me about the tracking you did for the Sheriff's Department at the murder scene? Did you find anything to help with the investigation?"

"I can't comment on that." Henry hoped that answer would discourage further questions. He should have known better. Hewlett was a reporter. Getting discouraged probably wasn't in his job description.

"Did you learn your tracking expertise in Colorado, catching all those cattle thieves? You were their most successful range detective for nearly ten years. Why did you leave your job?"

"Where did you hear that?"

Hewlett didn't relent. "Is it true?"

"Not exactly."

"How did you get the nickname of Whispering Smith?"

"Because I don't talk much." Henry turned and abruptly walked away. He crossed the street, quickly climbed into his truck and drove away before Hewlett had a chance to follow.

Henry drove backroads to Parsons Hollow Road, trying not to think about Carlie. The police car was gone, so he pulled off the road above the corral. Walking down the trail, he saw the yellow police tape was absent. Unlike his state of mind, the corral looked benign in the late morning light.

Henry paused under the large oak and pulled the notebook out of his back pocket. A blue jay jumped onto a low limb and squawked its raucous jay-jay at him, interrupting the stillness. As Henry neared the branch, the jay squawked louder, not intimidated by his approach. He smiled. The bird reminded him of Jimmy Lee.

The jay finally flew away, and Henry lingered in the shade, enjoying the relative quiet as he reviewed his notes. Several minutes later he left the shadows and entered the corral near the loading chute. Several sections of weathered fence rails were scattered on the ground. He stepped over them and approached the chute.

Glancing into the corral, he sensed something was different. He checked the sketch in his notebook to confirm that only one watering trough had been there. The second one was overturned, a salt block on top. He examined the first metal trough, finding a few inches of stagnant water and hundreds of dead insects. Deer tracks littered the ground, some were days old and some very recent. Cattle tracks were in abundance.

Henry studied the area. Beneath the oak, a textural difference in the soil attracted his eye. He began to walk closer when he caught movement in the rocks near the oaks. A pair of agitated chipmunks scurried for cover. He stopped. Nothing moved for several minutes. Finally, the chipmunks resumed their foraging. Henry scanned the rocks and trees skirting the corral. Nothing seemed out of the ordinary, but he couldn't shake the uneasy feeling that he was being watched.

After last night, he'd returned to the habit of carrying his pistol. Senses alert to his surroundings, he got on his knees and sifted the dirt through his fingers. He felt differences in the texture, something that could occur when a hole was refilled. He explored the ground with his fingers, finding it softer than the surrounding area. It was roughly a square, about the same width as a shovel.

Cattle tracks were everywhere around this spot, virtually concealing it. Henry glanced around the corral again. An idea struck him, and he was able to locate three more holes by looking for high concentrations of tracks and methodically poking the soil with a stick. Obviously, someone had tried to hide the holes with the tracks of cattle.

The cattle would have to be herded over these areas, and he'd seen no footprints. Not even indentations of buckets or traces of feed on the ground. He circled the corral, searching for human or animal tracks. He found only those of the cows. Something must be here. The movement of the cattle could not be explained otherwise.

Leaning against the fence, he stared thoughtfully at the bare ground, considering several possibilities. He made another circuit of the corral, looking for anything that didn't quite belong. Near the overturned trough, he found a scrap of burlap clinging to a rusted nail on a piece of wood. He slipped on his glasses and held the cloth between his fingers, examining it carefully. The fibers were packed with dirt.

Henry grinned.

Horse hooves and human feet covered in canvas or burlap wouldn't leave obvious marks. Searching the corral again, he found a faint fabric pattern stamped into the upper lip of a depression. The dirt-encrusted burlap mimicked smudged hoofprints. Now that he knew what to look for, he found several of the camouflaged prints scattered among the cattle tracks.

The chipmunks squeaked and darted into the rocks. Henry saw Louis Hannahan descending the trail from the road.

"Thought I'd find you here," Louis said.

Stuffing the piece of burlap into his pocket, Henry met him beneath the oak tree. "How'd you know where I'd be?"

"I *am* a detective," Louis replied, grinning. "Besides, Deputy Monroe said he saw you driving out this way."

"Keeping tabs?"

"Do you blame me?"

Henry wasn't sure how to respond to that, so he made

a noncommittal shrug.

"Thought I'd stop by," Louis said. "Just checked Aubrey's place. Nothing interesting, but we did find his truck parked there. It's not far from here. He must have walked to the barn."

Henry nodded. "Anything turn up at the barn?"

"Odessa took a look around and said everything appeared to be in order, though she did report what she called a prowler. Said one of the horses scared him by ripping off a piece of a denim. The forensics folks may have more to report later. Back to square one, I guess."

Henry pointed toward the corral. "I might have something."

"Saw you playing in the dirt."

"I found several holes. What's odd is whoever did the digging is playing cautious. They're using cattle tracks to hide signs."

Louis rubbed his chin and stared at the corral. "Anything in these holes?"

"I didn't get that far." Henry produced the fabric scrap and explained its use. He suggested they examine a few of the holes. Louis readily agreed, and they dug up the three. The depths varied, as well as the size. Two of them were empty. In the bottom of the third, Henry cut his finger on the edge of a rusted metal bucket. He sat back and chuckled.

"What's gotten into you?" Louis brushed his hands together.

"Buried treasure."

"Come again?"

"When I had supper at the Bar T the other night, this story about the North Carolina gold rush came up. Rory and Sally Ann found this old journal, and in it was a tale about a bandit and stolen money that was never recovered. They said Jimmy Lee and a couple of the wranglers had taken an interest in hunting it." Henry waved toward the corral.

"Could be what's going on here."

"You're thinking somebody's been out here, searching for a lost treasure, and keeping it secret? That's a lot of work." Louis got to his feet and looked across the dirt road. "You're also saying the cattle business may not be the McLeans after all?"

"It's possible the holes are related to some fabled treasure hunt, but it doesn't mean the McLeans aren't interested in the cattle. They're tucked away in a quiet place. Good opportunity for a thief."

"I'm curious why this particular place," Louis said. "And why it's secret. Maybe there's a motive here."

Henry didn't particularly care for Jimmy Lee, but couldn't see him killing for some treasure that may or may not be real. Others knew about it, too. "This would add a few more names to your list of suspects, including my father."

"I'm too close to most of the people in this town to dismiss anybody on personal feelings." Louis said. "Besides, I believe anyone is capable of killing. It's a matter of what provokes us."

For a second, Henry was back in the canyon in Colorado. The image of Conner's dead eyes floated through his thoughts. He quickly tucked the thought back in its hiding place.

Louis pointed toward the old road that wound down to the lake. "If Aubrey put his horse in the barn, how did he get back to the corral?"

"Aubrey preferred riding to walking."

"Then let's go with the assumption that someone else put the horse away. Where would Aubrey have left the horse?"

Henry studied the road. "If he was coming up from the barn, he wouldn't be able to see the corral until he rounded that stand of trees."

"Think you can find some tracks?"

Muddy Waters

Henry shrugged. It took him fifteen minutes to locate an area where a horse had been tied. He looked thoughtfully at the tracks. He recognized the tracks of McLean's horses, but there had been one, and sometimes two horses. In the meadow he'd found flattened grass where a blanket had been spread on the ground. Had Alva Jean and Aubrey met here? Rather than bring up that subject, he concentrated on the places where a single horse had been tied. He found a spot where he was certain the prints were Aubrey's.

"Aubrey was watching someone, or something," Henry said. "Whatever he saw, it appears to have held his interest."

"You said Aubrey was worried about the cattle." Louis crossed his arms over his chest. "If he was up here watching the cattle, and saw someone digging in the corral, then it stands to reason he also would have seen the cattle being used to cover up the holes. He mention anything to you about that? Would it make him think rustling?"

Henry shook his head. "Moving cattle around, but not stealing them isn't suspicious."

Louis frowned as he looked toward the corral. "Here's a thought. What if the person doing the digging isn't the same person hiding evidence of digging?"

"It would explain Aubrey's curiosity," Henry said. "But kills your theory that it's about cattle theft."

"I'm not ruling anything out just yet."

CHAPTER 19

Henry returned to Vernon's cabin a few hours later, where he paced in the small living room waiting for the phone to ring. After poking around the corral with Louis, he'd gone to retrieve his pickup from the police. Having nothing to focus on but Carlie and their upcoming meeting, he was in a surly mood. Things didn't improve when he tripped over Vernon's cat and bumped his sore shoulder against the doorframe. Fidgeting on the sofa wasn't much better.

Plenty of years had passed, and he reminded himself he'd moved on long ago. Seeing her again couldn't be that bad, could it? He scratched his stubbled chin and realized he needed to clean up before seeing Carlie, then wondered why he was so concerned about being presentable. The conflicting thoughts muddled his thinking.

He decided a hot shower would clear his head. Refreshed, with a towel wrapped around his waist, he inspected the large bruise on his shoulder. It was looking better, or at least less purple. He ran his hand over his face and tried not to gauge the passing of time in the bathroom mirror. The lines on his face stood out in the shadows of the harsh bathroom light. The scars on his upper body told a story, too. At least being in the saddle or working on the open range for weeks at a time had kept him tanned and muscular. Feeling like a narcissist, he turned away from the mirror.

He tried to concentrate on Aubrey's murder while

dressing, mentally ticking through his list of possible suspects for the hundredth time. His mind refused to cooperate. Giving up, he found an old Randolph Scott movie on television. Vernon's cat was happy with the choice, settling comfortably in his lap for a siesta. When the telephone rang, the cat bolted and knocked the phone onto the floor. Henry grabbed it and waited four rings before answering. No need to let her think he was in any hurry.

After a few formalities, Carlie invited him to meet at her house, which was located behind her parents' house. He remembered how to get there but let her give directions anyway. He told himself it wasn't because he liked hearing her voice.

Arriving about twenty minutes later, he parked beside the red Cherokee and steeled himself for whatever was ahead. What could she possibly have to say that would matter? The past couldn't be changed. If she wanted to apologize for being unfaithful, she was too late. He'd already forgiven her, because forgiveness was part of getting over things, wasn't it?

But it did matter. Especially how seeing her again had affected him. It had been unsettling, to say the least. He climbed out of the truck and looked toward the house. Carlie was seated in a plastic Adirondack chair on the porch. She rose, straightened the bottom of her blouse over her jeans.

Not trusting himself to walk a straight line under her intense gaze, he leaned against the front of his truck. His hand shook as he removed his hat. He gripped it tightly as he watched her cross the short distance to the truck.

"Thanks for coming over," she said. "I've been wanting to talk."

"There's nothing to say. It was fifteen years ago—"

"Henry, please."

He moved to the back of the truck and dropped the

tailgate. They sat side by side, their feet swinging a few inches above the ground. Part of him wanted to run, the other wanted to stay. He looked up at the star-strewn night sky, wishing he didn't feel so damned confused.

"The stars appear so large and bright here in the mountains," Carlie said.

"You should see them in Colorado."

"Oh, of course." Her voice was quiet. "I should have thought about that before saying it."

"They're still the same stars." Henry realized she was just as nervous. Thinking casual conversation might help them both, he dredged up something from their past. "Looking at stars from the tailgate of a pickup truck sounds like a line from some country song. Not that I would know. I'm still not into country music."

"You're kidding! How can you wear a cowboy hat? How do you survive out west without being a connoisseur of country music? I mean, what do your friends think?"

He recognized her teasing tone, even now. "I keep a Jerry Jeff Walker CD on hand, in case of an emergency. That's as close as I ever get."

"Impressive. His music has a high twang factor."

"Twang factor?" Henry could tease, too. "I don't know about that. *Mr. Bojangles* gets rock station airplay."

"Soft rock, maybe. And that's the Nitty Gritty Dirt Band version."

Henry shrugged.

"Where did that CD come from? The rock or country section?"

"Let's try again," Henry said. "Charlie Daniels Band?"

"Country."

"Don't tell me '*Long Haired Country Boy*' is a country song."

"Your first clue should have been the word 'country' in the title."

"ZZ Top?" Henry asked.

"Oh, be serious."

"They *are* from Texas."

They both laughed. Talk interspersed with laughter was all too familiar. It made Henry flinch. He said, "You don't really want to talk about music all evening, do you?"

Carlie shook her head. She was quiet for a moment. "I want to apologize."

"It was a long time ago." Henry shifted on the tailgate. "Don't worry about it."

"You don't understand—"

"What's to understand?" Henry interrupted, managing to say the words without the anger he felt. "You found someone else, that's all."

"It isn't all." Her voice sounded almost childlike. "It wasn't the truth."

Henry stared at her. He said nothing. He couldn't.

"All those years have passed and even now it still hurts." She sniffed and wiped a tear from her eye. "I lied about Tommy Blevins because I knew if I didn't, you would've thrown away your scholarship. Your happiness was important to me, and I knew you would never be happy if you stayed here. Not with the way things were between you and your father. I couldn't stand seeing how it affected you."

Henry stared in disbelief. For fifteen years, he believed she'd betrayed him. He had trusted her. Even as a young man he knew she was the one he wanted to be with, no question. Her lie had changed everything. He wanted to believe she was lying now, but knew she had no reason to lie. Nothing could erase the scars on his heart.

Carlie broke the awkward silence. "I don't expect you to forgive me. I just wanted you to know. Selfishly speaking, I guess this helps me deal with the pain of what I did."

Henry thought it should be comforting that she had suffered, too. But it wasn't. If anything, he felt worse knowing both of them had gone through hell needlessly. He wanted to tell her he had almost given up college to return home, of the many times he planned to come back and take her away from Tommy. It wouldn't matter now.

He jumped off the tailgate and opened the truck door. Carlie followed. She stood near him, inside the little circle of light emanating from the cab. His eyes met hers, and before she turned away he caught a glimpse of her pain.

"You probably think I'm awful," she said.

"I think," Henry spoke slowly, choosing his words. "You did what you thought you had to. Other than that, I don't want to think about anything right now."

CHAPTER 20

Henry pulled into the dirt parking lot of the Watering Hole Saloon and eyed the large, barn-like building with reservations. It sounded like the forget-your-troubles kind of place immortalized in the country music songs he said he didn't listen to. The number of vehicles in the lot indicated the bar was a popular hangout. His desire to feel the numbing effects of alcohol was strong, so he got out of the pickup.

He approached the entrance, feeling he'd been struck by lightning. His mind was spinning with a million what-ifs and an odd sort of mourning for lost time. Physical pain would have been better than the emotional chaos he was experiencing. He needed to ease the sting of Carlie's confession.

"Henry, is that you?"

He turned. Alva Jean pushed back her pink cowgirl hat and winked. Her sexy tank-top and tight-fitting jeans tucked into pink cowgirl boots made him feel uncomfortable. The idea of tequila shots until he was numb quickly faded from his thoughts. Nothing but trouble would come of this combination.

"Didn't expect to find you at a spring break bash!" She smiled slyly. "If you're here alone, you're welcome to come join me and my friends. The place is packed but we got a table."

He heard himself say that would be fine. She latched onto his right arm and practically dragged him toward the door. Perhaps this wasn't such a bad idea after all. Maybe she'd provide insight into Aubrey's life in Parsons Gap. It might keep his mind off Carlie, too.

They followed a young couple in matching black Wrangler jeans through the door. People congregated around every table. The bar occupying the long wall opposite the door was jammed two-deep with customers. The dance floor was packed while a live band pounded out near-deafening rockabilly music, making conversation below a shout impossible.

"What are you drinking?" Henry had to ask the question several times, finally he leaned in close and spoke loudly in Alva Jean's ear.

She mouthed the word longneck and Henry worked his way to the bar. He wedged his way between two women in tight-fitting Appalachian State T-shirts and ordered three beers as soon as he got the bartender's attention. Most of the patrons were college-aged and he felt out of place. He drank half the first bottle before leaving the bar, thinking it would be easy to slip out unseen.

Alva Jean appeared and attached herself to his arm. She grabbed one of the beers as she led him toward the back of the room, near restrooms labeled Fillies and Studs. Two couples and two empty chairs were squeezed around a small table. The band drowned out introductions as they played a tune Henry vaguely recognized. Both girls were young and blonde, similarly dressed in cropped shirts and tight jeans. Their hairstyles and earrings matched, and he wondered if they were twins.

While the girls giggled and whispered, their dates drank beer and looked bored. Occasionally they eyed the girls with mild enthusiasm. Henry finished his second beer. Placing the empty bottle on the table, he tried not to notice that college kids looked younger every year. They lined the walls, watching and waiting for an open table. Or a companion for the night, seeing the hungry looks on some of the anxious faces. Some of the young men were literally panting like hounds when a woman walked by them, which probably explained why they were still standing by the wall, alone.

The band started a slow song and couples flooded the dance floor.

"Wanna dance?" Alva Jean shouted into his ear. "My friends brought me here to have a little fun. They know I just love this band. I even dated the bass player in high school." She coaxed him to his feet. On the dance floor, she moved close and smiled up at him.

Being observant, Henry noticed things. Like how much she reminded him of Carlie with those even white teeth and inviting lips.

"By the way, my girlfriends back there think you are f-i-n-e." She waggled her eyebrows as she spelled out the word. Then she added, "For an older guy."

He wasn't sure if he should find that flattering or not. Her proximity and the faint smell of perfume almost made him forget the older guy comment. It was nice to hold her and feel the warmth of her body as they swayed slowly to the music. But nice was not where Henry's thoughts were going. Maybe the alcohol affected him more than he realized.

This was Aubrey's girlfriend. Carlie's little sister. She was out with friends, trying to forget the pain of loss. That sobered him. He breathed a sigh of relief when the band went into a fast tune and she no longer pressed her body against his. They danced through three more songs before returning to the bar.

Alva Jean held up two fingers. After he paid, she handed him one of the longnecks. He declined, and to his surprise, she downed one on the way. The empty joined the growing collection on the table. Alva Jean wiped her mouth with the back of her hand and winked at him as she started on the next bottle.

The quiet seemed unnatural when the band took a break. Near the main door, he saw Jimmy Lee talking with a raven-haired man whose thick-set features seemed familiar. Could this be Mauro? A redhead in tight jeans clung to Jimmy Lee's arm. When they turned to leave, he glared at Henry over the redhead's shoulder. Smirking, Jimmy Lee slipped a hand into her back pocket as they left.

The band started the next set with a slow song. Alva Jean grabbed Henry's arm when everyone at the table rose and headed for the dance floor. Once again, she pressed her body against his and nestled her head on his chest. She looked up, tears glistening in her eyes.

"I miss him," she said.

The tears tore at his heart. He told her Aubrey wouldn't want her to be sad. That it wouldn't be easy, but time would heal. Resisting the temptation to stroke her hair while he repeated the words, he settled for a brotherly pat on the back.

Henry took her hand. "Let's go outside and get some fresh air."

Alva Jean followed him outside and across the parking lot to his truck. She leaned against the truck and Henry was relieved to see she'd stopped crying. Before he could speak, she wrapped her arms around his neck, pulled him close and kissed him on the mouth. He disentangled himself with effort.

"I think we'd better keep this at the friend level." Henry stepped away from her. Alva Jean swayed, and he realized she was drunk. "Look, Aubrey was a good friend. When we lose someone, friends take care of each other and those they leave behind. I'm here to help, not to take his place."

She nodded, sniffing back tears. It wasn't long before she was crying again. Henry reluctantly reached out and took her in his arms, letting her bury her face in his shoulder. He closed his eyes and held her until the sobbing subsided. His shirt was wet, and she looked at him apologetically.

"You want to go back inside, or should I take you home?" Henry wiped tears from her cheek with his fingers.

"The band's louder than usual." Her speech was slurred. "Nothing I can't stand if you want to go back in and party."

Henry unlocked the driver's door. "I imagine it'll be a day or two before my ears stop ringing."

That elicited a weak smile. She opened the driver's side door and slid to the middle of the bench seat. Henry climbed in beside her and started the engine. Before he shifted into gear, she leaned in and kissed him. Her attempt to climb onto his lap was thwarted by the steering wheel. He gently pushed her back onto the seat. "We're not doing this."

"Oh, come on, Aubrey." She tried to launch a second attack.

Henry froze. Alva Jean did, too. Then she looked up at him with tears welling in her eyes. The dam burst, and she began crying uncontrollably. He held her close, blinking back his own tears.

"It's okay." The reassuring words were really for both of them. "It's okay."

"I thought I was doing so good." She hiccupped through the tears. "I miss him so much, and I thought this would take my mind off things for a little while."

"Distractions aren't always the best way to deal with things." Henry felt a little guilty about giving advice he wasn't following. "There comes a point where you just have to get on with your life while you heal."

Alva Jean's voice trembled. "Promise me you'll catch whoever did this."

Henry looked out the window into the darkness and

held her tightly, until her crying subsided. When it did, he gave her shoulders a quick squeeze. He wanted to tell her that he'd find Aubrey's killer, come hell or high water, no matter how long it took. Mostly he wanted her to know she wasn't the only one hurting. All he trusted himself to say was two words.

"I promise."

CHAPTER 21

"**J**esus, Henry. You're old enough to be her father."

Henry set his iced tea on the counter. He didn't need to see who had spoken. Jimmy Lee's mocking voice was easily recognizable. Della raised her eyebrows and turned away, busying herself filling a pitcher with tea. So much for idle conversation before the lunch crowd appeared. In the reflection of a glass picture frame, he saw Jimmy Lee behind him, flanked by two Bar T wranglers. Surely there must be work at the Bar T to keep them busy this time of day.

"I reckon you got lucky last night."

"That's none of your business, Jimmy Lee." Henry spoke quietly, not turning from the counter.

Jimmy Lee snorted. "I'll bet money on it. I know all about Alva Jean."

Henry felt his anger grow. He turned to face Jimmy Lee. "Then you don't know as much about her as you think you do."

"I know she's easier than a pop-top can."

Ordinarily, Henry would have let it pass. This morning he was feeling exceptionally irritable. Maybe it was Aubrey's death. Maybe it was this whole business with Carlie. Maybe it was because Alva Jean was standing in the doorway, listening to their exchange. Whatever the reason, Henry hit him.

In one quick motion, he had risen from the stool and struck Jimmy Lee's face with the back of his fist, a martial arts blow delivered with a snapping motion of the forearm. Jimmy Lee stumbled backwards into one of the wranglers, whose quick reaction prevented them both from falling to the floor. The other stood there, mouth open in surprise.

"You'll pay for that." Jimmy Lee wiped a trickle of blood from the corner of his mouth.

"You're welcome to try and collect." Henry stood there, fighting the urge to hit him again. "Right after you apologize to Alva Jean."

Jimmy Lee's retort was silenced by the wrangler's elbow in his ribs. He muttered something about a promise to his mother. Jimmy Lee glared at Henry. He reluctantly offered an apology to Alva Jean.

She immediately accepted.

The wrangler placed a hand on Jimmy Lee's arm and escorted him to a table in the back. The other wrangler shuffled along behind them, glancing over his shoulder at Henry, still open-mouthed. Henry sat down again, ignoring stares from the other patrons. Ice danced in his glass as Della refilled it.

"Can't say he didn't deserve that." She patted her hair.

Henry looked up from the glass as Alva Jean took the stool beside him. He managed a smile. "How are you this morning?"

She put her elbow on the counter and cradled her head in the crook of it. "Could be better, but that's what I get for drinking too much." She touched his arm. "Aren't many like you still around. You're a real jewel, Henry. Thank you for what you did."

"You're welcome." He didn't feel much like a jewel. After losing his temper, he was mentally kicking himself for allowing Jimmy Lee to get under his skin. Vernon had been right. Jimmy Lee was persistent.

Alva Jean smiled, a hint of a tear in her eyes. "I really mean it, Henry. You didn't have to do that."

Della nodded approvingly at Henry as she brought his order. She looked up when the cowbell jangled. "Oh dear, looks like they've been out all night." Her tone was hushed.

The McLean brothers spilled into the café, unkempt in dirt-streaked clothes. Beau wore a sleeveless chambray shirt that revealed a tattoo of a fire-breathing beast on his upper arm. He seemed to be doing his best to mimic the fierce look of the dragon. Add a few flames and his dark expression would have been a perfect match.

"They usually raise holy hell when they've pulled an all-nighter," Della said. "They party with some of those Mexican workers at the slaughterhouse and get stupid on tequila. Hard liquor just makes them meaner, if you can imagine that being possible."

Beau pointed at Jimmy Lee, seated at a table in the back, and nudged his brother. He said, "There's the two-timing little bastard."

Alva Jean rose from the stool beside Henry. "I'd better get to work."

Jimmy Lee got to his feet and faced the McLeans as they approached the booth. "Y'all got something you wanna say to me?"

The wranglers exchanged glances but remained seated at the table, their faces pale. Jimmy Lee stood his ground. Beau stopped in front of him, his thick-muscled body dwarfing Jimmy Lee. Henry gave him credit for not being intimidated. But in this case, it seemed Jimmy Lee was one of those people with more bravado than brains.

"I saw you with that woman last night." Beau's hands were balled into fists. "Odessa don't know about it yet, and you better hope when she finds out that she takes it well."

"Odessa dumped me, jackass," Jimmy Lee said. "Why should she care who I go out with?"

"That ain't the way I heard it."

"Well that's the way it is. Maybe you'd better get it

straight from your lying sister before you run off to kick somebody's ass on her behalf."

The café was silent. Beau's shoulders stiffened. He moved forward. "You mouthy little --"

"You want to mess with me, Beau?" Jimmy Lee snarled like a wildcat. "Go right ahead, but you better think. I'd hate for you to do something you'll be sorry for later."

Beau had taken a half step toward Jimmy Lee when Hugh put a hand on his shoulder. He nodded toward the door. Henry followed Beau's gaze. Louis Hannahan was standing just inside the door, watching the exchange.

"We'll talk about this later." Beau threw Jimmy Lee a menacing glare as he backed away.

"Problem, boys?" Louis approached the table.

Both Beau and Jimmy Lee shook their heads. Jimmy Lee shrugged and slid back into the booth, saying it was a misunderstanding.

Louis didn't press the issue. He walked to the counter and settled beside Henry on the stool Alva Jean had vacated. Della had a cup of coffee waiting. Louis had apparently seen the red mark on Jimmy Lee's jaw. He leaned toward Henry and asked if Beau had hit Jimmy Lee.

"Beau didn't touch him," Henry said. He stared at his glass of iced tea.

"Then who did?"

Della and Henry traded glances before Della finally spoke. "He just had a little lesson on manners is all."

Louis raised his eyebrows.

"He got what he deserved for making an insulting remark." Della winked at Henry. "And he has apologized."

Picking up on Della's inference, Louis looked at Henry. "You hit him?"

"He said something very unkind about a friend of mine."

"Making enemies fast, aren't you?" He sipped his

coffee. "Don't take it to heart. I heard there's a small contingency of people in town that still tolerate you. In fact, they've instructed me to invite you for supper tonight. Six o'clock. Patricia is very anxious to see you again."

Henry assumed Patricia was his wife. Growing up, it had always been Mrs. Hannahan. He'd never known her first name. "I'm not so sure it's a good idea."

"Before you decide, you should know both Carlie and Alva Jean were the ones who suggested it." Louis leaned a little closer. "Carlie finally told me about the whole Tommy Blevins thing."

Henry said nothing. Instead, he focused on his plate, where he fiddled with the toothpick in his sandwich. Alva Jean brought her father the lunch special and a slice of lemon pie. They ate in silence until Della approached with a pot of coffee in one hand and a pitcher of tea in the other.

"How's things, Della?" Louis pushed his coffee cup toward her.

She looked toward the door. "Getting better all the time."

They followed her gaze to the door, where Vernon stood with a small bouquet of wildflowers in his hand and a silly smile on his face. He crossed to the stool beside Louis, leaned over the counter to kiss Della's cheek and offer the flowers. Louis and Henry exchanged surprised glances at the unprecedented display of affection.

"Well, gentlemen!" Vernon beamed at them. "It won't be long now. The reign of the most eligible bachelor in the county is coming to an end. We've planned it for a week from Saturday, sort of small and simple, out at the ranch. You're welcome to join us."

"The rumors are true, then." Louis got to his feet and shook Vernon's hand. "Been wondering if you were going to invite anyone else to the big event. Congratulations. It's about time you made an honest woman out of Della."

"Hell," Vernon replied. "It was the only thing I could come up with to get Henry back in town."

Della frowned at him. "I take it the flowers are meant to make up for that remark?"

Vernon winked at her before taking the seat next to Louis. He looked at the gun Louis wore on his hip. "You're working today? Some new crime wave hitting Metropolis or something?"

Louis picked up his coffee cup. "Someone's breaking into cars in that downtown parking lot again."

"So why call in the big detective?"

"We're short staffed and everyone's plates are already full."

"So, it rolled uphill for a change," Vernon said.

Louis explained the problem as Della poured coffee. "The parking lots in town look nice with all that fancy landscaping. The town council is proud of them, but any idiot can see it gives thieves too much cover. The number of car break-ins has gone up significantly. Can't convince the council to make changes since the tourists rave about how beautiful the parking lots are. I don't mind saying this job was a lot easier before tourism came to town."

"My job has only gotten better." Vernon grinned as he stirred sugar in his coffee.

"You always were a lucky bastard."

Vernon asked Louis about his progress with the investigation.

"We are proceeding with our inquiries." Louis used his fork to emphasize each word.

"I just got the official response, didn't I?" Vernon said.

Louis nodded as he ate. His plate was empty and half the pie was gone.

Henry had been quietly eating his sandwich while they talked. He saw the McLeans scowl at Jimmy Lee as they headed toward the door.

Beau spoke loudly as they passed the counter. "He'd better watch that smart mouth of his or he'll get a shiny new boot up his ass."

Louis did a double take when he saw Beau's boots.

"Forget it." Hugh pushed the door open. "He ain't worth a boot cleaning."

"You got that right!" Beau replied with a hoarse laugh. Outside the café window, Beau paused to light a cigarette he had shaken from a red and white Marlboro pack.

Louis cleared his throat emphatically, eyes on Henry.

"I guess you can quit wondering which McLean I saw," Henry said.

"I'll see y'all later." Louis tossed money on the counter. "Except for you, Henry. I'd like your assistance."

CHAPTER 22

"You want me to do what?"

Louis pointed at the dirt-filled litter box Henry had placed on the floor of the interview room. "Walk across and step in it, normal-like, as you go along."

Beau jerked his head toward Henry. "What's he got to do with this?"

Henry had wondered the same thing, until Louis had given him the task of finding a way to compare Beau's actual footprints to photographs of those found at the crime scene. Henry had returned with a cat litter box and a bag of garden soil from the hardware store, and Louis issued a few hurried instructions before Beau arrived.

"Just do what I asked, please." Louis leaned against the table in the center of the room.

"Which foot?"

"Doesn't matter."

Beau scowled, and with an exaggerated sigh, pulled up his pantlegs as if afraid to get dirt on them. He walked through the box, leaving the imprint of his new Nocona boot. Beau backed away, and Louis nodded to Henry.

Putting on his glasses, Henry approached the fresh track. With slightly dramatic emphasis, he opened his well-worn notebook and turned pages until he found the one he wanted. Kneeling beside the box, he studied the track. He glanced from the boot print to the notebook and back, taking his time with verifying minute details. Louis told him to make it look good. Several minutes later, he closed the notebook and got to his feet. He glanced at Louis, who leaned against the table, sipping coffee from a Mayberry Sheriff's Department mug.

Henry bit his lower lip to suppress a smile. "I'd say it's the same track."

"In your expert opinion," Louis added.

"That's correct." Henry returned to the chair.

"What's this bullshit?" Beau glared at Henry.

Louis set the mug on the table. He folded his arms across his chest and frowned at Beau as if admonishing a child. "Not really your concern, but maybe you ought to know. Henry is a certified tracker. His expertise has been instrumental in helping solve several criminal cases in Colorado. I've asked him to help."

"Whatever," Beau grunted.

Louis opened a manila folder and handed Beau a black and white photograph of his boot track. "What you should be concerned about is where your boot track was found. That photo was taken at the scene of Aubrey Miller's murder."

Henry watched for a reaction from Beau, who didn't flinch.

"Do you want to tell me again where you were the night Aubrey Miller was killed?"

"You can't say I was there just because of a damned boot track. Maybe I was there the day before. Besides, I ain't the only man in town with new boots."

Louis turned to Henry, who briefly explained how the age of tracks was determined

"There's more evidence than the track." Louis picked up a second manila folder from the table. When Louis flipped it open, Henry was close enough to see it contained a receipt for automotive repair on a police department vehicle.

"Forensics report." Louis tapped the folder. "DNA. The results on the fresh cigarette butts found at the murder scene match the one I took from you outside the café."

"You think I'd kill my own cousin?"

"You said it, not me. I do want to know what you were doing there and what you saw."

Beau licked his lips. He glanced at Henry. "I wasn't doing nothin' wrong and I sure as hell didn't kill no one. I was waitin' on Hugh. My truck had a flat up on the road. Didn't have no spare, so I called Hugh on my cell phone. It took him an hour to get there."

"Did you see anything while you were waiting?"

"I saw Aubrey on a horse."

"One of your horses?" Louis asked.

"Didn't notice what horse he was riding. Only know he was riding one."

"Then what?"

"He hung around awhile, by that old corral. Thought I heard him talking to someone."

"Do you know who it was?"

Beau looked directly at Henry. "I was too far away to get a good look at him. After a few minutes, Aubrey rode away."

"Which direction did Aubrey go?" Louis asked.

"I don't recall."

Louis sighed. "Did he ride up the hill or down the hill?"

"I said I don't recall." Beau glanced at his watch.

"You remember anything else?"

Beau shook his head.

"What about Hugh? He see anyone on the road?"

"Didn't say."

Louis picked up his coffee cup and took a few sips. "Did you notice anyone around the cattle by the pines?"

"What cattle?"

"You said you waited there for about an hour. You didn't hear any cattle? They weren't even fifty feet away from you."

"Didn't hear nothing at all to do with cattle." Beau

rubbed his hands together. "And I know what they sound like."

"I imagine you do." Louis handed him a business card. "I appreciate your cooperation. You remember anything else, no matter how unimportant it seems, please let me know."

Beau paused at the door and glared at Henry a moment before directing his question at Louis. "Is he accusing somebody of stealing cattle? Aubrey told us what he does in Colorado."

"You got reason to worry, Beau?" Louis asked, raising his eyebrows.

Beau responded by slamming the door.

CHAPTER 23

Henry pulled his truck to a stop outside the Bar T Ranch. He'd been avoiding his father, and he was running out of excuses. He'd called earlier in the day and spoken with Sally Ann. She was delighted that he was visiting, and more than happy to let him look through the journal. Climbing out of his truck, he caught a glimpse of a wrangler pushing a wheelbarrow into the barn. Figuring he'd learn more about the digging from him than he would from Jimmy Lee, he entered the barn.

He paused to breathe in the smell of hay, leather and horse. He'd always been drawn to the big old barn, a sheltered place that was shady and cool even when the sun baked the earth outside. It was quiet, except for the chirping barn swallows darting among the rafters. Near the tack room, his gaze fell on the empty burlap sacks stacked by the tack room door. He thought about the burlap scrap he'd found at the corral. There'd been a stack in the McLeans' barn, too.

He scanned a collection of tools leaning against the wall – axes, shovels, and pitchforks. Could any of them have been the murder weapon? Among the tools, a metal detector was partially hidden by a saddle blanket. He glanced up the aisle and realized he was being watched. A dark-haired man leaned on a pitchfork outside the stall he'd been cleaning.

As Henry approached, the wrangler stepped around the wheelbarrow. "We've not been introduced, but I know you're Henry Smith." The young man spoke with a slight accent. "My name is Guillermo Flores."

"Pleased to meet you." Henry shook the offered hand, recognizing him as the one who'd caught Jimmy Lee at the café. "Haven't had a chance to see what the ranch has to offer, besides those signs down at the road. How's business?"

"Not bad. Lots of trail rides, especially on weekends. We have a few guests here for the bed and breakfast. Things pick up once school is out for summer." Guillermo looked at the floor. "I was sorry to hear about Aubrey Miller. He was a good man, no matter what Jimmy Lee thought. He could tell some great stories."

"Mostly lies, I'm sure." Henry gave him a wry smile. "Speaking of stories, I was told one about this place. Something about a bandit."

"You mean that so-called lost treasure?" Guillermo laughed and shook his head. He waved a hand toward the house. "We poked around. It was more of a joke than anything. For me it's a hoax, so I quit wasting my time. Jimmy Lee and Stan might still hunt for it, I don't know."

"Who's Stan?"

"Stan Breen. The other wrangler."

"Is he around?" Henry asked.

"He's off today and tomorrow."

"How'd you know where to look?"

"Jimmy Lee had copies of a diary," Guillermo said. "There was this thing in it about the moon and an eastern hill. This barn and that corral are east of the original part of the house. We had a look. Nothing out here but horse turds."

Henry chuckled. "You guide the trail rides?"

"That and some fly fishing. Vernon does a little seminar and I help out." Guillermo paused. "He says you fish. Are you as competitive?"

"I'm usually the guy catching the smaller ones." While Henry enjoyed the friendly competition, some days he'd rather just fish. "Maybe we could go, without the contest."

Guillermo smiled. "I'd like that."

Henry switched the conversation to horseback trips offered at the ranch.

"The usual stuff," Guillermo replied. "One hour up to half-day trips. Last year the new thing was an all-day ride, with lunch provided. Sometimes we'll do an overnighter for groups."

"Any of those rides use that old road to the lake?"

"Why do you ask?" Guillermo seemed more curious than suspicious.

"It shows heavy use. I know the McLeans have horses in that barn, but that doesn't account for it all."

"Odessa rents that barn from the Bar T. It was Jimmy Lee's idea, since it was empty." Guillermo cocked his head. "Does this have to do with the murder?"

"I'm not sure," Henry said.

Guillermo paused, perhaps waiting for him to elaborate. When Henry didn't, he said, "The longer rides follow that road. There are two loops off it we use."

Henry thanked him and turned to leave. Guillermo stopped him. "Jimmy Lee's comment was way out of line. He deserved what he got, and then some. You know his mother would have raised a few welts if she'd heard."

Henry nodded and went to the house. Sally Ann was in the dining room arranging fresh-cut flowers for the centerpiece. He was relieved to find Rory had gone away for the day on business. It removed the stress of his visit, and he released the breath he'd been holding.

"Will you stay for supper?" Sally Ann asked.

"I've been invited to dine with the Hannahan family tonight."

She gave him a knowing smile. "It would be nice to see

you and Carlie together again."

Henry thought it best to say nothing rather than betray his feelings toward Carlie.

"How is he?" Henry asked. He wasn't supposed to know about his father's cancer, so couldn't come right out and ask. Perhaps Sally Ann would bring it up.

"Your father?"

He nodded. "He looks, well, I don't know..."

"Old?" Her eyes twinkled with her smile. "It's become a bit of a dirty word around here, but we can't escape it. We all grow old."

Henry pulled out a chair and sat at the dining table. Through the big window, the creek in the valley below danced and shimmered in the sunlight. The water, like the rocks it streamed over, were oblivious to the flow of time. He thought about getting older. Where did he see himself in twenty years? Or thirty? Did that vision involve Parsons Gap?

Sally Ann hummed as she busied herself with the cut flowers. They sat in comfortable silence until she finished. She retrieved the journal from the office and showed him the passage. Moving the tattered piece of red ribbon that marked the page, he read the entry.

"Father returned from his trip north today and was very distraught. He would not tell Mother what bothered him. That evening I found him in the garden. He made me promise to keep a secret. Once I heard it, I felt my heart would burst. I could not break my promise, and so I am compelled to write the events here. A bandit held up Father's coach. Though he wore a mask, Father recognized his brother Jacob. One of the passengers had a gun and tried to shoot Jacob. Father shouted in warning. Jacob shot the man dead. When the man fell, his vest opened to expose a lawman's badge pinned to his shirt. Jacob

escaped. When the coach arrived in the next town, the passengers related the incident to the sheriff. Father was taken to jail as an accomplice. Jacob heard this news and arranged to meet with the sheriff to offer himself if Father was set free. The sheriff agreed. Father was freed. Before Father departed, Jacob told him to remember a curious quote. Father did not understand though Jacob said it would come to him directly. Father repeated the words as they were spoken to him. It was from Shakespeare and he was sure Jacob had mistaken the words. 'But, look, the moon, in rust mantle clad, walks o'er the dew of yon high eastern hill.' Father said it was morn and not moon, but Jacob insisted he remembered just as he had said. After Father left town, a crowd of unruly men broke into the jail and took Jacob. They hanged him from a tree outside the jail."

"That's the only place it's mentioned." Sally Ann offered to make photocopies of the pages. When she returned from the office, Henry immediately noticed her worried expression.

"Is something wrong?" He knew full well something was.

"You're getting this for Louis Hannahan, aren't you?"

Henry nodded.

"Does he think this has something to do with the murder?"

"I'm not sure what he's thinking." Henry felt dishonest saying those words, even if they were somewhat true. "All I know is that he's checking all possible connections."

"Jimmy Lee is the only one that's still interested in this treasure nonsense."

"It doesn't mean Louis thinks Jimmy Lee is involved." Henry hoped he sounded more convincing than he felt. He'd been thinking about that metal detector in the barn.

Muddy Waters

With the copied pages folded in his pocket, Henry intended to drive to Louis' office until he saw Jimmy Lee's black Chevy parked on the street in front of the Parsons Gap Brewery. An idea formed, and he wanted to see Jimmy Lee's reaction. He made a sharp turn into the city lot.

Henry entered the brewery and ordered a root beer as he glanced around the room. Jimmy Lee and Odessa were at a table toward the back, laughing and looking in Henry's direction. Apparently, they were a couple again. Frosty mug in hand, Henry settled at a table near the window. His back to Jimmy Lee, he opened the brewery menu.

"I see you ain't gone yet."

Like trout rising to a fly, Henry thought, suppressing a grin. Jimmy Lee loomed above him, wearing an expression indicating he was on the prod. That was nothing new.

"Why? Did you want this table?" Henry asked.

"That's not what I meant."

"You must mean Parsons Gap, then." Henry smiled and moved his chair around so that he faced Jimmy Lee. "You know I can't leave until after Vernon's wedding. I'm not so sure I want to go back. I'm starting to like the idea of coming home."

"Maybe I can change your mind." Jimmy Lee hooked his thumbs in his belt. "Besides, we've got a little matter that needs settling."

Henry chuckled, which only seemed to further aggravate Jimmy Lee.

"You think something's funny?"

"Why are you always trying to pick a fight with me, Jimmy Lee? We're family."

"You trying to insult me?"

"If I was, you'd know it," Henry said. "Now I can see you've got something on your mind. Sit down and we'll talk about it."

"This ain't something that requires talking," Jimmy Lee

replied.

"If you're upset about what happened at the café the other morning, I'm not apologizing. Honestly, I'm surprised you don't have better manners. I know Sally Ann raised you better."

"You're an asshole, Henry."

"I've been called worse." Henry pushed out an empty chair with his foot. Jimmy Lee eyed him as though he suspected some trick. "Have a seat. I'm glad you came over here. I've been wanting to talk to you and didn't want to do it in front of your girlfriend."

"She's not my girlfriend."

"Walking around with your hand in a woman's back pocket is just your way of being friendly, I suppose."

Jimmy Lee glared at him.

Henry took a long drink from the icy mug. "I'm curious about something. You wouldn't happen to own a metal detector, would you, Jimmy Lee?"

"What's it to you?"

"You might be interested in something I found up at that old corral."

Jimmy Lee's reluctance lost to his curiosity, and he slouched into the chair. He leaned in and spoke in a low voice. "What'd you find?"

"Holes mostly," Henry said. "Made me wonder, though. How'd you know where to dig?"

"I ain't telling you nothing about that."

"We'll try a new subject, then. Why did you report the cattle missing? Weren't you the one that moved them up there in the first place?

"Don't know where you got that idea because it wasn't me put 'em there." Jimmy Lee sneered at him, "But I'll tell you why I was worried. I heard your friend was a cattle thief, and he'd been up there a few times."

"Where'd you hear that he was a cattle thief?" Henry

glanced toward the back of the room. "Your girlfriend?"

"She ain't my girlfriend."

"So you said." Henry put his elbows on the table and leaned toward Jimmy Lee. "How often do you and Odessa go riding out by the lake?"

Jimmy Lee wasn't quite able to hide his surprise. "Who says we do?"

"Your tracks. Those horses you two ride are kept at that barn near the lake, aren't they? Aubrey told me Odessa sometimes rides with a boyfriend. I figure that boyfriend must be you."

"You got a point to all this bullshit?" Jimmy Lee tapped his knuckles on the table.

"I do," Henry said. "I think you put up Aubrey's horse after he was killed."

Jimmy Lee licked his lips and stopped tapping. His eyes narrowed. "You can't prove that."

"I don't have to prove it," Henry said. "But you might consider having a chat with Louis Hannahan before they analyze all the finger prints found out there."

CHAPTER 24

"**S**eems that bunch learned to lie before they learned to walk." Louis leaned back in his rocking chair. Henry sat in a matching chair on the wide front porch, watching a squirrel burying acorns in the Hannahan's wooded yard. The trees cast long shadows in the late afternoon sun, creating stripes across the grass.

Louis took a long drink of homemade lemonade. "I'm glad you were there. I think you helped put extra pressure on Beau."

Henry shot him a disbelieving look over his own glass of lemonade.

"Beau knows you saw him out there with those cattle," Louis said. "I figure you threw him off-balance. He's wondering what you've told me and what you haven't."

"I hope he doesn't lose too much sleep." Henry set his glass on the side table and glanced at the copied journal pages he'd been holding since they had gone to the porch. "Why is it you're allowing me to help with the investigation?"

A few moments passed before Louis answered. "I figured I had two options. I decided it's better to keep an eye on you than to wonder what you're up to."

"What was the other option?"

Louis grinned. "Putting you in jail."

Henry wasn't sure if he was joking.

"Besides," Louis said, "while there is no evidence or motive connecting you to the crime, I believe there are things you haven't told me."

Henry was working on a reply when Patricia opened the screen door and announced supper. As they rose from their chairs, Louis put a hand on Henry's arm. "I had enough of a fight staying on this case after my supervisor learned my daughter dated the victim," Louis said. "You do anything to mess up the trust I've earned, I'm going to be very unhappy."

When they entered the dining room, enticing aromas greeted Henry. The table struck him as a work of art, from the brightly colored tableware and napkins to wildflowers in a vivid blue vase. Patricia had aged little, and he began to wonder if there was something in the mountain water. She was a well-known artist in the region, and he remembered being impressed by her ability to combine simple sophistication with sincerity in both art and life. He had found those same qualities in Carlie. Random memories surfaced, making him smile. These weren't the usual clouded memories, and he felt more optimistic about the past than he had in years.

Louis pulled Patricia's chair out for her. His fingers brushed his wife's hand, and she smiled fondly at him. The subtle interaction between them made Henry realize how much they complemented each other. As a kid, he'd envied their children. They had what he didn't. A home filled with love. He was envious again, this time it was the affection they so obviously shared.

Henry wondered if he'd ever find that sort of happiness. He had dated several women over the years, but he approached relationships cautiously. If he found himself in danger of getting in over his head, he found a work-related excuse to keep him out of touch for weeks or even months. When he'd returned, if things weren't already over, it was easy to break off. He rationalized this pattern of behavior by telling himself she simply wasn't what he was looking for in a partner. Right or wrong, it had kept him heartbreak-free for many years.

"Is something the matter, Mr. Henry?"

Carlie's son, Jack, was staring at him from across the supper table. So was Alva Jean, who was seated beside him.

Henry shook his head. "Why do you ask?"

"I've asked three times if you'd pass the green beans."

He apologized and passed the bowl, trying to ignore the empty chair beside him. Carlie had been called out on an emergency shortly before he arrived. He couldn't decide if he was relieved or disappointed. In their first two meetings, he'd gotten off on the wrong foot. He wished for a better rapport but was uncertain how to approach it.

Carlie's son Jack was easier to impress. At first the boy had been shy. When he discovered Henry had lived in Colorado, questions about the Old West began to gush from the youngster. For a nine-year-old, he was an avid fan of cowboy films and had a wealth of movie trivia. It was an interest shared by Louis, too. Henry inadvertently discovered this by mentioning a few places where westerns had been filmed. The conversation turned to trivia.

"Yes, I've been to Monument Valley," Henry said, answering Jack's question about the setting of a particular John Wayne movie.

"What was the first western shot there?" Louis asked.

"*The Vanishing American*," Henry replied.

"I'm surprised you knew that."

"I read the brochure." He explained it was mentioned in the self-guided tour pamphlet.

Alva Jean gave Henry a thumbs up. "Finally, someone who can give these two a run for their money."

Louis winked. "How about Alan Ladd's first starring western?"

157

"I don't know that one," Jack said, his disappointment obvious.

"It's a trick question," Henry said. "Because it's also my nickname, Whispering Smith."

Louis had a not-so-subtle way of making it known he'd dug into Henry's background.

Patricia shook her head. "How about a subject the rest of us can enjoy?"

Alva Jean asked about the town's landscaping that eventually sparked a discussion on the threat of invasive species versus the benefits of native plants. Even Jack proved well-informed. Throughout the conversation, Henry eyed the empty chair. He tried denying his disappointment, but moments later when Carlie rushed in the back door, his delight was unmistakable.

After dinner, Henry offered to help with dishes but was chased out of the kitchen. Alva Jean herded him toward the den, where he found Carlie nestled on the couch, magazine in hand while watching television. Louis and Jack were nowhere to be seen, forcing Henry to consider the possibility of a setup. Unsure what to say, he stood in the doorway.

"Afraid I'll bite?" Carlie asked over her shoulder.

He was trying to come up with a clever comeback when he glanced at the television. Recognizing the buckskin-clad hero on the screen, he knew he'd been rescued by Shane.

"One of my favorites." Henry settled into the recliner, a safe and respectable distance from the sofa. He glanced toward Carlie, unable to see her face in the shadows. The only light in the room came from the flickering glow of the television and a dim lamp on a side table.

"This is Alan Ladd's best film in my opinion," Henry said. "But I've always been partial to his westerns."

"It's one of my all-time favorites." Carlie's eyes did not leave the screen. "This and *The Virginian*. 'When you call me that, smile.' I mean, what a great line."

"With Gary Cooper or Joel McCrea?"

"Joel McCrea, of course."

"Of course." He remembered the movie stills of Joel McCrea and other western film stars in her room, back in high school. Not the typical décor for adolescent females. Her father's influence, no doubt. They watched Shane climb into the saddle and head to town for the final showdown.

"This is the best part," Carlie said, continuing to stare at the television. "Jack Palance looks so sinister."

"That's because he's wearing black."

"Alan Ladd still kicks butt." She laughed and tucked her hair behind her ears. "Gosh, I sound like Jack."

Henry smiled and said he'd already noticed the resemblance.

Carlie peered at him. "You do look like Alan Ladd. Maybe it's got something to do with that roguish smile."

"Not only was he better looking, he was much shorter." He held his hand out about three feet from the floor, for emphasis. "I've got a few inches on him."

"How about Gary Cooper or Randolph Scott? Rumor has it you're a soft-spoken cowboy with a dangerous side."

"I may have been told I was soft-spoken, but I've never heard I was dangerous," Henry said. "Where'd you get that idea?"

"Besides a story or two I've heard, Alva Jean told me what happened at the café."

"That had nothing to do with being dangerous."

"It was still very gallant, and it's good to know chivalry isn't dead."

They watched the remainder of the movie in silence. After Shane rode into the sunset, Henry said, "I want you to know I understand your motivation for making up the story about you and Tommy. You were right, I would have stayed." He chose not to say more, though his mind was full of at least a thousand what ifs.

"You're back for Vernon's wedding." Carlie closed the magazine she'd been holding and laid it on the coffee table. "That must have taken some work on his part."

"When he asked me to be best man, I couldn't say no." Henry rubbed his hand on the recliner arm. "Would you consider going to the wedding with me? It's a week from Saturday."

"I can try, but no guarantees." She continued to stare at the television. "I'm on call. I've been looking for an associate to ease the workload. There's a new grad arriving for an interview this week. With any luck I'll have help soon."

Henry wished he hadn't asked. It was crazy to think anything could be salvaged from the wreckage of their past relationship.

"Maybe we could do something this Wednesday." She continued without giving him a chance to reply. "We close at noon on Wednesdays."

Henry began to feel a little more confident. "How long have you owned the practice?"

"Two years come August. I'd worked there a few years before Doc Johnston decided to retire. It was his idea that I buy him out."

"Must feel great being your own boss."

"I used to think it would be wonderful. Now I've got more worries and even less free time." She grabbed one of the throw pillows and hugged it to her chest. "Do you still rope?"

"Not competitively."

"You were pretty good in your rodeo days."

"That was a long time ago," Henry said.

"I remember that first championship, and those huge belt buckles you and Aubrey won."

"Talk about ancient history."

Carlie laughed. "You'd be surprised what memories

have been popping into my head lately. It's like high school was yesterday. Remember that time Vernon took us to the regionals in Raleigh? Those barrel-racer girls were hanging around you and Aubrey the whole time. I wouldn't dare tell you then, but they made me so jealous."

"I don't remember the girls hanging around," he lied.

"Well, you two seemed to really enjoy all the attention." Carlie looked at him. "That was also the first time you kissed me."

"Now I do remember that." Henry also recalled nearly choking with fear over the possibility of losing her as a friend with that kiss.

Henry watched the opening credits of *She Wore A Yellow Ribbon* on the television, wondering what the rest of the family was doing. The kitchen work should've been done by now.

"And in her hair, she wore a yellow ribbon!" Jack came bounding into the den, singing along with the movie score. Wearing a big grin, he jumped onto the sofa beside his mother.

"Jack loves John Wayne westerns," Carlie explained.

"I can see that." Henry grinned and looked at Jack. "I like them, too. Good moral fiber in those movies."

"See, Mom? Someone else in the world besides Grandpa likes John Wayne movies. Good moral fiber. I just like them because the Duke always wins."

"Almost always," Carlie corrected.

"Well, in *The Cowboys* the boys win for him." Jack eyed Henry. "You're a cowboy, right?"

"Sort of."

"Can you quick draw?" Jack demonstrated the quick draw with his finger and thumb held in the shape of a pistol.

"I'm not bad at it." Getting on his knees in front of the sofa, he held his arms out from his sides, like a gunfighter. Jack played along, moving the required distance apart.

161

With a mock scowl, Henry eyed his adversary. "This town ain't big enough for the both of us."

Jack's eyes narrowed. "Well, I ain't leavin' mister."

They faced each other, finger guns at the ready. The clock on the mantle ticked loudly. Jack's arm twitched and they drew simultaneously. *Pshhh, pshhh, pshhh!*

"You got me." Henry clutched his chest and toppled to the floor.

"Aha!" Jack crowed. He holstered his finger pistol. "I told Grandpa you'd know how. He said people don't do that anymore. We bet on it. Now I can tell him he owes me a dollar."

"If he gives you any trouble, you let me know." Henry got to his knees. He blew the smoke from the end of his finger pistol. "We'll make sure you get that dollar."

"Thanks, Mr. Henry! I can't wait to tell him." Jack bounced out of the den, forgetting about the movie playing on the television.

"You always were good with kids," Carlie said. "A.J. was fond of you. Mickey, too. He asked about you when he heard you were in town. I'm to say 'hello' for him."

While freshmen in high school, Carlie's little brother Mickey had developed an enormous crush on her best friend, Olivia. It had embarrassed Olivia to have a middle school boy following her like a lost puppy. "How is Mickey? Did he ever marry Olivia like he promised?"

Carlie laughed. "No, thank God. He got married almost six years ago. He lives in Charleston now. He and his wife have a little girl and a new son. Olivia, of course, is still looking for Mr. Right. This time in Raleigh. She's with some mortgage firm there. She's been married and divorced three times. We manage to get together about once a year."

Henry remembered Olivia being very fickle about boys, even in grade school.

"What about you?" Carlie said. "Do you have a family of

your own?"

He leaned back and stretched his legs, crossing them at the ankles. "Well, I– "

Carlie's pager beeped. "Duty calls," she muttered. "Excuse me."

She got up to use the telephone. Henry stared after her with a stupid grin on his face. He was caught red-handed by Jack, who entered the room just after she left.

"You like my mom, don't you?" Jack asked.

"We've known each other a long time."

"You smile at her like you like her."

Henry scratched his head thoughtfully. "Should I stop smiling at her?"

"I wouldn't if I was you. She likes your smile. She always has. I heard her tell Grandma."

"You shouldn't repeat everything you hear." Henry brandished both of his finger guns. "Sometimes it can get you into big trouble, Pilgrim."

CHAPTER 25

"You awake?"

"I am now," Henry growled into the phone. Darkness cloaked the cabin's interior, though light was creeping in the windows. "It's early. What the hell's going on?"

"We're going fishing," Vernon said.

"Fishing?"

"Yeah, fishing," he repeated. "I'll be there in fifteen minutes."

Henry had washed and dressed by the time Vernon arrived. He opened the door and invited his uncle inside. "What's gotten into you?"

"Fishing is supposed to be good therapy, ain't it?" Vernon paced the living room. "This wedding has gotten me so damned skittish. I'm afraid I'll bolt from the pasture if I see a big enough hole in the fence."

"Don't do anything drastic."

After Vernon followed him into the kitchen, Henry filled a plastic cup with iced tea. He took a gulp, hoping the caffeine would hit his bloodstream quickly.

"I thought you'd have outgrown that tea habit of yours by now," Vernon said. "Never heard of a cowboy that doesn't drink coffee."

"Just because I live out west doesn't make me a cowboy." Henry refilled the tea, then walked into the living room and grabbed his hat off a peg near the door.

"Sure it doesn't." Vernon looked at the Stetson and

rolled his eyes.

Henry eyed Vernon's battered straw hat.

"That's different," Vernon said. "It ain't a Stetson, only a cheap imitation."

"It's a cowboy hat. Emphasis on cowboy."

"Speaking of nonsense," Vernon said. "I hear you knocked Jimmy Lee on his ass."

"Where'd you hear that?"

They stepped outside and walked toward Vernon's pickup.

"Della said you were like a knight in shining armor." Vernon placed a hand against his cheek and gazed upward, like some grizzled damsel in distress. "She didn't say much other than Jimmy Lee deserved it."

"He insulted Alva Jean, and it wasn't very polite."

Vernon climbed into his pickup. "I hear you had supper at Hannahan's, too."

"Gossip gets around this town at record speed, doesn't it?"

"Saved the best one for last." Vernon rubbed his hands together and raised an eyebrow. "I hear you're sweet on Carlie."

Henry shook his head, amazed. "How did that one get started?"

Vernon laughed. "Forget about how, give me the dirt."

"There isn't any dirt. We talked, that's all."

"You going to see her again?"

Henry climbed into Vernon's pickup. "I've got another priority. I want Aubrey's killer brought to justice."

"You don't get it, do you?"

Henry shook his head. "But I'm sure you're going to tell me."

"Leave the clue chasing to Louis." Vernon crossed his fingers and said, "You and Carlie have been like this since you were kids. Everyone thought you'd end up together, as in the big fairy tale happily-ever-after together. Then, much to everyone's surprise, you forget all about her and run off to Colorado. Now you're getting a second chance. That doesn't happen every day, and you're fixing to blow it."

"You have no idea what you're talking about." Henry immediately regretted his angry tone. Had it been anyone but Vernon, he would have resented the intrusion into his personal life. He calmed his voice when he spoke again. "I did ask her to marry me. She turned me down."

Vernon stared at him as if he hadn't heard the words correctly.

"Let's go fishing," Henry said. "Seems I'm in need of some therapy, too."

As they drove toward the main highway, he told Vernon about Carlie's little white lie.

"Damn." Vernon shook his head. "I'd have left the state, too."

They rode the rest of the way in silence. Henry stared out the passenger window, soaking in the scenery and the earthy fragrance of the mountains. When they turned off the highway and onto State Road 1514, Henry glanced at Vernon. "We're fly fishing today?"

"Figured maybe I could out-fish you with a fly rod," Vernon said. "Besides, I haven't tried this creek in years."

Henry grinned, looking forward to the competition. They spent the better part of the morning on the river. It was a catch and release area, affording no evidence to support claims of who caught the largest trout. This was the topic of conversation for most of the drive home. Henry eventually conceded, but only to keep Vernon quiet for the remainder of the trip.

"That makes us one and one." Vernon beamed with obvious satisfaction. "You know we'll have to do a tie-breaker."

"Maybe we can squeeze in another trip before the

wedding."

Vernon groaned. "Why did you have to say the 'W' word?"

Henry couldn't help laughing. "You're worried about me and Carlie, but you're ready to forget Della?"

"Haven't you ever heard of 'Do as I say, not as I do'?"

"Be a man," Henry teased, "and make Della an honest woman."

"You know she's the one that popped the question?"

Henry chuckled. "I'm not surprised. She probably got tired of waiting on you to ask."

"I may have been slow coming to that idea."

"At least you both came to the same conclusion. No matter who asked, in my opinion you're a lucky man."

"You're right," Vernon said. "I sure can't think of anyone else I'd rather marry than Della. You may have cured my case of nerves."

"Now if I can cure your habit of always claiming you caught the biggest fish, I'd be a damned miracle worker."

"Asshole."

Henry remembered the last time he was called that name. "Say, what's with Jimmy Lee and Odessa McLean?"

Vernon shook his head and shot Henry a wry smile. "That boy enjoys playing with fire. Thinks he can play around on her and she won't know about it. I've told him he'd better learn to keep it in his pants or she'll cut it off for him. I imagine that's probably the least of his worries. Her brothers aren't very happy with his behavior, either."

"So I've noticed." Henry recalled the confrontation at the café. "Is he still hunting that lost treasure from the old journal?"

Vernon grew quiet. "He's been after it for months now. Sometimes he sneaks away from work to look in some new place he comes up with. I reckon he's obsessed. Lord only knows where he's decided to look this time."

He pulled onto the dirt drive to the cabin. Henry climbed out and waved as Vernon left in a cloud of dust. The cat greeted him when he stepped inside. After filling the cat's food bowl, he noticed a blinking light on the answering machine.

It was about an interview for a position at the Blue Ridge Parkway.

CHAPTER 26

Louis Hannahan parked the unmarked Tahoe outside Number 34 in the Vista Grande Mobile Home Park. A beat-up Pontiac sedan with oxidized paint and a flat tire sat in the drive. He climbed warped wood steps onto the dilapidated patio, glancing at three flowerpots filled with desiccated plant carcasses. A fourth pot, hidden behind a rusted barbeque grill, contained a cluster of thriving marijuana plants.

He rapped loudly on the metal door. Footsteps approached and the lace curtains parted. A plump female face, framed by curly hair, peered through the dirty window. "Who is it?"

"Detective Louis Hannahan." With one hand, Louis flipped open the wallet containing his credentials and held it up to the window. The door opened and the rest of the plump body came into view. She wore snug-fitting sweat pants and an oversized Appalachian State T-shirt. The odor of fried fish wafted onto the porch.

"Mrs. Breen?"

"It's Mizz," she corrected. "What do you want?"

"I'm looking for Stan." He slipped the badge holder into his pocket without taking his eyes off her. "Is he here?"

"He's working."

"When do you expect him home, ma'am?"

"How would I know?" Ms. Breen replied coldly. After a few seconds of biting her lip, she defrosted. "He got off work a little while ago, and it's not that far away."

"Mind if I wait?" Louis waved a hand toward a plastic chair on the patio.

"Is he in some kind of trouble?"

Louis shook his head. "I only want to ask him a few questions about something that may be related to an investigation."

She warmed a little more and opened the door. "You can come in. It's cooler inside."

Louis hesitated, uncertain of his tolerance for the odor of fried fish. He reluctantly stepped inside. The interior of the mobile home was clean and tidy. Ms. Breen flipped on the kitchen vent, then lit a scented candle on the kitchen counter before sitting on the sofa.

"I hate cooking fish inside," Ms. Breen said. "I prefer grilled fish, but Stan loves it fried. I try to fix it for him a few times a week."

"I'm with you." Louis involuntarily twitched his nose. "I prefer mine grilled."

"What is it you want to ask Stan? Maybe I can help."

Louis smiled to encourage her to be helpful. "Has he mentioned anything about hunting some treasure with Jimmy Lee Smith?"

"Oh, yes indeed." She laughed. "That was a few months back, though. He was excited at first, but after weeks of finding nothing he lost interest. Stan is always looking for ways to get a little extra income. Lately he's been learning to repair watches. He has half a dozen or so in his room that he's working on for friends."

"I'd say he's an industrious young man." Louis thought about the marijuana plants and wondered if that was another way Stan planned to add to his income.

Ms. Breen smiled. "I had hopes he'd attend college. His father offered to pay his way, but Stan wouldn't hear of it. He wanted to do it on his own, he said. I think he's just not ready. Eventually he'll go, and he'll let his father pay. He adores his father, which is much more than I can say."

"If you don't mind me asking, who is his father?"

"Oh, I thought everybody knew. It's Beau McLean."

Louis raised his eyebrows in surprise. Embarrassed at his reaction, he apologized.

"Don't you worry," Ms. Breen said. "That's what I get from most people."

Louis heard a car pull into the driveway.

"That's probably Stan now." She rose from the sofa and crossed to the door. "What can I say, Mr. Hannahan? I was once young and dumb, too. We had one of those short-lived high school flings. The careless kind. He pressured me to have an abortion, but I couldn't go through with it. When Stan was born, Beau started sending money. He's never missed a month up until Stan turned eighteen. He still comes by to visit as often as he can, more often now his father passed. Even attended Stan's graduation. I may dislike Beau, but you understand why I can't be upset with him. Besides his support all these years, he gave me Stan."

CHAPTER 27

The memorial service for a murder victim drew a crowd in the small community. Henry stood on the steps outside the church, watching mourners mill along the sidewalk like ants at a picnic. He recognized few people, which was fortunate. He wasn't in the mood for social chatter.

Death made him uncomfortable. He knew he was not alone in that respect. Beyond the usual philosophic thoughts on mortality, death conjured up unpleasant memories from his past, both distant and near. Losing his mother was the beginning. He could barely remember her face now, but he'd never forgotten the pain of loss. More recently, he'd had to come to grips with taking a life.

Turning, he entered the church. Louis stood inside the door, his greeting a slight nod. Henry wondered if he was there in an official capacity, or to pay his respects. When he realized he'd been squeezing his hands behind his back until his fingers ached, he tried to relax.

Henry sat down. Even while seated on the uncomfortable pew, his mind was miles away in an almost out-of-body experience. He felt numb and tried to convince himself it was his way of coping. The truth was he didn't want to admit anything could affect him so deeply. After his mother's death, he'd hit on a survival technique that served him well throughout his life. He'd formed an emotional wall and cultivated humor as a moat. Rarely had anyone or anything broken through. Now the moat was running dry and the walls were beginning to crack.

Aubrey's memorial service was seeping through one of the cracks. Despite his reluctance, Henry found he was beginning to move through the grieving process. Repressed anger was trying to reach the surface. The reverend's sermon droned on, briefly touching on the life of the deceased. With vehemence and increasing decibels, he asked if those in the audience were prepared for their own day of reckoning.

Henry wanted to leave, but he was stuck in the center of a packed pew near the middle of the small church. Had he been claustrophobic, he would have panicked by now. He tuned out the fire and brimstone. If Aubrey had a say, Henry knew he'd have wanted a huge wake with plenty of alcohol and loud music. He recalled Aubrey's infectious laugh, their infamous adventures as team ropers on the college rodeo circuit, and life after graduation. Those were good memories, something worth keeping.

Startled by a light hand on his shoulder, Henry looked up to see Sally Ann and his father behind him. Realizing he was the only person still seated in the church, he got to his feet. Sally Ann gave him a hug. Even Rory put a reassuring hand on his shoulder.

"You're welcome to come back to the house for lunch," Sally Ann said.

"Thanks, but I think I'd rather be alone for a while."

When Henry finally walked outside, the afternoon was bright with sunlight. A particular happy image had lodged in his mind and he knew where he wanted to go. Crossing to the parking lot, he climbed into the old Chevy, and drove toward Blowing Rock and the Blue Ridge Parkway. Once on the Parkway, he watched for the sign marking the riverside parking lot. The lot was empty. He stopped under a huge buckeye tree and sat in the truck for some time. He'd never been able to explain why, but this had been a place of solace, reflection and healing to him. He'd brought Carlie here, shortly after they started dating. She'd fallen in love with the place, too.

He looked out the windscreen and tried to see the river through the trees. They had grown considerably. The Linville River formed a large horseshoe here, surrounding the wooded park on three sides. He got out of the pickup and strolled toward the sound of flowing water. As the noise increased to a roar, he wished it would drown all thought and feeling. That didn't happen.

He climbed around a large tree leaning over the cut bank and perched on an exposed root. Clear water tumbled across the rock-strewn streambed, carrying the occasional leaf or stick downstream. Closing his eyes, he imagined the same current washing away the emotions he didn't want surfacing.

"I thought I'd find you here."

Surprised, Henry found Carlie standing on the bank above him. It crossed his mind he ought to pinch himself and make sure it wasn't a dream. Jumping off the root, he clambered up the bank. He stopped a few feet away and looked at her uncertainly.

"I'm so sorry, Henry." She moved forward and hugged him.

His father had always drilled into him that men didn't cry. But when Carlie took him into her arms, he wept. The emotions he'd been suppressing finally breached the surface. Not all of it was for Aubrey.

Carlie held him tightly and didn't say a word.

After several minutes he reluctantly pulled away and wiped his eyes on a handkerchief. "This is certainly a surprise," he said. "Apparently a much needed one."

"I'm sorry I didn't make it to the funeral. I didn't know about it until last night, when Dad asked if I was going. Then things got hectic at work." After a pause, she said in a quiet voice, "I should have been there."

He smiled. "Thanks. I appreciate that."

Carlie smiled back. "Would you like to get something to eat?"

"I'm not really hungry." His desire to be alone had vanished. "I wouldn't mind taking a drive, though. It's been years since I've been up here on the Parkway. We can stop somewhere a little later to eat."

Carlie offered to drive so Henry could play tourist. He grabbed a pair of sunglasses from his truck, locked the doors and climbed into her Cherokee. The drive north to Cone Manor was a short one. "Not a very scenic route," she said. "But there's a really nice view from the porch."

They sat in rocking chairs on the wide veranda without speaking for some time. Henry was captivated by the lake below and the blue-tinted mountains in the distance. After half an hour, they entered the house for a quick browse of the craft shop. Henry bought two bottles of water before they walked down the paved road toward the woods.

"You've been back in Parsons Gap for what, three years?" Henry asked.

She nodded. "Before that I worked a few years at a fast-paced practice in Charlotte to gain experience."

They stepped aside to allow a group of people on horseback to pass. Instead of continuing on the lake trail, they turned around and walked past the Manor toward the carriage barn.

"You knew from the start what you wanted to do, professionally speaking?"

"Pretty much," Carlie replied. "With the marriage turning out like it did, my work was all I really had to keep me sane."

"What happened with you and your ex?" Henry asked. "You can tell me to mind my own business."

"It's okay." Carlie swept her hair behind her ears. She

looked at the ground. "We started seeing each other in my senior year. We ended up getting married the next fall, after my first year in veterinary college. School was stressful and demanded a lot of my time, and we grew apart. Actually, I don't think it would have mattered in the long run. The divorce was final shortly after the beginning of my junior year."

Carlie stopped to examine a clump of yellow wildflowers beside the trail. "Looking back, I can see lots of reasons we shouldn't have married. And lots of reasons why we couldn't get along after we did. They say hindsight is twenty-twenty, don't they?"

"Does Jack get to see him?"

"He's visited once or twice, before he moved to Fayetteville. Last I heard, he was a CPA there. It's been a couple of years now. Being a father wasn't something he embraced. Now he's remarried, has two kids, and seems happy with family life. Jack knows, but I don't know if he resents it. He doesn't like talking about his father."

"Must have been tough. A single parent going to college."

"My parents were great," Carlie said. "I couldn't have done it without them. They were always encouraging me to hang in there. Didn't want me to give up my dream, and all that. It involved sacrifices, though. They practically raised Jack. I still feel guilty about deserting my kid for the bigger part of two years while I finished school."

"Seems like things turned out fine. He's a good kid." Henry took a last look at the valley before they reached the Cherokee. "You consider Parsons Gap your home now?"

"Absolutely." Carlie answered without hesitation. "When I first left for college, I didn't ever want to see this town again. That all changed while I was gone. It's true you have to be away from something before you gain appreciation for it."

Henry was beginning to appreciate a lot of things he'd been away from.

Carlie drove them across Linn Cove Viaduct and into the Stack Rock parking area. "Feel up to hiking another short trail?" Carlie stopped the Cherokee near the trailhead.

"Absolutely."

She parked the vehicle and led the way along a worn, root-strewn path to a wooden walkway near a huge boulder. They paused on the wooden platform to look up at it.

"This has always been one of my favorite places," Carlie said. "The view isn't great when the trees have leaves and it's not quiet with the parkway bridge so close, but I still like it."

Henry considered the house-sized stone towering above them. "It is a nice rock."

Carlie laughed and beckoned him to follow her across the walkway and down the steps to another rock with a large flattened area on top. She climbed onto it and sat cross-legged. Henry joined her. The boulder nestled against an old pine tree, literally in the shadow of the larger rock.

"What about you?" Carlie asked. "Where's home for you now?"

"I used to think my home was anywhere but here." A cool breeze blew past him from the creek below. "Or anywhere my father wasn't. I thought I really loved living in Colorado, but I'm starting to see things differently. Like you said, being away makes appreciation grow."

"What do you miss most about North Carolina?"

"Lightning bugs."

She laughed. "Why lightning bugs?"

Henry shrugged. "I saw some the other night. Made me feel like a kid again. I used to chase them, before my mother died. Back when I was happy."

Carlie didn't comment. Henry realized he'd told Carlie more about his inner workings than he'd ever told himself.

For several minutes, there was only the gurgle of the creek and the rustle of leaves in the breeze.

"What are your plans, Henry?"

He looked up at the towering rock, as if it might have an answer. "I'm really not sure. I miss spending time with Vernon. He's not getting any younger, and I may have some regrets about my relationship with my father."

"What sort of regrets?"

Wishing he hadn't spoken the words, he could only shrug his shoulders. It was something difficult to explain, something that recently surfaced. It had been buried deep, right next to where he'd hidden those tears for so many years. Feeling suddenly embarrassed, he lost willingness to be open and honest.

"Dad says you've helped with the investigation."

He was surprised she'd moved the conversation away from the too-personal, like she'd read his mind. It was unsettling. "Either that or go to jail," Henry replied.

"You're joking, right?"

"He thought I was trying to find Aubrey's murderer on my own."

"And were you?" Carlie asked.

Henry started to answer but she stopped him. "It's better if I don't know. As long as Aubrey's killer is brought to justice, it doesn't matter to me."

"I won't argue that."

Carlie smiled. "From the way he went on about your tracking abilities, I'd say he was pretty impressed. My parents never admitted this until you'd gone away to college, but they were both very fond of you."

"They've obviously got good taste." Henry pointed down the trail. "Where does this go?"

"There's a footbridge over Stack Rock Creek. It's not too far ahead. The trail goes on from there to the Linn Cove information center. Beyond that I'm not sure."

Muddy Waters

"Want to go to the creek?"

"Why not."

Henry climbed off the rock and turned to help her down, but she was already beside him. This time he led the way, the roar of water growing louder as they hiked. The trail turned sharply to the right where a footbridge spanned the creek. Henry stopped in the middle of the bridge. Water spilled over the rocks behind and above the trail, bouncing through a jumble of smaller rocks littered with logs and debris before passing under the footbridge and disappearing beneath the trees. The sound was mesmerizing, even with the occasional roar of an automobile passing above them on the viaduct.

"This is a beautiful spot." Henry put his hands on the bridge railing and leaned over to look at the creek below.

Carlie placed her hand on his arm and squeezed lightly. "I hate to leave, but I'm getting really hungry."

"I'm about three calories from death myself."

CHAPTER 28

"I'm hoping you can help connect some dots." Louis straightened his tie before lifting a floral teacup for a sip.

Henry tried not to laugh. He sat at an outdoor table at the Tea Room, a small café in the tourist section of town. Fresh-cut flowers and an artfully arranged plate of croissants decorated the table. The garden was bordered by a privacy fence and accented by flowering plants, flowering vines, and potted plants. As charming as he found the surroundings, it didn't seem appropriate for two men discussing murder. Unless Miss Marple was joining them.

"Connecting dots. I'm your man." Henry poured tea from the teapot into a matching floral cup. After stirring in a packet of sugar, he selected a strawberry-cream cheese croissant. The delicious buttery flavor of the croissant changed his mind about appropriate places to discuss murder.

"Hope you don't mind it here," Louis said, waving at the plate. "I'm meeting my wife here in half an hour or so." He explained that Patricia was the featured artist for the weekend's Art in the Garden. "The first dot is about Jimmy Lee, he stopped by my office yesterday morning to explain how he'd found a saddled horse at McLean's barn the morning after Miller's death."

"Does he have an alibi?"

Louis flashed a mischievous grin. "Jimmy Lee claims he and Odessa had been riding out by the old cemetery. They'd intended to watch the sunset, but they got into an argument. She got pretty upset and rode off. Jimmy Lee rode back to the barn a little later. He says it was dark when he finished putting up his horse. He felt bad about their disagreement, so he went to Odessa's place to apologize. They spent the rest of the evening making up."

"Probably best not to dwell on those images."

"Jimmy Lee went out to feed the horses early the next morning and the horse was there. He figured it was Odessa's, so he unsaddled it and turned it into the pasture. Odessa confirmed they were together both before and after the disagreement."

Henry picked up his teacup. If Jimmy Lee was that worried about his relationship with Odessa, he probably wouldn't be murdering anyone over a non-existent relationship with Alva Jean. "Didn't he pay attention to the horse?"

"Says he was in a hurry to get to work. Both were bay mares and he didn't look closely." Louis fixed Henry with his serious look. "Jimmy Lee finally told me you suggested he come see me. How did you know?"

"I was at that barn." Henry didn't elaborate, and he hoped Louis wouldn't ask. "There was a bridle looped on one of the saddles. Everything else was organized and hung in its place. Aubrey was a little obsessive-compulsive in that respect. If Aubrey had put the horse away, the bridle would have been on a peg. Since you didn't mention any odd fingerprints being found, I figured it had to be someone who went there often. Aubrey told me Beau and Hugh rarely ride, which left Jimmy Lee or Odessa. I guessed correctly."

"Lucky you." Louis drained the tea from his cup and set it carefully on the matching saucer. He told Henry about his visit with Ms. Breen.

"What did you do about the marijuana plants?"

Louis laughed. "I told him they'd better be gone before

I sent a deputy out on patrol. He nearly tripped over his own feet getting out the door to get rid of them."

"Breen is unlikely, and Jimmy Lee and Odessa gave each other an alibi. Not that I trust them." Henry told him about his chat with the wrangler, Guillermo Flores. "I didn't ask him where he was on the night of the murder. He didn't seem interested in some treasure that probably doesn't exist."

"Same with Breen," Louis said. "Either they're both lying, or I'm running out of suspects."

Henry spread his hands. "Who does that leave? The McLean brothers?"

"I see these cloak and dagger discussions have now gone public." Patricia had approached the table unnoticed. Both Louis and Henry rose from their chairs. Henry took her arrival as his cue to leave, and offered his chair as he made his excuses.

"You want to ride out to the old cemetery and have a look around?" Louis asked. "I promise not to give you hell about interfering with the investigation."

Henry considered this. Several days had passed and he doubted he'd find anything useful in the way of tracks, but it still might be worth a trip. "I'll let you know."

He walked toward his pickup, thinking about yesterday's telephone interview. His impression that it was a mere formality made him uneasy. Things were changing faster than anticipated. If the job was offered, was he ready to commit? With his mind occupied, it wasn't until he climbed into the truck that he noticed the .38 caliber bullet sitting on the dash.

CHAPTER 29

Henry avoided the Bar T Ranch house and walked directly to the barn. Hoping to locate one of the wranglers about borrowing a horse, he was happy to find Guillermo already saddling up for a trail ride. Guillermo greeted him with a smile. Near the corral, Henry saw a group of people anxiously waiting to mount up.

"*Buenos dias*," Guillermo said.

Henry acknowledged him with a nod. "I'm looking for an old cemetery, not far from where the McLeans keep their horses."

"I think I know the one," Guillermo said. "We pass close to it on this ride."

"Is there a horse available to get me there?"

"There's a pinto in the third stall that's too rambunctious for the public. I'll saddle him for you, and you can join us."

"No need, I can handle that." Henry looked toward the corral where two wranglers helped group members climb into saddles. "Looks like your hands are full enough."

Guillermo followed the glance and chuckled. "I've had worse." He pointed out which tack to use for the pinto, then led his horse to the corral. Henry saddled the gelding and joined the group as they prepared to hit the trail. He followed Guillermo and his eight riders along a two-track dirt road between fenced pastures.

The creak of leather and occasional jingle of the bit were familiar, relaxing sounds. He thought about the bullet on his dashboard. He'd left the truck windows open while meeting with Louis. It could have been random, but he doubted it. Someone didn't want him poking around. Beau McLean was his first pick. His irritation at Henry's part in the boot track comparison was obvious. Did it follow that Beau killed Aubrey and was afraid of being caught?

The pinto grabbed his attention when he balked at an overpass on Parsons Hollow Road. The trail narrowed under the bridge, then ran parallel to a small creek. It took a few minutes to gently urge the horse forward. He caught up with the group on the south side of the old corral, where the trail crossed the meadow and joined the rutted dirt road toward McLeans' barn.

Guillermo had stopped the group in the shade offered by a stand of pines. He waved Henry to the front. "The trail you want forks off to the west in about a hundred yards. Keep going for half a mile, until you see a rocky ridge. The graveyard will be below it, on the right, past the foundation of an old church."

Henry patted the horse's neck and asked in Spanish, "You know a man called Mauro?"

"I don't know him personally, though I know of him," Guillermo replied. "He works at the slaughterhouse. The kill floor is a perfect place for that one. Not a nice man."

Henry touched his hat as he reined the pinto onto the trail.

Once out of sight, he got the holstered pistol from the saddlebag and slipped it onto his belt. He kept a cautious eye on his surroundings as he rode. The directions were easy to follow. He used a lead rope to tie the pinto to a tree. Finding no prints around the church foundation, he moved on to the cemetery. As he suspected, rain had washed away any sign of Jimmy Lee's visit. He walked among the scattering of gravestones and read a few inscriptions on the more ornate ones. Parsons and Moon were the predominant names. Several graves were marked only with brick-sized stones.

The pinto tossed his head and pricked his ears toward the trail. Crouching behind a headstone, Henry waited. He relaxed when he spotted Guillermo and the trail ride crowd coming out of the woods. Mounting the pinto, he trotted down to meet them.

"Find what you were looking for?" Guillermo asked.

"Too much time passed." Henry rode beside him, talking casually, until the trail narrowed. He dropped back, lost in thought until two women caught up where the trail widened again.

"Didn't we meet you at the Watering Hole Saloon?" one of the riders asked. "You're Alva Jean's friend, right?"

Henry recognized them, wondering again if they were twins. They were dressed alike, this time in plaid shirts with tight jeans tucked into pink-embossed boots. The only difference was one had a ponytail and one wore her hair loose.

"Did your friend ever find you?"

"Which friend?" Henry asked.

"Never told us his name. He was a Mexican, though." The ponytail woman whispered the word Mexican as she cut her eyes at Guillermo. "Not cute like him."

"Kind of thick in the chest?"

"I think so." The ponytail bounced when she nodded. Henry remembered seeing a man talking to Jimmy Lee

that could have been Mauro. But Mauro worked at the

McLeans' slaughter plant. What was the association?

CHAPTER 30

When the clock hit six that afternoon, Henry was seated at a table in the Watering Hole Saloon. He'd returned from his ride to find a message from Carlie. The other veterinarian interested in working at her clinic had arrived early, and Carlie wanted to show him the sights in Parsons Gap. He wasn't sure a saloon was the place to start, but he was happy to be invited.

The place was empty compared to his last visit, and the waitress had taken his drink order as soon as he sat down. The root beer arrived in a brown bottle, accompanied by a frosted mug. Though the label proclaimed it as Parsons Gap Brewery's finest, Louis had been right. It tasted nothing like he'd gotten at the source.

Henry put on his glasses and examined the placard on the table. The night's entertainment was to be provided by The Road Apples. Pictured in cowboy hats, pearl-snapped shirts and jeans undoubtedly meant they performed country music.

"Come here often, cowboy?"

Henry looked up, delighted to see Carlie smiling at him. Her hand lightly touched his shoulder. Beside her was a tall young man he guessed was the prospective veterinarian. He was taking in the large room with an expression of mild shock, as if he'd never been in a barn-sized redneck bar before.

"Well, it's not really the sort of place I usually frequent." Henry replaced the placard and got to his feet. "But I hear they've got great country music."

Carlie laughed and introduced Dr. William Danner. His curly, dark hair and fine features reminded Henry of one of the Greek gods. He imagined Dr. Danner would catch the interest of quite a few young ladies in the saloon tonight.

"If he's interested in the associate position at the clinic, he should see what he's in for. Alva Jean recommended this place. She'll be here soon. Nothing like birth by fire."

Henry shook William's hand, then pulled out a chair for Carlie.

"What's that you're drinking? Dark beer?" William asked after they were all seated.

"Root beer," Henry said. "A friend of mine told me this place serves the second best frosty mug in town."

William laughed. "I guess I'll play it safe and go for a beer, then."

While they waited for Alva Jean to arrive, Henry asked William about himself. He'd grown up in Durham and would be graduating from veterinary college in May.

"Initially, I'd considered employment at a practice in the Raleigh-Durham area," William said. "I realized I didn't want to stay in the city, so I began looking in the mountainous region of the state."

Carlie's practice appealed to him because it was small animal work rather than wrestling with horses and cows. He had arrived a few days early to spend time getting to know the area.

"I didn't expect it, but Dr. Hannahan graciously offered to show me around."

"Oh please. Call me Carlie."

"Well hello, Henry!" Alva Jean appeared at the table.

She greeted the others, smiling brightly when introduced to Dr. William Danner. It was obvious she'd captured William's attention. When the band started playing, it was no surprise William asked her to dance.

The Road Apples weren't as loud as the previous band, and conversation was possible without shouting. Henry listened attentively as Carlie chatted about William's interest in the job. As she spoke, he found he enjoyed listening, no matter the subject. He didn't even care if they talked for that matter.

The band started a slow song and Carlie scanned the dance floor for Alva Jean and William. The stage lights danced in her eyes and bounced off her auburn hair. At that moment, Henry knew his heart was lost. He also realized he'd been holding his breath. "If I promise not to step on your toes, would you dance with me?"

"Yes, I'd like that," Carlie said. "Don't try to fool me. Alva Jean told me you could dance."

He stood and offered his hand. Her hand was strong and warm in his. Sliding an arm around her waist, he moved toward the dance floor.

"I really enjoyed our day on the Parkway," Henry said. "It was good medicine, and it helped me through a rough time. I can't tell you how much I appreciate you being there."

While they danced, he caught her looking at him, the faintest hint of a mischievous smile on her lips. The song ended. She grabbed his hand and led him to their table.

Carlie moved her chair close and leaned toward him. "Tell me something. I've been wondering why such a nice, good-looking, and intelligent guy like you isn't married with ten kids."

"Who says I'm not?" Henry smiled and took a sip of root beer.

Her eyes widened.

"Two or three maybe," He said. "Not ten."

She frowned, but still looked at him expectantly.

"Probably because none of the prospective wives had the foresight to tell me I was good-looking and intelligent."

"Don't forget modest."

"That, too." Henry's finger wiped water droplets on the root beer mug. "Maybe I never found what I wanted. Besides, who said I was nice?"

"A girl has ways of getting information."

"Does she, now?" He studied her face a moment, then gave her a mischievous smile.

"What are you thinking about?" She pushed her hair behind her ears.

"You don't want to know." He hoped she wasn't as intuitive as her father. "It would dash the illusion that I'm nice."

"You just don't want to tell me."

Henry shrugged. "I was wondering if a clever pick-up line would ever work on you. And if so, which one would it be?"

"Is this for personal gain, or your own curiosity?" Carlie asked. "Don't even think of saying for old time's sake. I'll kick you in the shins."

Henry assured her it was mere curiosity. They traded pick-up lines, trying to recall the dumbest one they'd heard. The band had played at least three songs before he realized how much time had passed. When the band began playing *Long-Haired Country Boy*, they both laughed.

"Now I'll have to admit it. If a band at this saloon is playing the song, it must be country." Henry shook his head. "To think I've been misguided all these years."

Carlie's laugh was one he really liked hearing. She looked away. "Alva Jean and William seem to be enjoying themselves."

Henry turned toward the dance floor. "Isn't it unfair to loose Alva Jean on him so soon?"

"I'm not that desperate for an associate." She ordered a light beer when the waitress passed. "We'll see what the evening brings."

He wished for another slow song, but the band had taken a break. Alva Jean appeared at the table with an odd look on her face, grabbed Carlie's hand and dragged her to the Fillies' room.

"Something wrong?" Henry asked when William returned to the table.

"I just found out about Alva Jean's boyfriend," William said. "All I did was ask her if she was seeing anyone. She told me he'd been murdered, then started crying. I feel absolutely terrible. Someday I'll learn to keep my mouth shut."

"You had no way of knowing."

"I still feel bad. I mean, she's just so... so great. I called Dr. Hannahan last night when I got in, and Alva Jean answered the phone. We talked for almost an hour." He flashed a brilliant smile. "I was just a little curious, you know. If I was to accept this position and perhaps she wasn't seeing anyone... Well, I would hope there'd be an opportunity to get to know her better. Not that it's a deciding factor. Of course, with her being the sister of my employer, it might be ill advised."

"Alva Jean is a wonderful person. Ill-advised or not, she'd be worth the risk." Henry emptied his root beer. He wondered how soon country living would make William drop the formal speech. "That's just my opinion, of course."

William nodded. "It sounds silly, given I've just met her, but there's something special about her. About them both, really. Pardon my open curiosity... Well, you and Dr. Hannahan, I mean Carlie, are pretty serious I take it?"

"We're just old friends."

He looked surprised, and his cheeks flushed. "I'm sorry, I didn't mean to assume. The way you two interact, I just thought –"

A loud crash interrupted them. People scattered, revealing the source of the racket. Jimmy Lee was pinned against the wall by Beau's left hand on his throat. In Beau's right was a broken beer bottle.

"Ain't no reason to get so upset!" Jimmy Lee's words echoed in the sudden silence.

Carlie and Alva Jean had returned to the table. Carlie leaned toward Henry, an alarmed look on her face. "Oh my God," she said. "Beau might kill him. Or make him wish he were dead."

Beau waved the broken bottle in sweeping arcs in front of Jimmy Lee's face while Odessa cheered. Realizing no one was inclined to stop them, Henry crossed the room. "Hold on, Beau," he said. "Why don't we talk, before things get out of hand?"

Beau turned toward him and blinked. Henry caught a whiff of hard liquor.

"You'd best mind your own business." The words were slurred, but the menace in them was clear.

"It is my business." Henry's voice was quiet. "You see, he's family."

"Not that he'll admit." Odessa scowled at Henry before turning to her brother. "I say we show this bastard what happens to people who stick their nose where it don't belong!"

She launched an unexpected kick. Henry avoided the full force of the blow, but her boot still landed solidly against his ribs. It knocked the breath out of him and sent a jolt of stinging pain through him. He was momentarily stunned. Beau let go of Jimmy Lee and jumped at Henry with the bottle. Half-hitting and half-slicing, the jagged glass cut Henry above his eyebrow.

Beau grinned wickedly and stepped back to admire his handiwork, giving Henry time to recover. When Beau came at him again, his drunkenness made him careless. He waited until Beau was close, then slapped the bottle away and followed with a vicious kick to the knee. When Beau bent to grab his leg, Henry landed a backhand blow to his face. Beau was hurting, and only halfheartedly swung a fist at Henry's head. Henry easily ducked under the punch and kicked him in the groin.

Beau groaned and dropped to the floor. Enraged, Odessa charged. This time Henry didn't underestimate her. Dropping his shoulder as she rushed in, he flipped her over his back, dropping her onto a table. She bounced into the chairs then onto the floor with a loud crack. Spouting profanities, she rolled and cradled her left arm.

"Holy shit!" Jimmy Lee's voice came from somewhere behind him. "Did y'all see that?"

"Hey man, you're bleeding." Someone offered Henry a bar towel. He looked away from the fallen McLeans and realized blood was dripping down the side of his face and onto his white shirt. Suddenly dizzy, he sank into the chair he'd been holding and pressed the towel to his forehead.

Something thumped behind him. Turning, he saw Carlie waving a cue stick at a man huddled on the floor. People gathered around, blocking his view. They slapped him on the back and spoke words he ignored. He searched for Carlie in the pressing crowd as two deputies pushed their way through. They bombarded him with questions. Before he could work out a response, Carlie answered for him.

"He's going to need some stitches." One of the deputies looked at the wound on Henry's forehead. "He looks a little pale, too. Maybe we need to call an ambulance."

"No need," Carlie said. "The hospital is only a few miles from here. It's easier to drive there ourselves."

"But you're a – "

"Animal doctors know a little about humans, too." Cool hands lifted the towel, examining his forehead. Carlie urged him to his feet. She led him out the door to her Jeep Cherokee. She and William flanked him in the backseat.

Muddy Waters

Alva Jean took the driver's seat.

By the time they arrived at the hospital, Henry's head was throbbing. William helped him inside, gripping his arm to keep him steady. Henry removed the towel to fumble with his wallet, trying to find his insurance information. One look at the blood-soaked towel and the room started spinning. His knees buckled, and he hoped William could support him because he didn't want to fall on his face in front of Carlie.

CHAPTER 31

Henry awoke in a strange room with a pounding headache. Light was streaming in the window and he wished someone would close the blinds. He touched the thick pad of gauze on his forehead, vaguely remembering the doctor suturing his wound. As his mind cleared, he recalled agreeing to spend the night at the Hannahan house.

"How are you feeling?" The voice startled him. Louis was standing in the doorway, silhouetted in the light from the open door. Henry had to squint to see his face.

"I'm not dead," Henry replied. "But this headache sure makes me wish I was."

"You're lucky. What made you want to tangle with the McLeans?"

"It certainly wasn't intentional." Henry sat up carefully. He spotted his jeans and white shirt folded neatly on a chair in the corner. Both had been washed.

"Carlie called from work and wanted me to look in on you. She's on her way over."

Louis left, and Henry got out of bed. Using the chair for balance, he dressed slowly. His side ached nearly as much as his head.

"I thought you'd still be in bed," Carlie said from the door.

Henry looked up from tucking in his shirt. "Your father rousted me."

"He was supposed to check on you, not wake you."

"I needed to get up anyway." He touched the bandage on his head. "I owe you an apology."

"Why on earth would you owe me an apology?"

"I didn't mean to ruin the whole evening."

"You didn't ruin any more than I did by hitting a guy with a beer bottle."

"Who was he?"

"McLean's foreman. He had a cue stick, and it was obvious what he intended to do with it."

A thought occurred to him. "William didn't get scared off, did he?"

"The opposite." Carlie laughed. "He thought it was very exciting."

"Well, I apologize just the same."

"When I said Beau might kill Jimmy Lee, I had no idea you'd jump into the thick of it."

"I didn't plan on it, that's for sure. I assumed Beau might be capable of rational thought."

"Not when tequila's involved."

"Della tried to warn me about that," Henry said. "I should have paid closer attention."

"A lot of people were glad to see someone get the best of Beau. He's done some serious damage in fights. I was really worried when you went over there."

Henry touched the bandage on his forehead, wondering what he'd been thinking last night.

"Mom has breakfast ready," Carlie said. "I've got to go. I'll see you later, okay?"

"I look forward to it." He thought he sounded too enthusiastic. He pulled on his boots and found his way to the kitchen.

Patricia greeted him with a glass of iced tea. "Breakfast?"

"No thank you, ma'am." Henry took a seat beside Louis at the large breakfast bar.

"If you need anything, just ask. I'll be upstairs in my studio."

Henry thanked her and reached for the tea.

Louis pointed to the bandage. "How many stitches?"

"I don't know exactly." Henry wished his head would stop throbbing.

"Well, you'll always have something to remind you of this trip."

Henry was afraid laughing might hurt. "Not my idea of a souvenir."

Louis sipped his coffee. "Ran into Hugh early this morning. He told me Beau has a badly strained knee. Looks like he'll be hobbling around on crutches for some time. And Odessa's none too happy about a broken arm."

Henry cringed at the thought of hurting a woman. "I'm not very proud of myself for that."

"She would've broken your arm given the chance." Louis pushed away his empty breakfast plate. "It was a tough call. At least you didn't have to punch her."

"That's doesn't make me feel any better."

Louis shrugged. "Forensics didn't find any blood on that saddle Jimmy Lee took off the horse. Miller wasn't near the horse when he was hit. But we knew that from the tracks around the body. Or lack of, as you put it."

"That raises a couple of questions, doesn't it?"

"Does it?"

"If you think like a cowboy," Henry explained. "A cowboy wouldn't get off a horse if he didn't have to. So why did he? Was it for a closer look at something he found curious?"

"Like what? There weren't any tracks supporting that."

Henry considered another scenario. "What if Aubrey was doing the digging?"

"There were no open holes." Louis rubbed his chin. "How would Aubrey have known about this treasure thing, or where to dig? Through Odessa? That points to Jimmy Lee. Are they lying about the alibi?"

"That's why you get paid the big bucks, detective."

"My life is so much simpler when you're not around. You give me too much to worry about. Maybe we'll drive out to the old cemetery tomorrow, if you're up to it." Louis finished his coffee then checked his watch. He got up and put his dishes in the sink. "Speaking of worrying, I'm concerned about Carlie."

"What about her?" Henry tried not to sound alarmed.

"I don't want to see her get hurt." Louis opened the back door to leave. "Let's just leave it at that."

CHAPTER 32

Louis Hannahan spent most of Monday morning reviewing the Miller file. He sat at his desk and read through all the statements, then read them again. He did the same with his notes. The only thing he'd gotten out of it was a headache. He foraged in his desk drawer for a bottle of Tylenol. He washed two tablets down with cold coffee and wondered why people drank it on purpose.

What was he overlooking? Since he already had a headache, now was as good a time as any to revisit the McLeans. He arrived at the slaughterhouse office shortly before two o'clock, where he was greeted by a primly-dressed secretary. Louis showed his credentials and introduced himself before asking to speak with Beau.

"He hasn't returned to work yet." Her words were clipped, efficient.

"How about Hugh?"

"Do you have an appointment?" she asked.

Apparently, his being a detective didn't impress her. "Ma'am, I'm investigating a murder. I don't *need* an appointment."

With an exaggerated sigh, she pushed herself to her feet. "I'll tell him you're here."

She disappeared out the door he'd just entered. A few minutes later, she returned with Hugh on her heels. Dark circles under his eyes hinted at the extra work his brother's absence had caused. It occurred to Louis that he should feel sorry for Hugh, but he couldn't. The McLeans had cost him many sleepless nights throughout his career.

"Hello, Mr. Hannahan. What brings you out this way?" Hugh's casual words conflicted with the fear in his eyes.

"Just want to ask you a few things." How many times Hugh had entertained policemen with questions?

"My office is just over here." Hugh glanced at his secretary. "Please hold my calls."

Louis felt her eyes on him until they entered her employer's inner sanctum. Hugh closed the door softly behind them.

"Ask away." Hugh offered Louis the small chair in front of his desk.

His headache had not subsided, so he didn't waste time on putting Hugh at ease before getting to the point. "You know those cattle near that old corral? Did Beau tell you how long they'd been there?"

Hugh had a lousy poker face. Louis could see the wheels turning as he worked out a response. "Yeah," Hugh finally said. "Maybe six months."

The unexpected honesty threw Louis off, and it took a few seconds to regain his line of thinking. "Isn't that about the time your cousin arrived in town?"

Hugh frowned. "What does this have to do with investigating Aubrey's death?"

"Did Aubrey or Beau mention seeing anyone digging in the corral?"

"Not that I remember."

"When did Aubrey start riding your horses?"

"I showed him around town a day or two after he got here. The barn was one of the places we stopped. He asked if anyone rode them, because they looked rough to him. Odessa's the only one ever messed with them, and that wasn't often. Until recently, that is."

"You ever get complaints about Aubrey riding the horses?"

"Only from Jimmy Lee." Hugh almost spat the name. "Whining little bastard was worried Aubrey might catch him and Odessa fooling around."

Louis coughed, hoping to dislodge that image from his mind. "You see anything when you drove out to meet Beau that night? Another vehicle? Someone walking? Even if it doesn't seem important, I'd like to know."

Hugh shook his head. "I was the only one on the road."

"One more thing. Where can I find Odessa?"

"At home, I guess." Hugh added, "She ain't able to work until her arm heals."

Louis thanked Hugh for his time and left, smiling at the secretary as he passed her desk. Once in the Tahoe, he scribbled a few notes. He wasn't sure he'd gotten anything useful from Hugh, but the record might help later. After grabbing a chicken sandwich at a fast-food restaurant on his way through town, he drove to the Bar T Ranch. Jimmy Lee was climbing into his pickup when Louis arrived.

"Got a minute to talk?" Louis asked from the Tahoe.

"Do I have much choice?" Jimmy Lee paused by the open truck door. "I thought you was happy with what I told you the other day."

Louis got out of his vehicle. "That was the other day."

"Is here okay or do we need to find a dark room with a bare light bulb?"

"This will do." Louis rubbed his eyes as he struggled to hide his annoyance. "When you and Odessa went riding, did you ever see Aubrey at the corral?"

Jimmy Lee shook his head.

"Ever see him talking to anyone at the McLean's barn or the trail there?"

Again, the head shake.

"Were you the one poking around that corral for this so-called lost treasure mentioned in the journal?"

Jimmy Lee folded his arms across his chest. "I'm not

stupid."

Louis bit his tongue, suppressing an unprofessional remark. "I didn't ask if you were stupid. I asked if you were digging."

"Why would I? Just because some airheaded girl wrote it in a journal don't mean it's real."

"Do you know of anyone who might have been looking for it?"

Jimmy Lee shifted his feet. "No idea."

"Not even a theory?"

"Nope."

Louis lightly tapped his knuckles on his holster. "How about we try something easier. Who else knew about that story in the journal?"

Jimmy Lee shrugged. "Anyone at the ranch, I suppose."

"How about the wranglers?"

"I reckon so."

"Didn't two of them look for a while?"

Jimmy Lee shrugged again.

"What about the ranch guests? Any of them know?"

"Can't say for sure. Momma may have mentioned it to some of them."

This was like talking to a brick wall, except brick walls didn't lie. "Why did you report the cattle as stolen?"

"Because of Aubrey. Odessa told me he was a cattle thief. It was kind of a joke on him, to keep him far away from any cows. I wanted him out of our hair, if you know what I mean."

Louis didn't want to know what he meant. "If you'd never seen him around, why'd you feel the need to keep him 'out of your hair'?"

"He was riding up there, wasn't he? Who knew when he'd show up?"

This was getting him nowhere, though Jimmy Lee wasn't as bad as the McLeans when it came to lying. He considered taking him in for questioning to see if that would shake the truth out of him. Since his headache had grown along with his frustration, he decided to call it a day. A tall glass of iced tea and an hour or so in a rocking chair on the front porch was sounding good. He could relax and think about the case in relative peace.

"Any more questions, or can I go now?" Jimmy Lee asked. "I've got things to do."

"I'm trying to solve a murder," Louis said with forced patience. "Would it hurt you to be less of an asshole, and maybe a little more cooperative?"

Jimmy Lee snickered. "If I acted any different, people would think something was wrong, wouldn't they?"

CHAPTER 33

Vernon settled on the sofa with the television remote and flipped through the channels. "The doc says take it easy, so what are you going to do with yourself?"

Henry wondered the same thing. He touched the bandage on his forehead. Sadly, his uncle's visit was the highlight of his afternoon. "Besides go stir-crazy?"

Vernon's channel surfing began to annoy him. Television was something Henry rarely watched, especially daytime programs. He didn't care who anyone slept with and he wasn't good at guessing grocery prices. He tried to think of a way to distract Vernon from the TV. Maybe it was time to bring up the job at Blue Ridge Parkway. He was about to mention it when a soft tap on the front door stopped him.

Vernon answered the door. "Look what the cat dragged in."

Carlie stepped inside the cabin. "How you feeling?"

"Other than bored, not bad." Henry grinned. A clump of pet hair clung to one leg of her scrubs and an ominous dark stain decorated the front of her shirt. Even in dirty work clothes she was a ray of sunshine. He barely heard Vernon make an excuse about needing something to drink before disappearing into the kitchen.

"Bored means better." Carlie placed her shoulder bag on the coffee table. "How long before that bandage comes off?"

"Should've done it already," Henry said. "I was afraid to

see what it looks like."

"May I?"

Henry nodded. She frowned as she carefully removed the bandage.

"Is it bad?" Henry gingerly touched the swollen skin around the sutures.

"I'm just used to things with fur."

"Are you saying my eyebrow's been shaved?"

Carlie laughed. "It's still there." She sat on the sofa and pulled a paper bag out of her purse. "Dad sent some movies to help break the monotony of recuperation."

"That's thoughtful." Henry said, "What'd he send?"

"I didn't look, to tell the truth."

He reached into the bag, pulled out the first movie and smiled. He held up *Whispering Smith* and said, "Your father has a twisted sense of humor."

Vernon came back from the kitchen with a handful of chocolate chip cookies. "Della's making supper. Looks like you're in good hands, so I'll stop in again tomorrow." At the door, he winked at Henry before closing it.

Henry looked at Carlie. "Have you eaten?"

"I came straight from work," she replied. "Lunch was hours ago."

"There's a pizza in the freezer, and we've got movies."

They sat at the kitchen table while they waited on the pizza. As he poured two glasses of iced tea, Henry asked about Dr. William Danner.

"I have high hopes, both in his abilities and in his desire to join the practice," Carlie said. "Unfortunately, he's got other offers. I'll know something next week, one way or the other."

When the pizza was done, he cut it and placed a couple of slices onto paper plates. He grinned as he handed one to her. "Not exactly the Ritz."

They sat on the sofa, watching Alan Ladd as a railroad

detective on the trail of his best friend.

"This nickname of yours," Carlie began. "Is it because you're like this character, quiet but dangerous?"

"I certainly don't see myself that way."

"Then the Whispering Smith thing is because you look like Alan Ladd?"

"I look nothing like him."

"Why protest?" Carlie laughed. "I think he was kind of handsome. Besides, it doesn't matter how you got it. Most everyone in town will be using it before long, if they aren't already."

"Why's that?"

"The way you handled the McLeans. This is a small town. Imagine the talk."

Henry felt his face flush. "I wouldn't say it was a clear victory. I did end up in the emergency room."

"Odessa and Beau have battle scars that are far worse. You only needed a few stitches." Carlie touched his forehead.

Henry felt the soft coolness of her hand. Suddenly, his mouth was dry and his heart thumped in his chest. She looked into his eyes and he thought seriously about kissing her. He leaned closer. A yellow ball of fur bounced onto Henry's lap, startling them both.

"Vernon's cat," Henry said. "He pretty much comes and goes as he pleases."

"I've noticed." Carlie watched the cat leap from the sofa onto the coffee table. She looked back at Henry. "Henry–"

Her pager began to beep with increasing loudness.

CHAPTER 34

"If you really want to come along, I won't object to the company," Carlie said. "As long as you're following doctor's orders."

"I've rested all day," Henry reassured her. "It'll do me good to get out."

"Fair warning, this might be grisly. It sounds like a cat with an abscess."

"I'm sure I've seen worse." He touched the sutures in his forehead and chuckled.

Darkness had fallen long before they arrived at the veterinary hospital. Carlie opened the door and turned on the lights. She locked the door before going into the treatment area to switch on more lights. Henry sat behind the reception desk and watched for her clients.

Carlie took the other chair when she returned. "How did you end up as a range detective?"

"Not quite what I started out to do," Henry said. "You remember that I wanted to be a park ranger or a game warden? I landed a few summer jobs with the U.S. Fish & Wildlife Service. They were always temporary, never permanent, so I also worked as a hunting guide. This hunter that regularly hired me suggested I look into the local rancher's association. They paid for law enforcement training in exchange for a two-year commitment. Been at it ever since." He looked at her and smiled. "I suppose I got sidetracked."

"Don't we all?" She stared out the front window as she

spoke. "Is your job dangerous?"

"In spite of the stories Aubrey told, most of the work is mundane. Even when I'm out on the range, things are pretty uneventful."

Headlight beams struck the window as a vehicle turned into the parking lot. Carlie unlocked the door and greeted the clients, a man and a young girl he introduced as his daughter. Henry recognized the newspaper reporter, Wayne Hewlett.

Wanting to avoid Hewlett, Henry stayed in the reception area while the cat was examined. He walked around the room, surveying the displays of pet food and other products. He was standing in front of a large poster announcing a breakthrough in heartworm and parasite control, when the exam room door opened. He found himself face to face with the reporter.

Closing the door behind him, Hewlett watched his daughter shuffle to a chair. "Don't worry, honey. Elwood is in good hands with Dr. Hannahan."

The girl nodded but didn't appear convinced. Hewlett turned to Henry. "I think we got off on the wrong foot the other morning. I've been known to be aggressive when pursuing a story."

Henry leaned against the wall and folded his arms on his chest.

"It's a huge story," Hewlett said. "Death is one thing, but murder is a whole other animal. It's something that doesn't happen here, that's why people are upset and nervous. There's only been one other murder in the town's history. Imagine the story if the two were connected."

"Connected how?" Henry asked, suddenly interested.

Carlie poked her head around the exam room door. "Mr. Hewlett, I'm going to need to sedate your kitty after all. You want to pick him up in the morning?"

Hewlett glanced at his daughter. "We'd rather take him

back tonight."

"He'll need to stay in his carrier until morning," Carlie replied. "I don't want him hurting himself while recovering from sedation. If you're okay with that, you're welcome to wait."

Hewlett nodded. "That's fine."

From somewhere behind her, the cat snarled and growled. Carlie looked at Henry. "Would you mind lending a hand?"

"Don't pay him no mind, Mr. Hannahan," Hewlett's daughter said to Henry. "He's always like that around strangers."

Carlie waved Henry to follow her into the spacious treatment area, where the cat sat on a table in what she called a squeeze cage. The cat hissed and spat, then clawed at him through the bars. Henry looked at the cat, then at Carlie, hoping she wasn't asking him to hold the cat.

"Let's get to work, Mr. Hannahan." She explained how the cage worked, which involved pushing a movable panel inward until the cat was pressed into a more confined space. Henry pushed while Carlie used a small syringe to inject the cat, who protested with a high-pitched yowl.

Within minutes, the cat was docile. Carlie pulled on a pair of exam gloves, shaved the cat's fur and cleaned the quarter-sized wound. "Just a simple abscess that looks uglier than it is. Most of it drained on its own. The ones that don't can be messy. Smelly, too."

He didn't want to see a messy one. His stomach was already protesting. Once finished, Carlie gave the cat an antibiotic injection and placed him in a cardboard box with the words "Pet Wagon" on the side. Henry closed the box, making sure the top was secure. He placed it on the floor. Carlie scribbled in the treatment record, then offered a tour.

"This place is bigger than I expected," Henry said.

"We've had to add an exam room and put in another

treatment table. We draw a lot of clients from the surrounding communities. The staff is great, and that really means a lot. Word of mouth beats advertising."

"I'm impressed."

Carlie smiled, obviously proud of the hospital. The cat began to move around in the box. "Time to let the Hewletts rescue Cat-Zilla from my evil clutches." As Carlie moved toward the door, she pointed at the box. "Watch yourself."

Henry saw a large paw swiping at him through one of the ventilation holes. The razor-sharp claws were less than an inch from his leg. He moved, and Cat-Zilla yowled.

"Smile when you call me that," Henry said to the cat.

After Carlie finished talking with Hewlett and his daughter, Henry picked up the box and offered to carry it to their vehicle. Once outside, he spoke to the reporter. "What did you mean about the murders being connected?"

"I didn't say they were." Hewlett helped his daughter climb into the car. "It's just odd they happened within a quarter mile of each other."

CHAPTER 35

It was after nine when Henry awoke, feeling slightly dazed from a restless night plagued by nightmares. He'd even dreamt about Aubrey's murder. The killer was dressed like the Grim Reaper, hovering at the edge of his dream, seen and unseen, drifting between two murders decades apart. Henry got up and walked sleepily toward the kitchen, nearly stumbling over Vernon's outstretched legs. His uncle was seated on the sofa, looking through the movies Carlie had brought.

"Morning," Henry yawned.

"Back at ya," Vernon said. He waggled his eyebrows. "How was your evening?"

"She had an emergency call."

"Better luck next time." He held up a movie and grinned. "I see she's looking after you."

"Actually, Louis sent those."

"Quit avoiding the subject," Vernon said. "What's going on between you two?"

"I helped Louis with a little tracking."

He rolled his eyes. "I meant with Carlie."

"Oh," Henry said. "We're just friends."

"Are you happy about that?"

Henry shrugged, feigning indifference.

Vernon shook his head. "Boy, you're dumber than you look. And you look pretty dumb right now."

"What are you trying to say?"

"You're in love with that woman. Even I can see that,

217

and I'm thick as a plank when it comes to matters of the heart." He frowned at Henry. "What is it you're afraid of?"

Henry knew he'd give himself away if he said anything. He stared at the patterns in the old wood floor, resigned to enduring his uncle's little tirade.

"Or maybe we're talking about something a little more serious here," Vernon said. "She scares you, doesn't she? You're afraid of taking a chance."

That went to the bone, and Henry mentally recoiled from the words.

"So what if she turned you down the first time you popped the question." Vernon shook his head. "I think this is more serious than you realize, son. Don't you believe for a minute that putting it off and going back to Colorado will make those feelings go away."

"Aren't you supposed to be at work or something?" Henry turned away and stared out the window. Maybe this would turn out to be part of the bad dreams from last night. Any minute he'd wake up and find his world was back to normal again.

"Look, I'm saying this because I don't want you to end up a crusty old bachelor like me. A few years down the road, you'll start being angry with yourself about letting her get away. Maybe you'll get lucky and find someone to keep you company in your golden years, when you're too old and tired to worry about heartbreak. It sucks to find happiness when you don't have much time left to bask in it. Trust me on that one."

"I really don't care to discuss this right now."

Vernon's voice softened. "You ought to tell her how you feel."

Henry was silent for a few moments. "What if she doesn't feel the same?"

"I don't believe that, and neither do you." Vernon jumped to his feet. "I've got places to be." He was out the door before Henry could reply.

Henry wandered into the kitchen to make breakfast before attacking the day. Armed with iced tea and jam-smothered toast, he sat back in the kitchen chair and sighed. He didn't want to dwell on Carlie, so he contemplated Hewlett's words. What if he was on to something, and the murders were connected? His thoughts were interrupted by the ringing telephone.

"Hello?"

"When you going to see her?" It was Vernon, nagging again.

"Too busy right now, trying to enjoy some peace and quiet."

"Damn if they ain't right. You can lead a horse to water, but you can't make him drink." Disappointment was obvious in Vernon's voice. "Just as well. She probably isn't worth giving up the job that nearly got you killed anyway."

"Why did you call?" Henry grew irritated, but it had little to do with Vernon.

"Is my wallet on the coffee table?"

Henry looked. "Yes, it is."

"I'll be by in fifteen minutes to pick it up."

"Don't expect to find any money in it." Henry hung up the phone.

Not wanting to be there when Vernon returned, he dressed, grabbed his truck keys and went out the door. He wasn't sure where he was going, he just drove. It wasn't surprising that he ended up on the Blue Ridge Parkway. The Rolling Stones blared from the speakers. Rays of sunlight filtered through the trees lining the road as he drove. Mick and the boys sang about not getting what you want, but it was the word need that got Henry's attention. It explained the ache in his heart when he thought about going back to Colorado. He swore loudly and slapped the steering wheel.

After high school, he'd believed falling in love was

something that would never happen to him again. He thought about Aubrey and how happy he'd been to move back. How he'd found someone and how, for the first time, he'd really thought about settling down. And how his time was gone before he could enjoy what he'd found.

Henry parked in the next overlook. Hours slipped away as he sat on the tailgate and gazed at the bluish haze hanging over the mountains. It was dark when he returned to Parsons Gap. Turning into the Hannahan place, he parked beside Carlie's Cherokee. He climbed out of his truck and walked to the front porch, careful to avoid the dozens of moths dancing around the light. The curtain in the window to the left of the door moved slightly. After what seemed to be the longest minute he'd ever endured, the door opened.

"Henry," Carlie said, her expression neutral. "What are you doing here?"

Feeling like a high school kid on a first date, he removed his hat and shifted his feet nervously. Words bounced around in his head but none of them came together to form a complete sentence.

"Would you like to come in?" She asked, rescuing him. "I'll get us something to drink. Make yourself at home in the living room. I'll be right back."

The house wasn't as small as the outside appearance suggested. Two rooms were along a hallway that led to a large kitchen. A small room off the living room had been made into a home office. He glanced at the tidy desk as he made his way to the sofa. The house was quiet and he remembered Carlie was on call, so her son would be next door.

He settled onto the small but comfortable sofa and glanced around the room, every detail burning its way into his mind. Wicker chairs and hardwood floors gave the space warmth. A bowl containing seashells sat on the coffee table.

Framed black and white photographs of seaside scenes hung on the walls. The room had an airy feeling, more like a beach house than a home in the mountains.

She handed him a glass of iced tea then sat in a wicker chair. One sleeve of her white Henley shirt slipped down to her wrist, and she shoved it back into place. Crossing her arms, she fixed him with an intense gaze. "You didn't come here to drink tea."

His thumb rubbed the side of the glass. "I came here because I wanted to talk about us."

"Well, that's good. It's been on my mind, too." Her face was still unreadable.

"Tell me what you're thinking." Henry hoped she might save him the trouble of working out what he was going to say.

She stared at the floor. "I don't think we should see each other anymore. You'll be going back soon... and I just think it would be for the best."

Not what he'd expected, so it was now or never. Henry took a deep breath. Speaking from the heart was not something he was accustomed to doing. "Before you close the door on us seeing each other, I want you to know I'm in love with you." Henry plowed ahead. "There are no guarantees things will work out for us, but I want to give it a shot."

Carlie seemed genuinely surprised, which made him wonder what she'd been expecting.

"I'm accepting a job on the Blue Ridge Parkway. Meaning Parsons Gap will be my home." He paused to take a sip of tea. "I'd like to know what you feel, not what you think."

"I don't know what to say," Carlie said.

"I'm not asking you to decide anything right now." He was relieved that he'd managed to say what he felt.

"But—"

He held up his hand. "All I ask is that you don't invent some story to try and make me leave."

An awkward silence fell heavily between them.

Henry got to his feet. "I'd better go."

Without looking back at her, he opened the door and walked onto the porch. Behind him, he heard her rise from the chair.

"Henry, wait."

He turned. Carlie stepped onto the porch and stood in front of him. "It seems I'm doing okay with explaining what I think, but not how I feel."

Placing her hands on the back of his neck, she pulled his face down to hers. Their initial kiss was a tentative one. The subsequent kisses grew less hesitant. Henry was acutely aware of an almost electrical shock as he circled his arms around her. He felt a shiver when he drew her close and she pressed her body against his.

"I'd like to be romantic and carry you to the bedroom," Henry whispered the words. "But I'm not sure where it is."

Carlie took his hand and showed him the way.

CHAPTER 36

Beau McLean liked to gamble. Cards were his favorite, and he considered himself quite good at poker, especially five-card stud, the game he was now playing. But he'd been losing steadily and was down a few hundred dollars already. Not a lot of money by his usual standards of late, just more than he'd brought to tonight's backroom game at the Wooden Nickel.

The full house staring back at him promised a change of luck, but to stay in the game he'd need more cash. He'd cash a check if he hadn't told his brother he'd quit gambling. To make things worse, the only check he had was on the company account. If he cashed that here, Hugh would find out and rightly assume he'd broken that promise. He was between a rock and a hard place.

This seemed to be the case more and more often these days. The family business was making money, but it kept them too busy to enjoy the fruits of their labor. Hiring Aubrey had eased the workload. The downside was his salary had cut their profit. With Mauro's help, Beau had found a way to supplement the meat market with the stolen cattle. Then Aubrey had to go and get himself killed. Now Hannahan was breathing down their necks about the murder and the rustling. Thanks to Smith, no doubt. Smith was also responsible for him being unable to work for a week or two.

He stared at his cards and wondered how much truth was in Aubrey's stories. Beau still hadn't figured out how

Smith got the best of him and Odessa at the Watering Hole. They were both on the floor before Mauro even had a chance to cross the room. They'd all blamed it on the tequila.

Next time Beau would be sober, and take great satisfaction in some payback. Though that bastard Smith certainly deserved it, he'd gotten tight with Hannahan and his daughter. Anything too obvious might land them in a pile of law problems. Hugh could worry about the plan. He was the smart one, and there was time to think on it while Beau's knee healed. Right now, he had more than enough trouble to handle. Like the latest stunt his son had pulled. Stan's mother might have been taken in by the lies, but Beau knew better. His son was a thief. Luckily there was an upside.

"I'm folding," Beau said with disgust. He tossed his cards on the table and pushed back his chair. Without another word, he left the bar.

On the drive home, his cell rang. "Yeah?"

"I got your message. Can you meet tonight?"

Beau grinned. "Sure. Where?"

"At the corral."

"I can be there in a half hour."

"Make it forty-five."

"All right." Beau closed the phone and smiled.

His little cash problem was about to be solved. If things went quickly enough, he might be able to rejoin that poker game tonight. He drove his pickup slowly across town, unable to keep the grin off his face. His first stop was Odessa's horse barn. He parked in the grass on the side of the barn, where it was hidden from the road, then made sure nobody else was there. This wasn't the time for surprises. Beau reached for his crutches and limped into the barn.

His ticket for a shake of the money tree was in a brown

paper bag hidden under a stack of grain sacks. After a last glance around the barn, he grabbed the bag and stuffed it in his jacket pocket. He slipped outside and climbed into his truck. The road to the corral was rough, but he'd driven it before. And it sure beat walking down that trail from Parsons Hollow Road with crutches.

Ten minutes later, he stopped under the big oak and shut off the engine. As an afterthought, he took the pistol from the glove box, jammed it in his belt then got his crutches and limped toward the corral. A big owl flew from one of the fence posts, making him jump. He dropped one crutch to grab the pistol, tripped over it and landed on his bad knee. Swearing profusely, he almost didn't hear someone come up beside him.

Beau looked up. "You're early. You got the money?"

"Depends. You got the item?"

"Of course." He patted his jacket pocket.

A blinding white flash was the last thing Beau saw.

CHAPTER 37

Henry awoke shortly after dawn with Carlie's head nestled in the hollow of his shoulder, her hair spilling across his chest. Sunshine was finding its way through the blinds and the room gleamed in the light. Their lovemaking had been slow and passionate, each one taking time to rediscover the pleasures and delights of the other. Afterwards, they'd laid in bed whispering and laughing, caressing and teasing. They'd made love again before finally falling asleep.

When Carlie rolled onto her pillow, Henry slipped out of bed. For a moment he just stood there, watching as she slept. There was a difference, one he'd forgotten, in being with a woman he cared deeply about. The emotional involvement seemed to amplify the physical pleasure to something more intense, and far more gratifying, than the brief satisfaction of a one-night stand. The hollowness of the typical morning after had been replaced by a warm, comfortable feeling that centered in his chest and radiated outward.

He forced himself to look away. He located his boxers among the clothes scattered on the floor and stepped quietly into the bathroom. Carlie was awake when he returned. She snuggled into the blanket and smiled sleepily. He leaned against the doorway. "Morning."

"Good morning," she mumbled. "What creatures on your boxer shorts? Armadillos?"

Henry glanced down. "Hedgehogs."

"Cute."

Henry sat on the bed and brushed a tendril of hair from her cheek. His fingers traced the line of her jaw and neck and toyed with the small pearl on her gold necklace. He remembered giving her that pearl on her sixteenth birthday. "You're beautiful, you know."

"Hmm. I had no idea you were so romantic."

"I'm full of surprises."

Carlie took his hand in hers and squeezed tightly, then touched the scar on his side. "How did you get this? Was it when you had to kill someone in the line of duty?"

"No, it wasn't." He wondered just how many stories Aubrey had told.

"Does it bother you to talk about it?"

Henry found himself telling her about that night in the canyon, right up to finding Conner tying a bandana around his own leg. There he hesitated, thinking about how he was going to say what happened next. He'd never really talked about it to anyone outside the inquiry. That had been detached. Cold. This felt almost cathartic. "I told him to drop his rifle. He didn't. He tried to shoot again."

Carlie shivered.

"How about I make you some breakfast?" Henry leaned over, intending to kiss her.

She stopped him and reached up to touch his forehead.

"You look a little flushed, and I know you didn't rest much last night," Carlie said, her concern obvious. "Maybe we shouldn't have—"

"No," Henry replied. "We definitely should have."

Loud knocking on the front door interrupted them. Carlie slipped into her robe and headed down the hall as Henry grabbed his jeans from the floor.

She opened the door. "Good morning, Dad. What's going on?"

"Is Henry here?" Her father's voice boomed. "I need to

talk to him."

Henry was surprised that Louis knew where to find him. Then he recalled his pickup parked outside, making it obvious to the world he had stayed the night. He slipped on a t-shirt before walking barefoot down the hall. Louis stood in the living room, his expression grim.

"Was he here all night, Carlie?"

"I don't think that's any of your business."

Louis paused, his face registering surprise. "I didn't mean it that way. It's police business."

"He was here all night," Carlie said defiantly.

"What time did he arrive?"

"Right after dusk."

"I'm standing right here," Henry said.

"Beau McLean was murdered last night. The rest of the McLeans are on the warpath. They're really hot to get the guy who did it."

"You make it sound like I should be worried," Henry said.

"A couple of peculiar things were found at the murder scene."

Henry didn't like the sound of that. "What happened?"

"Beau left home yesterday afternoon and never made it back. Deputy Monroe found his truck early this morning at that old corral off Parsons Hollow Road. Beau's body was near it, shot once in the chest. The murder weapon was found near the scene. We ran the registration number." Louis fixed him with that intense stare. "Funny thing. It's your pistol."

"I don't think that's funny."

"Where and when did you last see that pistol?"

"It was in my truck the night I went to the Watering Hole Saloon and got this little souvenir." Henry pointed to the sutures in his forehead. "I don't know who drove the pickup to the cabin, or when, but that's where it's been parked until yesterday."

"That would have been Alva Jean or William," Carlie said. "She gave the keys to Dad, and he gave them to you when he dropped you at the cabin the next morning."

"Was it locked when you got in it yesterday?"

Henry nodded, recalling Vernon's badgering and how distracted his thoughts had been yesterday. He should have looked in the truck. Had his carelessness cost a life? "I didn't check for the pistol."

Louis glanced at Carlie before speaking to Henry. "Maybe it'd be best if you come outside with me."

Henry stepped onto the porch, thoughts on Mauro's unsuccessful surprise party and the bullet on his truck dash. Henry didn't know whether it had been about stolen cattle or murder. Was framing him the new plan? What did they think he knew?

"This was unintentional," Louis said in a low voice, "but the McLeans heard about the murder weapon on their police scanner. They know who owns it. As in they want you dead."

If he thought the McLeans weren't level-headed before, the effect of their brother's death could make them dangerously unpredictable.

"There's something else." Louis stared at the porch rocker as he spoke. "I hope your intentions here are nothing but honorable with Carlie. Do something stupid, and I might just kill you myself."

Carlie came to the door and smiled at them through the screen. "Are you harassing Henry?"

"Only a little," Louis admitted. "Guess I can't say much. You're quite capable of looking out for yourself."

She looked at Henry. "Did you tell him you're staying in Parsons Gap?"

"Didn't get a chance." He caught her father's surprised expression.

"Don't pay any attention to him," Carlie said. "He's like an old bear at times. You should've heard him growling when Alva Jean began dating."

Inside the house a telephone rang. Carlie excused herself to answer it.

"I may not be proud of the circumstances," Louis said. "But you do have an alibi."

"That depends on the time of death. We fell asleep around midnight. A few hours later, I got up to put an extra blanket on the bed. Carlie didn't wake up. I don't know if she would have awakened had I stepped out."

"You're too damned honest." Louis shook his head. "Did you do it?"

"Do what?"

"Step out and kill Beau," Louis replied. "What other 'it' do you think I'm talking about?"

CHAPTER 38

The crime scene van and two patrol cars were parked under the pines whose long shadows cast dappled sunlight on the corral. Louis stopped the Tahoe and glanced at the police tape fluttering around an area that included Beau's pickup. The time of death had been estimated between 10:00 pm and midnight, so the alibi was concrete. That didn't change the fact someone had tried to pin Beau's murder on Henry. He glanced at Henry, sitting quietly in the passenger seat, and wondered if he was still holding back information.

"If I'd wanted to kill a McLean, it'd be Odessa. She kicks like a mule." Henry rubbed his side. "And I certainly wouldn't have been stupid enough to leave my weapon at the scene."

Louis had to consider all possibilities, and he didn't feel Henry was taking the situation seriously. "Maybe you were trying to throw me off."

"What would be my motive?"

Louis shrugged. "You tell me."

"Let's say it's possible, but unlikely, that Beau killed Aubrey Miller. I somehow figure it out, lure Beau to the corral and kill him with my own pistol."

"Which you leave at the scene."

"Like a big fat calling card."

"Another explanation is someone is hoping to slow you down or stop you. If you're arrested and put in jail, that would do the trick." Louis added, "You must be close to finding out something."

"I've no idea what that 'something' is."

"Let's go take a look." Louis climbed out of the Tahoe and looked toward the corral. A faint mist still hung in the morning air, giving the place a spooky feeling. The tarp covering Beau's body near a section of dilapidated fence did not help. Henry came around the truck and stood beside him.

"I used to like this place," Louis said. "Good place to come and enjoy the solitude. Kind of gone sour now."

Henry remained silent.

"See where the body was found? Looks like somebody waited up there." Louis pointed at an opportunistic pine growing among a jumble of rocks. "Until Beau showed up. We put tape around there to keep traffic to a minimum. Maybe things won't be too trampled this time. The pistol was found next to the body, but not in the victim's hand."

"How did the killer get up there?"

"That's what I'm hoping you'll help me learn."

Henry looked toward the rocks. "Were there any tracks on the trail?"

"None that we noticed." Louis followed Henry to the corral, nodding to Deputy Monroe. A crime scene technician joined them.

"The coroner gave me a better idea on the time of death," the technician reported. "Ten o'clock, plus or minus half an hour."

While Henry examined the ground, Monroe approached Louis and spoke in a low voice. "I thought Smith was the number one suspect."

"His gun being here doesn't automatically make him the 'number one' suspect," Louis said. "Besides, he's got a solid alibi."

"Which means you've already verified it." Monroe sounded disappointed. "Who was he with? A woman?

That's the easiest alibi to get, isn't it? A man with his looks could get a woman to lie for him easy enough."

"Mr. Smith is here to help us do some tracking." Louis gave Monroe a look that he hoped made it clear the subject was closed. He walked away from them and toward Henry, who was glaring at Monroe.

Louis overheard the technician whisper to Monroe, "You idiot. Didn't you hear Smith's vehicle was found at his daughter's house?"

Louis approached Henry and hooked a thumb toward the crime scene people. "They're waiting for you to take a quick look at the ground around the body. There were a lot of tracks."

He followed Henry across the dilapidated fence and into the corral. Monroe had just joined them when a bullet kicked up dust between them. They all dove for cover at the crack of a gunshot from the direction of the road. Three more bullets peppered the ground. Henry and Louis dropped behind a small collection of loose boards near the fence, while Monroe crouched behind an overturned water trough with his weapon drawn.

"Damn it!" Louis rolled to his side, right hand clamped to his upper left arm. Blood oozed between his fingers. He dropped his pistol in the dust beside him. "Jesus that stings."

The technician's eyes widened. "Holy shit! He's bleeding."

"You hit?" Henry crawled toward him, grabbing the pistol on the way.

"No, a nail got me." Louis fumbled with the tear in his sleeve. He glanced around, assessing the situation. The shots had ceased. The crime scene crew huddled behind the old loading chute. Monroe looked shaken, but he'd gotten on the radio to call for assistance. Louis scanned the area close to the road and thought he saw someone moving around.

Henry had noticed the movement, too. "It's Odessa McLean."

Louis looked again but saw nothing. "How –"

"Hey, Hannahan!" Odessa shouted. "All I want is the bastard that killed my brother. I've got no quarrel with the rest of you."

"Nothing breaks the ice like a line from a low budget movie," Henry said with a wry smile. "Sounds like she's looking for me."

"Apparently." Louis wondered how Odessa managed to shoot the rifle with a broken arm. If that's what accounted for her poor accuracy, he decided he should be thankful.

"Dear God," Monroe said. Sweat was dripping down his forehead and off his nose. "Someone ought to get that gun away from that crazy bitch before she kills one of us."

"We just need to buy some time," Louis said. "Backup should be arriving soon."

"Hannahan, did you hear me?" Odessa shouted.

"I heard you." Louis kept his voice calm. "You know I can't do that. You also know this won't accomplish anything."

"Send him out! That's all I ask."

"Why not drop the gun and we'll talk this over?"

"Not until you send Smith out," Odessa replied.

Louis glanced at the blood soaking his shirtsleeve. He spoke to the others in a low voice, "Got anything to bandage this?"

Monroe had been watching the rocks from the lower edge of the trough. He turned and shook his head. Henry pulled out his shirttail, intending to tear off a strip.

"Wait." The technician tossed him a handkerchief. "It's clean."

Henry looked toward the road again. "She's pretty much got us pinned down."

"Aren't you Captain Fucking Obvious," Monroe growled.

Henry tied the handkerchief around Louis' arm.

"I suppose you'd just run up there and take her gun away," Monroe said.

"Not exactly," Henry said. "But I sure wouldn't be cowering behind a water trough waiting for someone else to do it."

"Why you mouthy little shit. I ought to—"

"Monroe! Knock it off," Louis hissed. He turned to Henry. "You have an idea?"

Henry paused as if thinking over options. "One of us could move along the outside of this back fence to the creek, through the culvert, and cross to the other side of the road. The trees over there would provide enough cover to get in close behind her."

Louis considered this. "You'd have to be pretty stealthy to manage that."

"You got that right," Monroe said. "All those McLeans hunt and fish. They know their way around the woods. She'll nail your ass before you cross the road."

"I can do it," Henry said.

Louis glanced at him. "I can't let you."

Henry shrugged. Monroe stretched his legs. The thwack of a bullet into the earth close to the water trough made him jump. "Jesus Christ!"

Louis was distracted for a moment, but it was enough. When he looked around, he saw Henry following the fence line toward the creek.

"Monroe," Louis said over his shoulder. "Fire a few shots her way, but space them out so she has to find cover."

At the first shot, Henry started running. After three shots, he was at the creek and out of sight. Odessa didn't return their fire, so they waited. Several minutes passed.

"Nothing's stirring. Think I winged her?" Monroe

peered at the hillside.

Louis glimpsed Odessa through the trees, hands in the air and walking down the trail toward them. "I'll be damned."

Monroe edged his head around the trough. "Now how in the hell did he do that?"

Odessa stopped at the corral. Louis got to his feet, not bothering to brush off the dust covering his clothes. Monroe, gun still drawn, stood and watched. Henry handed over her rifle, as well as the pistol, then turned away from Louis' glare.

"What makes you think Henry killed your brother?" Louis asked.

"Police scanner," she said. "Heard it was his pistol they found. Heard he was here, too." Louis stared at Monroe, hiding the anger they both knew was there. Monroe was the one responsible for the information being public. "Start with assaulting police officers, and have the responding deputies transport her."

Louis refused Henry's recommendation that he go to the hospital. Once Monroe and the CSI tech were out of sight, he wheeled on Henry and hit him on the jaw. The unexpected blow knocked Henry off balance, causing him to stumble backward and fall to the ground. His hat spun off and landed in the dust beside him with a loud plop.

Surprise showed on Henry's face, but he stayed on the ground. Louis glowered at him for almost a full minute, contemplating whether to speak before his anger dissipated. Finally, he offered Henry a hand up.

"I guess I deserved that." Henry rubbed his jaw.

"Don't ever pull a stunt like that again." Louis said. "Now, let's take a look at these tracks."

They walked toward the rocks where he thought the killer had waited. Monroe rejoined them. Louis saw him glance at Henry's dusty jeans and face, where a slight discoloration was evident on his jaw. Ignoring Monroe's open curiosity, he focused on where Henry was examining the area.

The space enclosed by yellow police tape was littered with tracks. Henry put on his glasses and studied the ground from different angles. He pulled a notebook out of his pocket and jotted down notes after each observation.

"What are you writing down?" Monroe asked.

"Nothing, really. It just impresses the law enforcement people who are watching."

"Ha, ha," Monroe said without humor.

Louis tried to hide his smile. He watched Henry continue to work away from the rocks and up the hill to the ridge road. The trail must have been a difficult one to follow if Henry's slow progress was any measure.

"You noticed that somebody waited here, didn't you?" Henry asked.

"Looks like the killer was expecting him."

Henry nodded, his expression grim. "Is there any doubt the two murders are connected?"

"Not in my mind." Louis felt confident that attempted blackmail had gotten Beau killed. He wished he knew what knowledge or evidence he'd possessed.

"The killer stayed mostly on hard ground and rocks," Henry said. "But it's still obvious someone passed through here."

As Henry followed the trail across the dirt road, Louis stayed with him. Just south of the pines where the cattle had been after Aubrey's murder, he found more tracks. "A horse was tied over there. Came in from the south on that trail."

"The one from the lake?" Louis asked.

"Yes, from the lake," Henry said. "I can track it, but I can tell you it's the bay mare."

Monroe scoffed. "You got all that from tracks."

"I've tracked these horses before. I recognize the left front shoe."

"That and the help of a rabbit's foot." Monroe had mumbled, but he stood close to Louis.

"Monroe," Louis said quietly. "I want to see you in my office as soon as we get back. Meanwhile, I don't want to hear anything else from you unless it relates to this case."

"Yes, sir." Monroe looked away.

Henry led them to an area where the horse had been tied. Louis told Monroe to notify the crime scene team.

As Monroe scurried away, Louis turned to Henry. "We'd better take a look in the barn."

Henry pointed at the blood-soaked bandana tied to his arm. "I think a doctor better take a look at your arm."

CHAPTER 39

The emergency room nurse recognized Louis. After notifying the doctor, she rushed him into an exam room. Henry sat in the waiting area across from a woman with two small children. He regretted that decision when he saw both had snotty noses and honking coughs. The youngest kept slipping away to offer a share of his half-eaten sucker to anyone making eye contact. Finding an outdated fishing magazine, Henry buried himself in an article about fly-fishing in Florida until Louis returned.

"You know I had to get eight stitches in my arm?" Louis gingerly touched his arm.

Henry touched his own sutures. "We're practically blood brothers."

Getting to his feet, Henry walked toward the exit.

Once they were outside, Louis said, "Brothers or not, we may end up fighting over which one of us has a better motive for wanting to kill Odessa McLean."

"How about getting something to eat before we have this fight? I missed breakfast."

Louis followed Henry to the Tahoe, complaining about the investigation moving forward without him. "Monroe said all three of McLean's horses were at the barn. One was tied inside, still saddled. He said forensics is there, and everything's under control, but I feel like I should be out there. Was there anything else you needed to do with the tracks?"

"Nothing that can't wait." Henry lied, knowing Louis

wouldn't rest otherwise.

When they entered the Corner Café, several breakfast patrons gawked at them. Henry realized he and Louis looked like they'd just left a battlefield. Dust clung to their clothes, and Louis still wore the ripped, blood-stained shirt. Once they settled at the counter, the crowd's attention returned to their plates.

"Aren't you two a sight?" Della patted the countertop. "What can I get y'all to drink? Looks like you could use something stronger than what we serve here, but you'll have to make do."

Henry ordered sweet tea.

"Make it two," Louis said.

Della brought the drinks and leaned on the counter. "I heard all about what happened to you." She pointed her pen at Henry's sutured forehead, then looked at Louis. "It's you I'm wondering about. And since you're here, I'd hate to see the other guy."

"It wasn't a person." Henry tried not to smile.

Della looked surprised. "Then what – "

"It was a nail," Louis said in a quiet voice.

"A rusty one. Attached to a very big piece of wood." Henry did his part to make Louis seem heroic.

"Did this nail up and hit you on its own, or did someone help it?" Della asked.

"I fell on it."

Louis didn't elaborate, and Henry couldn't help laughing.

"I hope you're suffering from shock or low blood sugar," Louis said. "Or you might find yourself walking home."

After they'd placed their orders, Henry asked, "Any leads who might have killed Beau?"

"You mean since the number one suspect has an airtight alibi involving my daughter?"

Henry fidgeted with the silverware while Louis drank

iced tea.

"I'm glad to hear you're staying in Parsons Gap," Louis finally said. "Got a job lined up?"

"I'm considering a couple of options."

"You're not bad at police work. Tracking especially."

"I suppose I could try my hand at it," Henry said. "But I've heard some of the detectives in the local investigations division are real bastards."

"Smart ass." Louis took out his wallet and found a business card. "Here, I've got a friend looking for temporary help. It's a start and could lead to full time."

Henry read the business card Louis handed him, surprised to find it was the same person who'd interviewed him a few days ago. It made him wonder if Louis had inside information.

"You ought to give him a call."

"I've met him," Henry admitted.

"I know."

Della brought their breakfasts and whisked away to seat a group of customers entering the café. Louis looked toward the door where Wayne Hewlett was peering inside. "He must have gotten wind of a breaking story."

"My goodness, that man is a weasel." Della had reappeared to refill their glasses. "He's probably wanting to ask you about that parking lot. He was in here the other day when Vernon came in, fit to be tied. His truck was broken into while he was downtown picking up some things for the wedding. They even took the corsage."

Louis shook his head. "We've been trying to work on that problem with the city council. They're not being very receptive. Security cameras will cost them a bundle. They don't seem to understand how just trimming the hedges lower would help."

"Makes sense to me," Della replied. "Maybe I ought to run for city council."

"That's not a bad idea. Never hurts to have civic leaders who can think logically." Louis turned and looked toward the door. "I'd better pacify Hewlett before he blows a gasket."

"Good luck." Della grabbed two pitchers of tea and headed off to make her rounds.

Louis stepped outside and spoke briefly to the reporter. Henry watched Hewlett twitch his head a few times before scurrying away.

"He wanted to know more about the incident with Odessa." Louis reclaimed his seat at the counter. "I promised him a press release this afternoon."

After finishing breakfast, Louis drove to the corral where Henry had left his truck. Before he climbed out, Louis placed a hand on his shoulder. "Look, I'm sorry about what I said earlier today. About doubting your intentions."

Henry nodded.

"But not about killing you."

CHAPTER 40

"**H**ey, cowboy." Carlie stood on the porch, smiling at Henry as he climbed from his truck. He'd remembered Wednesday was her half day at work and had driven to her place in hopes she'd be home. Telephoning would have been easier, but then he'd have to imagine what that smile looked like. Seeing it in person was much better.

"You are just the person I want to see," he said.

"I am?"

Henry stepped onto the porch and slipped an arm around her waist. "I'm in a bind. I need a dinner date for Friday night at the Bar T Ranch. I asked that pretty new waitress at the Corner Café to go, but she's washing her hair. Could you fill in?"

"I don't know," Carlie said. "I was thinking about doing laundry."

Henry gave her a long kiss.

"Since you put it that way." She laughed and invited him inside.

They sat at the kitchen table, drinking iced tea and discussing Vernon's wedding. She'd already asked the USDA veterinarian to cover emergencies on Saturday afternoon. The conversation turned back to events of the previous day.

"I'm not so sure you and Dad should play together anymore," Carlie said. "You're supposed to be taking it easy, and both of you end up getting shot at. He's just as guilty, asking you to track."

"The tetanus shot was probably the worst thing that happened to him yesterday."

She laughed. "He really hates needles."

He had wanted to see her last night, but Monroe had kept him occupied until dark. After a few fruitless hours of tracking, the deputy requested he write a statement to enclose in the report. At least he'd managed to call Carlie before falling asleep on the sofa.

"The good news is you two bonded over the experience," she said.

Henry smiled and lifted his glass of tea.

"What really happened?" Carlie reached across the table and put her hand in his. "All Dad would tell me was the usual 'helping with his inquiries' or some other cop-talk."

"Short version," Henry said. "The police found my pistol at the scene and it's probably the murder weapon."

"Sounds slightly incriminating."

Henry told her very little about Odessa shooting at them. "Louis thinks someone wants me out of the investigation."

"You're too close, and it's worrying someone."

"He, or she, wouldn't be nearly as worried if they knew I haven't a clue." The theft of his pistol from his truck bothered him. Narrowing it down to when and where it occurred might help. His guess was the Watering Hole Saloon parking lot, right after the fight. He recalled seeing several likely suspects there, including Jimmy Lee and the slaughterhouse foreman, Mauro.

The front door opened, and Carlie let go of Henry's hand. She offered an apologetic look as her son dumped his backpack onto a kitchen chair. "You're home early."

"Grandma picked me up from school." Jack grabbed an apple from the bowl on the kitchen table. "Hello, Mr. Henry!"

He shuffled to the living room with his backpack, where he flopped onto the sofa.

"Since you made your father off limits, what are the chances I could take you and Jack fishing?"

"Depends on where." Carlie held up her pager. "Why don't you ask Jack yourself?"

Henry finished his glass of tea before rising from the table. Jack was in the living room, using the remote to flip through the channels.

"I was thinking about trying a little fishing at the lake this afternoon, only my usual fishing buddy isn't available. Want to fill in for Vernon?"

Jack turned off the television and jumped off the sofa. "I sure do!"

Henry whispered, "Think we might be able to talk her into going, too?"

"She hasn't been in years," Jack replied. "If you ask her, I bet she'll go. Like I said, she likes you a lot."

Half an hour later, the three of them drove to the lake in Henry's pickup. It was the same lake he and Vernon had fished, near McLean's barn. He parked in the dirt lot by the lake and climbed out of the truck. He handed two containers of worms to Jack and grabbed the fishing poles and a tackle box from the truck bed.

"How'd you know to get bait?" Jack grabbed the worms.

Henry shrugged. "I was planning to go anyway."

"With three fishing rods?" Jack asked suspiciously.

"Lucky I had extras."

Jack glanced at his mother. "I think he planned the whole thing, don't you, Mom?"

"It does seem a little fishy, I admit," Carlie said.

Jack poked Henry in the ribs. "Did you hear that?"

"Let's hope it gets even fishier," Henry replied. He and Jack walked down the bank. He handed Jack a fishing rod

247

and a container of worms. It didn't take him long to find a fishing spot to his liking. Henry had to smile, remembering how much he'd enjoyed fishing as a boy.

"He really likes you."

Henry turned around. Carlie stood on the bank above him, hands in the back pockets of her blue jeans.

"What about you?" Henry asked.

"I really like you, too."

"I meant, are you ready for a fishing pole? But I'll go with your interpretation."

She moved down to the lake's edge, accepting the offered fishing pole. Henry had already rigged the line and baited the hook.

"There are a lot of single parents around these days," Carlie said. "My co-workers talk. Most of them think having someone new in their life means the kids are going to be excluded. Children worry, too. Jack was a little concerned when you started coming around. This shows him you have no problem including him, and we both want you to know it's appreciated."

Henry had no idea how to respond because he'd never considered excluding Jack. Call it a package deal, but he'd accepted that without question. Out of the corner of his eye, he saw Jack moving into some cattails to work out a snag in his line.

"I'd better go see if he needs help." Henry trotted over with the tackle box, arriving as the line broke free. Jack had lost the float, sinker and hook.

"A fish took the float under right away, but you see what happened," Jack said.

"Must be a good hiding place for fish. Under a log or something." Henry glanced out at the lake. While he helped Jack rig the pole, he thought about the dirt road coming from Parsons Hollow Road and the old corral. The only thing he knew about the murder years ago was that the suspect was never caught because he'd disappeared. Jack cast again, dropping about twenty feet out. Henry watched the concentric ripples slowly dissipate across the surface of the lake. Medium-sized trees lined the opposite shore, and he wondered if they would have even been there twenty or thirty years ago.

"Is that the same place you got snagged the first time?" Henry asked.

"No, that was more to the left. I gave up on that spot even though I had lots of bites there."

"They'll find the bait, I'm sure." Henry walked toward Carlie, nearly tripping over his own fishing rod.

"What's got you so preoccupied?" she asked.

Henry shrugged. "Fishing, I guess."

"I can tell your mind is churning over something." One hand on her hip, she cocked her head. "You've got this funny expression that's not quite a frown and not quite a smile. I remember it from years ago, when you were trying to work out a problem. It's about these murders, isn't it? What's got you thinking?"

Henry looked at her for several seconds before he spoke. He was surprised how well she still knew him, even after years apart. Outside of the law enforcement circles, he'd never found anyone interested in discussing ideas and theories on a case. He could get used to this.

"It's Aubrey's death." Henry still wasn't comfortable saying the word murder in the same sentence as Aubrey's name. "I wonder if it's somehow connected to the previous murder in Parsons Gap."

"What do you mean?"

He told her what Hewlett had said about the murders occurring within one small area, and if that might be the connection. Henry's knowledge of the earlier death was sketchy. "From what I've understand, the co-worker was never located. I wonder if it's because he never left."

"Meaning, he's still living around here?"

Henry shook his head. "Not living."

Her expression changed to one of comprehension. "You think Aubrey figured this out?"

"It's more likely he found something that would point to the missing man," Henry said. "The guy had a vehicle that's never been located. Jack's snag over there got me thinking. This lake isn't very far away."

"Has the lake ever been searched?" Carlie asked.

"That's something your father might know."

She glanced behind him. "Looks like Jack was busy while we sat here chatting."

Henry turned. Jack was carrying a small stringer of bluegill, trying not to drag the last few along the ground. Henry quickly grabbed a plastic bucket from the back of the pickup and scooped water out of the lake. Grinning proudly, Jack dropped the stringer of fish into it.

Jack was all for a fish fry. Carlie was agreeable, as long as she didn't have to clean or cook them. Henry offered, and once they returned to the house, he and Jack began cleaning the catch. Carlie brought out a pan of saltwater for the cleaned fish and announced she was going inside to enjoy a bath.

"Why do girls like taking baths so much?" Jack asked when she was gone.

"Do they?" Henry pulled a fish out of the bucket and began to clean it. "I've never paid much attention."

Jack shrugged. "Mom does anyway."

"Well, I guess the why doesn't matter. It makes them smell nice, and that's a pretty important thing."

Henry gutted another fish, and when he passed it to Jack, the boy looked up at Henry. "You make my mom smile a lot. She's happier than I ever remember." Jack scaled the fish then dropped it into the bowl of clean water. "You aren't going away, like my dad, are you?"

Henry met Jack's gaze. "I plan on sticking around."

"Like you planned on having three fishing rods in your truck?"

Henry smiled. "Yeah, just like that."

"Awesome."

Henry handed him another fish.

"You're way cooler than my dad," Jack said.

"I'm not trying to take his place, you know."

"So what if you do?" Jack said. He added angrily, "He's a big jerk and I hope I never see him again."

"He may be a jerk," Henry said. "But he's still your father. My father is a jerk, too. For most of my life, I thought I hated him. It's taken me a long time to figure out that I really don't. I may not like that he's a jerk, but I've learned that's who he is. I can't change that he's my father and I can't stop him from being a jerk. My attitude is what I can change. Accepting that he's a jerk just helps me deal with him."

Jack slowly scaled the fish, his face serious. "I guess that makes sense."

Henry was surprised by the emotional maturity of a nine-year old. Pointing his knife at the two fish he'd just cleaned that had yet to be scaled, he said, "You're falling behind. I suppose you're expecting me to take up your slack."

Jack laughed as Henry helped remove scales. Once that was done, they took the fish into to the kitchen. Carlie emerged from the bath and came into the room, leaning between them to look at their catch.

"You're right," Jack said to Henry. "Baths do make girls smell nice."

Carlie eyed both of them, openly curious.

"Jack caught a lot of fish." Henry washed his forearms and hands in the kitchen sink.

"I see that." She looked at Jack. "And now someone

smells like fish. How about you take a shower before supper?"

Jack wasn't enthusiastic, but he was hungry. He hurried to his room to grab clean clothes before darting into the bathroom.

"I hope he takes time to actually wash." Carlie was still in her bathrobe, her damp hair hanging limply in her face.

Henry moved a strand of hair away from her lips and kissed her. "You're not wearing anything under that robe, are you?"

Carlie smiled at him mischievously. "I guess I'd better get dressed before you lose control."

Henry playfully slipped a hand inside her robe. She made a familiar little noise that prompted him to grin. "I don't think I'm the only one in danger of losing control."

While Carlie dressed, Henry made dinner. They sat at the table, eating and laughing. He was conscious of how comfortable he felt here. A few weeks ago, the idea of him embracing domestic life would have been ridiculous.

After he and Carlie finished the dishes, Henry said, "I'd better be going. I want to stop in and see your father."

"We'll go with you," she said. "Jack sleeps over there when I'm on call."

"Whoa, aren't you staying over?" Jack asked. "It's all right if you do. I know you won't act like some jerk who just wants to get my mom in bed."

"Jack!" Carlie stood in the doorway, her face red with embarrassment. "Where do you get such ideas?"

"School," Jack replied. "You're not the only single parent, you know."

CHAPTER 41

"**W**hat do you know about the rock hunters?" Henry asked as he entered the den.

Maps, books, and scribbled notes were scattered across the coffee table. Louis looked up from the yellow legal pad on his knee. "The what?"

"It looks downright scholarly in here," Henry said.

"You've been hanging around this place too long, you're picking up a

Southern drawl." Louis pushed the notepad aside and pointed at the map. "I've been trying to make sense of that quote from the journal, 'But, look, the moon, in rust mantle clad, walks o'er the dew of yon high eastern hill.' I'm not having much luck."

"What are you looking for?" Henry sat on the sofa and glanced at the map.

"Moon Creek. I thought there was one around here, but I can't locate it. Maybe I need an older map. Patricia may know. She grew up here, and I remember her grandfather telling all sorts of stories about the history of the area. This is going way back, when Patricia and I were first married."

"Since we're on the subject of history, I'm really curious about that rock hunter's murder."

"Ah." Louis leaned over and slipped a folder from under the map. He opened it and handed Henry a copy of a newspaper clipping. Henry fished his glasses out of his pocket and read the article.

Muddy Waters

August 7, 1970. Woman Found Dead – Police Investigate Possibility of Foul Play

Tragedy befell an archeology student working at a site near Parsons Gap. Sheriff J.E. Wallace told reporters this morning that a woman's body had been found at the site, located northeast of Moon Creek. The woman was identified as Barnetta Marie Bridges, 23, of Chapel Hill, a promising student of archeology at Duke University. Miss Bridges was assisting Dr. Calvin Saunders, also of Duke University, with research on early indigenous peoples of the area. She apparently died from a blow to the head. Sheriff Wallace says the police are investigating the suspicious death. Her colleague, Dr. Calvin Saunders, could not be located for questioning. It is believed Dr. Saunders, 28 of Raleigh, has fled the area. Police are asking anyone with information to call the sheriff's office.

"I see why you're looking for Moon Creek." Henry removed his glasses. "Calvin Saunders was never found?"

"Not even a whisper." Louis shook his head. "I read the original report on microfiche. I've got someone printing it for me tomorrow. Also found some information on the autopsy results, aside from the report. It indicated the woman had been struck on the left cheek. She apparently fell, hitting the right side of her head on a rock. That's what killed her. Turns out she was pregnant, less than six weeks."

"Saunders?"

"It was generally suspected. They'd been working the dig off and on for three months. Witnesses heard them arguing in town the day before about a diamond ring. Sounded like a lover's spat."

"A rock!"

"What was that?"

"A diamond was often called a rock." Henry glanced at the map. "It doesn't make sense that someone is only trying

254

to keep some silly treasure hunt a secret. What other reasons are there for not wanting anyone poking around?"

"Finding something they shouldn't," Louis replied. "Where are you going with this?"

Henry stretched his legs. "What if Calvin Saunders never left the area?"

"I'm not sure I follow."

"What if Saunders *couldn't* leave the area," Henry looked at Louis.

"Because he was dead." Louis whispered the words. He leaned back in his chair, fingers steepled. After a few moments, he tapped the map. "You think he's buried up by the corral somewhere?"

"It would explain the need to keep the digging at the corral secret. And, it would explain why a person digging there may have stumbled across something."

"It makes sense," Louis said. "But I don't like the implications. We're talking three deaths, one past and two present. All connected."

"Four if you count the lady rock hunter."

"Archeologist," Louis said. "They were archeologists."

"Okay, four if you count her."

Louis rubbed his jaw. "Aubrey had been riding up there on a regular basis. He probably knew who was digging. He figures out why and decides to try it himself. Old man McLean used to have a lot of old maps. Aubrey finds a promising place to dig for this treasure, and he gives it a try. Only he finds something else entirely. So how do the cattle fit in?"

Henry arranged his thoughts before continuing. "Why not say Jimmy Lee is the treasure hunter, though I think several people were searching without telling others. There's the matter of the cattle Jimmy Lee said he didn't move there. Let's say he's telling the truth. Jimmy Lee digs the holes, the killer comes along later and uses the cattle to hide the evidence. By camouflaging the digging, there's a better chance of keeping it secret."

"Everyone at the ranch knew about this treasure hunt." Louis steepled his fingers and touched his chin. "Hits a little close to home, doesn't it?"

Henry stared at his boots. "Yeah, it does."

"Through Jimmy Lee, or the cattle they intended to steal, the McLeans learned of the digging. They could figure out what Jimmy Lee was doing." Louis smacked his hand against his leg. "So Beau tried his hand at digging where Aubrey did. That could explain his death."

"Except Beau was found with a pistol, not a shovel." Henry said. "There were no fresh holes or signs of recent digging. I think your first thought was right. Beau was trying to blackmail someone."

"That doesn't paint a pretty picture."

"It doesn't. When you look at who knew about the treasure and who would've been around in 1970, it really narrows the field." Henry immediately regretted voicing those thoughts.

Louis rubbed his cheek and nodded. He spoke quietly. "I've got a metal detector. You want to have a look around that old corral?"

"Are you two about done with your cloak-and-dagger discussion?" Patricia asked from the doorway. "I was thinking of a slice of peach pie with ice cream."

Henry followed them into the kitchen. They sat at the counter, where Louis asked about Moon Creek.

"The name of that creek was changed years ago." Patricia placed pie and a scoop of ice cream onto three plates. "In the seventies, if I recall. You know how a few well-intended citizens get a wild hair and decide to rename something for a locally famous person. I remember there being a small general store near the creek. We used to go there when I was a child." She placed the platter on the counter. "I believe it was called Moon General Store something or other because the Moon family ran it. They'd lived in the area for generations. I think the original Moon was a blacksmith or something.

"Where would the archeological site have been?" Henry asked.

"That I'm not sure about."

"It might have had something to do with Native Americans," Louis explained.

"Oh, that would probably have been across the creek, on the west side of the railroad. There used to be talk of an old village or burial mound there."

"What railroad?"

"It's long gone. The old grade is now Parsons Hollow Road."

"Well, now, that makes sense." Louis looked at Henry. "You certainly wouldn't want to bury a body in an active archeological site."

CHAPTER 42

Louis was awakened by the telephone at half past five the next morning. He sat upright and glanced around the dark room. Had he been dreaming? The telephone rang again and he realized he hadn't. "Hannahan."

He glanced at Patricia. She had somehow slept through the noise.

"It's Henry." The voice on the other end sounded tired, distant. "Sorry it's early, but you did say to call if I found anything."

Louis had to think for a moment before remembering Henry had gone to the corral with a metal detector.

"It's all right." Louis was wide awake now. "What've you got?"

"I found one of those little picks archeologists use."

"Yes?"

"It was on top of some human remains, and it's a perfect match to the hole in the skull." Henry paused. Louis thought he heard him yawn. "We were right, there was something out here a metal-detector could pick up. I called Monroe, as instructed. The remains have been removed and we're all finished out there. A positive ID hasn't been made, but Calvin Saunders' wallet was in what was left of the trousers. I'm with Monroe, doing the paperwork now."

"I'll be in the office in twenty minutes. Can you wait around?"

"If I'm asleep, just nudge my chair."

Louis got out of bed and quickly dressed. At the

bedroom door, he looked back at Patricia. She was still sleeping, so he blew her a kiss before leaving the room. He usually enjoyed the fifteen-minute drive to his office. It gave him time to think and sort out things he needed to do during the day ahead. This morning, the time served to fuel his increasing anxiety.

It wasn't helped by the presence of Ms. Breen and her son waiting for him outside his office.

"What can I do for you two this morning?" Louis wished he'd taken time to get coffee from downstairs. He had a feeling it was going to be a long day.

"It's Stan that's got something to say," Ms. Breen replied.

Unlocking the door, Louis offered Ms. Breen the desk chair. He waved Stan toward an uncomfortable one against the wall. Perched on the edge of his desk, Louis clasped his hands together and waited. Ms. Breen folded her plump hands in her lap, fixing her son with a look that left little unsaid.

Stan squirmed in his chair. His face looked ashen, and his lips trembled. "It's about my collection of watches."

CHAPTER 43

Henry squeezed Carlie's hand as they were welcomed into the Bar T Ranch house by Sally Ann. Much of the stress about seeing his father was gone, and it had to do with Carlie. Somehow, she kept him grounded. They followed his step-mother into the expansive living room where Rory and Jimmy Lee sat in leather chairs. Two glasses of beer were on the table between them. Both men rose from their seats when Carlie came into the room.

Jimmy Lee offered to get drinks and disappeared into the kitchen. Henry watched Carlie take in the room and comment on how much the renovation had changed the place. She told Sally Ann how much she loved the open, airy feeling. "And I've always admired that fireplace."

"So have I," Sally Ann said. "When we began planning the renovations, we agreed it had to stay as is. The guests love it, too."

"Do you have lots of guests?"

"We're nearly full," Sally Ann said. "It's high season, with school being out. We're booked through October."

"Providing these murders don't discourage them," Jimmy Lee said. He returned from the kitchen with two glasses of iced tea.

The awkward silence was broken by Sally Ann. "Supper is almost ready. Why don't you bring your drinks into the dining room?"

"Isn't Vernon going to be here?" Henry glanced around the room.

"Off with Della somewhere," Rory said. "Her people are having a get-together. Getting ready for the big day."

"I can almost hear the clank of a ball and chain." Jimmy Lee laughed at his own joke as he walked toward the dining room.

Rory caught Henry's arm before he left the room. "Can I talk with you a moment?"

Henry reluctantly followed him into the office. Rory sat on the edge of the desk before speaking, a mannerism Henry surprisingly recognized as one of his own.

"I understand you're planning on staying in Parsons Gap," Rory said.

Henry nodded. "Yes, sir."

"Would you consider working at the Bar T? Sally Ann and I have been talking about this for a while. We're getting busier each season. We need someone to help coordinate outdoor activities."

Henry tried not to stumble over his words. "I have no idea what that would involve."

"That's all right," Rory replied. "We're working on it as we go. Basically, we need someone to plan and lead outdoor activities, like fly fishing."

He thought about how to respond to the offer. Working for his father wasn't something he was ready to do. Then there was Jimmy Lee. "I don't think me working here is such a good idea."

"Before you decide, know that Jimmy Lee suggested it," Rory explained. "And you'd be working for Vernon."

"I really appreciate the offer," Henry said. "I'd like to talk it over with Carlie before making a decision."

"I understand." Rory actually smiled at him. "There's something else."

Henry steeled himself and waited for the bomb to drop about his father's cancer.

"I may not know how to show it, and may have never

said it, but I do love you, Henry. I've always been proud of you."

Henry was shocked and could only stare at his father. He felt he should make some comment, but his mind was spinning and unable to focus on forming a sentence. To make things worse, Rory was watching him expectantly. Did he expect his little revelation was going to erase the past like some sort of magic wand? Henry bit back a caustic remark as he turned to leave the office, putting an end to the conversation. Just like his father.

He stopped in the doorway, determined not to be just like his father. "That's a lot to digest."

"Then let it settle."

Following Rory into the dining room, he was grateful his chair was next to Carlie. He fought the urge to pinch himself, to make sure this wasn't a dream. Instead, he reached under the table and held Carlie's hand. The way his heart beat faster when they touched was more real than anything a pinch could accomplish.

Dinner with his family was more pleasant than he'd imagined. After dessert they migrated back to the huge room, laughing and continuing various threads of their supper table conversations. Rory had been relating a story of some hunting trip to Carlie and was now showing her a photograph on the mantle. Henry settled on the sofa, across from Jimmy Lee, as Carlie enjoyed the story. He grudgingly acknowledged that Rory was very good at spinning tales. Whatever his father had said made her laugh. Henry smiled, liking the way her head tilted back when she laughed.

Jimmy Lee snorted. "Damn, you'll be the next one hooking up to a ball and chain."

Henry could think of worse things. "Thanks for suggesting me as coordinator."

"Don't get warm fuzzies over it," Jimmy Lee said. "It

ain't because I like you. I did it because keeping it family is what's good for the ranch."

Jimmy Lee rose and walked to the kitchen for another beer, leaving Henry alone on the sofa. Rory was returning the photograph he had been holding to its place on the mantle. Carlie glanced up, and something about the fireplace caught her attention.

"Is this the original fireplace?" she asked.

Rory nodded.

She pointed at the plaque high above the mantle. Henry got to his feet and joined them at the fireplace. Jimmy Lee wandered over too, beer bottle in hand.

"You said it's never been altered or moved, right?" Carlie asked.

"It's the original. The bigger part of the house was added on the original cabin."

Carlie glanced at Henry. "What was that Shakespeare quote you and Dad have been talking about, with the moon?"

It was Rory who recited the quote. "But, look, the moon, in rust mantle clad, walks o'er the dew of yon high eastern hill."

"Mantel." Carlie pointed at the plaque above the fireplace. "A.H. Moon & Sons."

Rory and Jimmy Lee exchanged glances. Jimmy Lee left in search of a ladder and a screwdriver. Returning, he climbed up and began prying the plaque away from the stone. It came off easily enough. Sally Ann handed him a flashlight. He peered inside the hole, then reached in and retrieved an oilskin bundle. He handed it down to Rory, who waited until everyone had gathered around the coffee table before unrolling it. They stared silently at the crude map drawn on the leather.

Jimmy Lee cocked his head. "I recognize some of these landmarks. This is Ripshin Lake, that's the Elk River, and that mark right there." He stabbed at the map with his finger.

Rory finished for him. "Is now at the bottom of Watauga Lake."

"Yeah," Jimmy Lee said. "Ain't that a bitch?"

CHAPTER 44

Sally Ann placed a basket of hot biscuits and a jar of homemade strawberry jam on the breakfast table. "Have you considered the job offer?"

"Yes and no." Henry reached for a biscuit. He glanced at the newspaper by his father's chair. "I've thought about it, then thought about it some more. The decision isn't an easy one. You would know why more than anyone."

"You could always work summers for the National Park Service and the ranch in fall and winter," Sally Ann said.

"That's a thought." It was the same thing Carlie had suggested. He put a thick layer of jam between halves of the biscuit. The front-page headline caught his attention and he pulled the newspaper closer. According to the story, the sheriff's department was actively conducting a search for Cal Saunders' remains in the old corral. He wondered if Louis had intended for this version of the story to flush a killer. Louis had called him earlier this morning to tell him the dental records confirmed the body was Calvin Saunders.

"It's so odd that the article about Nettie would appear on Vernon's wedding day."

Henry looked up from the newspaper. "Nettie?"

Sally Ann pointed at the newspaper. "Well, Barnetta was her name. Barnetta Bridges."

"Did you know her?"

"I'd only met her a few times, but she was the sweetest girl. What a tragedy, Vernon finding her dead like that. You see, Vernon was going to marry her. That's why it's so odd."

Henry's mind was numb. "What do you mean, he found her?"

"She and Vernon had been serious for quite a while, as I recall. He had just given her a ring, a nice little diamond. Asked her to marry him. She'd said yes, of course. He went to see her on a Friday, after the work on the dig was done. He came back later in such a state, saying she was dead. Rory got him calmed down then called the sheriff."

"Wasn't there another archeologist?" Henry asked.

"Vernon said he saw him driving away when he pulled into the camp."

"But he couldn't have—" Henry jumped to his feet, his muscles tensed. My God, he thought, not Vernon. This must be a mistake. Someone else must have been there. Anyone but Vernon.

A door slammed somewhere in the house.

"Where is Vernon now?" Henry hoped his voice wasn't trembling as much as he felt it was.

Sally Ann gave him a strange look. "He was just here. Maybe he's gone outside."

Henry ran toward the door and looked out, ignoring Sally Ann's barrage of questions. Vernon's truck was parked by the barn, but Vernon was nowhere in sight. The hair stood on the back of his neck, and Henry was hesitant to step outside.

"What's going on?" Sally Ann asked him again.

Henry stared out the door, weighing options. He could give Vernon a chance to get away. Even as he contemplated it, he knew it wouldn't happen. As a range detective, he'd never consider it. He knew precisely what he'd have done if Vernon had stolen cattle in his territory.

"Call the police." Henry made eye contact with Sally Ann. "Ask for Louis Hannahan and tell him what you just told me. Stay inside the house and away from the windows."

"Henry, will you please tell me what's going on?"

"Just do what I asked you." He spoke with a little more force than intended, but Sally Ann jumped toward the kitchen without another word.

He wanted a weapon, but his pistol was still in police custody. Remembering the gun collection, he ran into the living room. The old .30-.30 lever action rifle was there, the one he learned to shoot with as a boy. He used a dining room chair to reach up and took it off the wall. Then he went to the kitchen, looking for Sally Ann. She was just hanging up the phone.

"They patched me straight through to Louis," she said. "He's on his way. He said to tell you to sit tight, and to say he means it. Henry, what—"

"Where can I find ammunition for this rifle?"

"In the safe, I think."

Henry followed her to the office and impatiently watched her open the safe. She handed him a box of cartridges as he heard the main door open and close. Footsteps approached the office. Henry signaled Sally Ann to stay quiet by placing his forefinger over his lips. There wasn't time to load the rifle. Pushing Sally Ann gently behind him, Henry leveled the rifle at the doorway and waited.

Henry nearly scared Rory out of his wits.

"What the hell's gotten into you?"

Taking a deep breath, Henry tried to ignore the familiar tone. "Did you see Vernon out there anywhere?"

"No, I didn't." Rory's voice was edged with anger. "What are you doing with that rifle?"

Henry checked the rifle to make sure it was safe to use. He heard the sound of a vehicle coming up the driveway. He went to the door in time to see Louis' unmarked Tahoe pull in beside Rory's truck. A second unmarked car was parked there, too. Henry loaded the rifle while watching the barn and corrals for Vernon.

"I'm talking to you, Henry."

Henry didn't turn around to face him. Eyes still on the barn and corrals, he took a deep breath and tried to stay calm.

"You hear me?"

Henry gripped the rifle so tightly that his knuckles turned white. Finally, he wheeled on his father. "Don't push it."

Rory stood there, pulling at his mustache. Henry knew it as an indicator of a high level of irritation. Not wanting to set off a powder keg, he took a deep breath before speaking.

"I'll explain later." He spoke with an edge to his voice that seemed to surprise his father. He'd even stopped tugging his mustache. In a slightly softer tone, Henry said, "For now, you'll just have to trust me."

CHAPTER 45

Louis climbed out of the Tahoe, glancing toward the house before walking cautiously to the barn. He'd seen Henry just inside the door and hoped he'd stay there, out of the way. Monroe waited near the large barn door, holding a radio close to his ear. Louis joined him and overheard the garbled radio transmission. "...On horseback ... toward the ridge ... lost under the trees."

"Can you repeat?" Monroe barked into the radio.

The second attempt was even more broken. Monroe tried to raise a response a few more times before shrugging his shoulders. Monroe walked to the outside corner of the barn, checking for better reception. He stared absently down the hallway of the barn, wondering how he was going to tell Rory and Sally Ann about this. Hearing the faint scrape of a boot in the dirt behind him, he whipped around with his pistol drawn.

Henry was standing on the opposite side of the barn door. Louis exhaled and lowered the pistol. Then he saw the rifle Henry carried casually in the crook of his right arm.

"What are you doing with that?" Louis asked.

"I should be asking you that same question." Henry eyed the pistol.

"The simple answer is that Wayne Hewlett broke the story too early. It's certainly complicated things."

Henry said nothing.

"I thought we'd be able to do this without a problem," Louis said. "Now he's figured out we've made the connection. He was here in the barn when he saw Monroe coming up the drive. Now he's grabbed a horse, but he's been spotted and I imagine we'll be closing in soon. I only hope he gives up without a fight."

Henry still didn't speak.

"I only confirmed it this morning. Stan Breen was arrested. Seems his watch collection was a bunch of stolen ones, all taken from cars in the city parking lot. He told me about breaking into Vernon's truck. There was a watch in it with an inscription on the back. Turned out it belonged to Cal Saunders. He saw your pistol but didn't touch it. Stan gave the watch to Beau, hoping he would take it to the police and say he found it. When word got out that Beau was dead, Stan came forward."

Henry ran his fingers through his hair, frowning.

"We also found a large wrench, recently buried." Louis' voice echoed in the empty barn. "We think that was used to kill Aubrey."

He watched Henry, trying to get a read on his emotional state. He seemed calm as he walked toward the tack room and placed his rifle against the wall. Plucking a coil of rope off a peg, Henry leaned against the wall. He shook out a loop and played at catching the knob on the tack room door. "Where's the rest of the cavalry?"

"Setting up checkpoints."

For several minutes, neither spoke. The mobile phone on Louis' hip rang. He flipped it open and answered.

"We've lost him."

"Say that again." Louis listened to the explanation, closed the phone and swore. He looked at Henry. "They've lost him. Slipped through by going into a thick canopy of trees. The helicopter crew lost him."

"Do you need a tracker?"

"I won't ask," Louis said. "Not under these circumstances."

"You don't have to ask." Henry's voice sounded strangely quiet. "I'm offering."

Louis weighed the options. He didn't want Vernon to get

away. He was well aware that Vernon knew the area well and was an experienced outdoorsman. If he continued to evade the helicopter, he could easily lose himself in the national forest. From there he could wait it out and choose when to make his escape. Setting Henry on his trail would actually be his best bet.

"I'll accept your offer."

Henry got to his feet, suddenly business-like. "You ride?"

Louis nodded.

"This could take a while. We'll need water and maybe some food." Henry picked two horses from the corral behind the barn. Louis knew enough about horses to be drawn to one of them, a long-legged sorrel mare with a conformation for endurance. Henry kept the other, a spirited paint gelding. He asked Louis to go inside for food and water as he tied the horses near the tack room. Louis hesitated, afraid Henry might go after Vernon on his own. He decided to trust him and went to the main house.

The horses were saddled and ready when Louis returned. Henry quickly stuffed their provisions into saddlebags. He then coiled the rope and hung it over the saddle horn. From a peg on the inside of the tack room, Henry grabbed a dusty scabbard for the rifle. Louis touched his arm as he attached it to the saddle.

"I think it's best you keep that rifle in the scabbard." Louis wasn't sure how Henry would handle confronting the man who'd murdered his best friend, even if it was his uncle. "Don't use it unless I tell you to use it."

Henry nodded, and without a word he mounted the paint. Louis patted the sorrel before he climbed into the saddle, enjoying the familiar smell of horse sweat and leather. He pointed toward the trailhead on the south side of the barn. "He went that way," Louis said, absurdly feeling like a sidekick in a low-budget western.

CHAPTER 46

Louis kept up with Henry's brisk pace until they reached Parsons Hollow Road. As they neared the bridge, the trail narrowed and they slowed to a walk. At a fork, Henry returned to an easy gallop and didn't drop the tempo until they reached the church ruins. This was where Vernon had reportedly ducked into the woods. Henry leaned from the saddle to look at the ground.

Louis watched him work, wondering if Vernon had any idea Henry was the one following his trail. He also wondered how desperate Vernon had become. Louis had to assume he was armed. Three people were dead already, would more deaths matter? The possibility of an ambush wasn't far from his thoughts. If the stories he'd heard about Henry were true, he couldn't have chosen a better man for the task. This was Henry's kind of game, and he hoped Vernon wouldn't be able to outfox him.

They left the wide trail and entered national forest lands. They kept the horses to a walk for nearly an hour. Henry halted the paint and dismounted. After a quick look at the ground, he squinted up at Louis, shading his eyes with his hand.

"I figure he'll ride fast for a short distance, then maybe throw in a change of direction or two before he starts hiding his trail."

Louis nodded but said nothing.

"How do you want to work this?" Henry glanced around. "Want me to run him into the ground or take it with caution? Might even be able to surprise him, but I wouldn't count on it."

"Is there any particular advantage to either approach?"

"Not really." Henry got a bottle of water from the saddlebag. "There are certainly disadvantages. He may panic if he's pushed, on the other hand he may try an ambush if he's got time to plan."

Louis dismounted and stretched his legs. He chewed his lower lip as he eyed Henry. "I'm leaving it up to you. You're the one with experience doing this sort of thing."

Henry mounted and rode ahead. Louis followed, amazed how Henry managed to keep an eye on the trail while avoiding low branches that threatened to knock him from the saddle. The thick canopy of trees abruptly opened into a large meadow with a creek flowing down the center. They dismounted by the creek and allowed the horses a little water. Henry rummaged in the saddlebag and offered Louis a Snickers bar.

Louis had just torn the wrapper off when Henry's horse raised his head sharply and whinnied. Vernon came out of the trees a few hundred yards away. Seeing them, he quickly urged his horse into a gallop and started across the meadow.

Henry jumped into the saddle, holding back the anxious paint while Louis tried to mount. The sorrel was nervously circling Louis as he tried to get a foot in the stirrup. Holding the left rein tighter, Louis managed to shove his toe into the stirrup and swing his leg over the saddle. Henry bolted ahead, leaving Louis in the dust, until he gave the horse its head and caught up.

They raced across the meadow side by side, leaning over the necks of their horses as the wind tore at their shirts. Louis found it exhilarating. The fast pace and the excitement of the chase made him feel he'd been born a hundred years too late. But he didn't have time to really contemplate that. Henry was shouting at him.

"Lay low against the horse to make a smaller target, in case he shoots."

Louis leaned forward, watching Vernon circle towards them slightly before dashing into the timber less than a hundred yards ahead of them. Crossing the last fifty yards at a slower gallop, they entered the trees cautiously. The band of trees thinned almost immediately and they halted at the edge of a steep, rocky slope. A solid slab of smooth rock was under their hooves. Henry leaned over in the saddle, searching the ground. He jumped off the paint for a closer look.

When Henry looked up, Louis knew from his expression he'd lost the trail.

CHAPTER 47

Henry had been fighting his emotions, knowing he needed to remain calm if he wanted to find Vernon's tracks. He glanced back at Louis, tugged his hat brim and tried not to scowl. He leapt to the ground, handed the reins to Louis, and began moving in ever-widening circles. Three blades of freshly bent grass caught his attention. He knelt and pressed his fingers into the soil, feeling the depression left by the hoof. Vernon had covered the hooves with a thick cloth to mask the trail across the rock. It also muffled the sound of horseshoes on stone.

When had Vernon found the time? Henry looked around cautiously and wished Louis had allowed him to wear the pistol. He felt uneasy. Had Vernon been watching them, waiting until they were close before he showed himself? That would mean Vernon wanted them to follow. Henry studied the trail, his thoughts whirling with possibilities.

Vernon had headed for the large rocky area ahead. Masking the trail hadn't mattered in the meadow, where broken twigs and leaves and bent grass revealed his passing. Following it across stone would slow things down a little. Henry looked at the expanse of rock. It appeared to extend quite some distance, and a recent downpour had removed most of the debris normally present. That left little to show the passing of a horse.

The steep hill beyond was scattered with small boulders, dead trees and limbs, and in some places, gravel-sized stones. From here, the drop off looked impassable. Henry walked half the length of the slab, kneeling here and there to study possible tracks. He got to his feet and looked at Louis.

"It looks like he's buying time." Henry glanced around warily, fidgeting with a twig he'd picked up. "Could be he's just trying to put some distance between him and us, but I got a feeling that's not the case."

Louis began eyeing the rocks and trees suspiciously.

Henry examined the ground for signs of Vernon's exit point. He paused briefly at a couple of areas with promising trail signs that turned out to be deer trails. At the end of the stone, he found nothing and began to walk back to his starting place. He turned and looked down the slope, realizing it was a natural stairway of stone. He stared at it for a full minute before moving deliberately down the rocky steps, searching. About a third of the way down, he found several dislodged pebbles and a trace of crushed grass.

He pointed at the base of the hill. "He went down here."

"That's pretty steep," Louis said.

Along the bottom of the slope, rocks and tree branches had accumulated in patches. Henry spotted a stretch of bare ground among the debris. From where he stood, he thought he could make out three hoof-sized depressions.

"Think we can make it?" Louis asked.

"Vernon made it," Henry said quietly. "But that's not what I'm worried about."

Louis glanced at the slope then back at Henry. His face was expressionless, but there was something about his eyes that made him glad Henry wasn't on his trail.

"What bothers you then?" Louis asked.

"That slope is exposed, and he's had some time."

Henry didn't voice the question. Would Vernon shoot one, or both of them? His eyes searched the hillside for likely hiding places. There were simply too many. He took the paint's reins from Louis. "I suppose he's less likely to shoot me. How about you set up behind those rocks and cover me with my rifle."

Louis grabbed the weapon and led the sorrel into the meadow where he tied it to a sapling, well out of sight. He returned to the hillside where Henry waited.

"Wish me luck." Henry climbed into the saddle. Lifting the reins, he slowly rode to the edge. He stopped the paint and scanned the timber edging the bowl-like area. With a deep breath, he urged the horse over the edge.

The horse was sure-footed and Henry gave him his head. About halfway down, he realized it wasn't as bad as it looked from the top. He let out the breath he'd been holding. Suddenly the horse jerked beneath him. He heard the report of a rifle as the paint lurched forward onto its knees.

Kicking his feet free of the stirrups, Henry hit the ground on his heels. He skidded a few feet before falling on his backside a short distance away. The paint tried to get up, but Henry scrambled toward him and got on the uphill side. He grabbed the reins to control the paint's head. He tried to locate Vernon's hiding place as he reached for the saddlebag.

"Leave it be, Henry." Vernon's voice came from behind.

Henry held onto the reins but kept his hands in sight. He hoped Louis was paying attention.

"Where is he?" Vernon asked

"Up there somewhere." Henry glanced over his shoulder. "Looking for another way down. He was afraid to ride down the slope."

Vernon glanced toward the meadow.

"The best thing you can do is give yourself up."

"Best thing for Louis, maybe. Not so good for me. I aim to get myself lost. Get on your feet and back away from that horse."

"He'll try to get up if I do."

"I only nicked him," Vernon said. "He'll be all right."

Henry let go of the reins and watched the paint struggle to his feet. The horse shook his body vigorously before moving a short distance away to put his nose into a clump of grass. He saw a trickle of blood high on his haunch, which twitched continuously as he grazed. Getting slowly to his feet, Henry turned to face Vernon, hands held at shoulder level.

Crouched between a couple of big rocks and a shrub, Vernon was practically invisible. "Stay where you are."

Henry felt his anger rising. Not only had Vernon shot a good horse, he was responsible for the deaths of at least two other people. One of them someone Vernon had watched grow up. Now his uncle was aiming a rifle at his chest. Henry felt betrayed. He could understand Vernon wanting to save his own skin, but at what cost?

"Louis!" Vernon shouted. "I've got Henry. Drop your gun and come out so I can see you."

There was no reply.

"He may have gone back for the others," Henry lied.

"And leave you to the wolves?" Vernon added, "Or perhaps it's the other way around."

"Vernon–"

"Don't say anything, Henry. This is difficult enough."

Henry noticed an animal-like wildness in his uncle's eyes, similar to one he'd seen in the eyes of a mountain lion cornered by hounds. For the first time in his life, Henry felt fear. The fear worsened when he thought of Carlie. Mentally wrestling his emotions, he fought to think clearly. He glanced around, assessing his situation. Louis had his rifle. Other than a couple good-sized limbs and a few rocks, he saw nothing useful. Then he saw the rope on the ground a few feet away. It must have slipped from the saddle when the paint fell.

"Show yourself, Louis!"

"You'd think a man from Utah wouldn't get nervous about rocky hillsides," Henry said, wondering what was keeping Louis. "No telling how far he rode to find a way down here."

"Louis, I'm waiting!"

Louis' reply was a bullet that hit the rock near Vernon's shoulder, sending a shower of splinters into his face. Vernon pulled the trigger in surprise, the bullet careened off a rock up slope. Henry dove for the rope. Once his fingers encircled it, he rolled behind the boulder that sheltered Vernon.

Henry pressed himself against the rock, knowing Vernon wouldn't be able to see him without exposing himself to Louis. With Louis above, Vernon's only possible escape route was downhill to the shelter of a stand of pines. Henry carefully shook out a loop in the rope. The shrub rustled as Vernon tried to peer around the rock and locate him. He waited.

"Give yourself up, Vernon," Louis shouted. "It's over."

Vernon fired once, and dashed out from between the rocks. He passed Henry as the rope sailed out, the loop settling over his shoulders. Setting his feet, Henry jerked the rope. Vernon fell backwards, landing hard on his back. The rifle flew from his hands.

Keeping the rope tight, Henry picked up the lever-action rifle in one hand, swinging it John Wayne-style to chamber a round. The barrel came down, aimed squarely at Vernon's chest. His finger was on the trigger, and he dropped the rope to steady the muzzle.

"You son of a bitch," Henry said in a quiet voice. "You're not even sorry, are you?"

Behind him, he heard Louis making his way down the slope.

"That first morning we went fishing, you weren't

nervous about the wedding." Henry fought to control his anger.

Vernon must have sensed the anger, too. He started to speak but stopped.

"Henry," Louis said softly.

Henry didn't look up, didn't take his eyes off Vernon. After what seemed an eternity, he moved the muzzle of the rifle away from Vernon. Louis stepped in, searched him then slipped on handcuffs. He read Vernon his rights, helped him to his feet then followed him up the slope to the meadow. Henry made sure they both reached the top of the hill before he headed down the slope to look for Vernon's horse.

He found it tied behind a growth of scrubby oaks. Checking the cinch, he climbed into the saddle. He gathered the reins of the limping paint and led it up the slope where he met Louis under the pines. Removing the buckskin's bridle, Henry placed the rope around the neck of Vernon's horse. He tied the other end to Louis' saddle horn. Together they helped Vernon into the saddle.

"Sorry it took me so long. I didn't have a clear shot," Louis said. "If I moved he'd have heard me. I picked up on *The Man from Utah* movie reference right away, and knew you only needed a distraction."

"It worked, that's what matters." Henry examined the paint's wound. It didn't look serious, but he was reluctant to ride him. The horse was willing enough to follow the other horses, so he loosened the cinch and looped the reins over the saddle horn. Then he climbed on the sorrel, behind Louis.

"For a minute there, I thought you were going to pull the trigger," Louis said.

"So did I."

CHAPTER 48

Rory stared into the fireplace, looking much older than his sixty-two years. Vernon's arrest had deflated him. Henry was still feeling prickly from their earlier confrontation, but felt he should reach out in some way. Something. Anything. He just couldn't think of a gesture that would suffice. What reassurances could he give a man he felt he barely knew? Feeling awkward and inadequate, he stood by the office door with his hands in his pockets.

His hesitation was rewarded by interruption. Louis entered the room from the kitchen. His eyes met Henry's briefly before he crossed the room to the fireplace. Placing a hand on Rory's shoulder, he said softly, "I'm sorry."

"That stupid bastard." Rory held an old black and white photograph of himself and Vernon as boys, standing with their father and grandfather in front of a log house. Well over fifty years old, it was the last photograph taken of his grandfather. Rory replaced the photo and turned to Louis. "What did he tell you about Nettie?"

"That he was in love with her, that they'd been seeing each other for a number of months. He claims he didn't know, but apparently she was already engaged to Saunders. Nettie had told him Saunders didn't approve of any sort of distraction on a dig, so she and Vernon saw each other secretly. Usually on Fridays, because Saunders went to town every Friday to run errands.

"According to Vernon, Saunders came back early, caught him and Nettie together and started ranting about how she was going to be his wife. Saunders was blind with anger. He and Nettie had words, and eventually Saunders slapped her. She fell, hit her head and didn't move. Saunders blamed Vernon for the argument and came after him with a shovel. The only thing Vernon found to defend himself was a pick."

"Why didn't he just turn himself in?" Rory asked. "Sounds like self-defense."

Louis shrugged. "Vernon said Nettie was pregnant, and she'd told Vernon it was his. A few weeks earlier he'd been drinking and had words with Saunders, which ended up with Vernon threatening to kill him. He was scared, so he buried Saunders across the road from the archeology site. Hid the car in the lake, like you thought." He glanced at Henry. "When he told the police he'd seen a car leaving fast, they assumed Saunders had killed her."

"What about Aubrey?" Henry could forgive Vernon for Saunders' death. That was self-defense. Not Aubrey's.

"Apparently, he knew Jimmy Lee was up there digging around, so he decided to try his hand. Vernon had gone up there one evening, intending to move the cattle over the digging spots. Aubrey was there. He'd found a watch and showed it to Vernon. It had the engraving, 'to C.S. from B.B. with love.' Vernon panicked."

"Stupid bastard," Rory repeated. He turned to stare into the empty fireplace.

Louis turned to Henry. "How you feeling?"

"I'd rather not feel anything right now." Henry went to the liquor cabinet he'd seen Vernon raid not long ago. He grabbed a bottle of whiskey from the back of a shelf and three glasses from the cabinet. Waving the bottle at Louis in invitation, he slowly crossed the living room to the twin sofas.

He placed the glasses on the coffee table, opened the bottle of Scotch whiskey and poured two fingers in each glass. Rory crossed to the sofa, snatched up his glass and unceremoniously downed the amber liquid. He refilled the glass before turning to Henry. He raised his glass. "I'm glad you're home, son."

Louis raised his glass and quickly tossed back the whiskey, wincing as he set it back on the table. Henry drank last, coughing when the whiskey burned his throat.

"Don't choke on it, damn it!" Rory said. "Never was much of a hard liquor man, were you?"

"That stuff is potent," Henry croaked.

Louis picked up the bottle and refilled their glasses. He looked at Henry with the slightest hint of a smile on his lips as he raised his glass. "Here's to Whispering Smith."

Henry choked on that drink too, but the numbing warmth in his stomach was worth the brief burning in his throat. He reflected on all that had happened in the past few weeks. A lot of things had muddied the waters of his life since he'd arrived in Parsons Gap. Facing the things he'd run away from fifteen years ago had allowed him to discover that deep down, this place was where he'd rather be.

"I'd better get back to the office." Louis got to his feet. Henry thought he looked a little worse for wear. "Rory, you let me know if there's anything I can do."

Nodding his thanks, Rory followed Louis to the door.

Rory returned to the fireplace. He lifted his eyes to the old photograph. "I'm still trying to figure why Vernon told you I had cancer, when it was him all along. I knew he'd been going to see a doctor. He told me it was his heart."

"How's Della taking it?" Henry asked.

"Sally Ann said she's holding up well. He'd told her it was terminal, so she'd accepted that she wouldn't have him long." Rory shook his head. "You know he'd signed his share of the ranch over to Della? He wanted her to have something when the cancer took him. You may laugh at this, but I think she's going to be a great addition."

Muddy Waters

Henry remained by the sofa, eyeing the whiskey bottle. He wished Carlie was here with him now, like that day at the river. Once again, he and his father were alone in the room and once again he had no idea what to say. Taking a deep breath, he crossed to the fireplace. Henry gave up on finding the right words and simply put a hand on his father's shoulder.

❄ ❄ ❄

Thank you for reading.
Please review this book. Reviews help others find Absolutely Amazing eBooks and inspire us to keep providing these marvelous tales.

If you would like to be put on our email list to receive updates on new releases, contests, and promotions, please go to AbsolutelyAmazingEbooks.com and sign up.

About the Author

Candace J. Carter is a South Carolina-based writer. She received a Doctor of Veterinary Medicine degree from Iowa State University following military service. She spent much of her professional career with the U.S. Department of the Interior, and has worked with several threatened and endangered species in both Colorado and Florida, including the black-footed ferret, Florida scrub-jay, and four species of sea turtles. She is retired from the National Park Service.

Muddy Waters is her first published mystery.

www.ingramcontent.com/pod-product-compliance
Lightning Source LLC
Chambersburg PA
CBHW070443030726
47503CB00004B/865